MY
SISTER'S
HUSBAND

BOOKS BY NICOLA MARSH

The Scandal
The Last Wife

MY SISTER'S HUSBAND

NICOLA MARSH

bookouture

Published by Bookouture in 2020

An imprint of Storyfire Ltd.
Carmelite House
50 Victoria Embankment
London EC4Y 0DZ

www.bookouture.com

ISBN: 978-1-80019-014-6
eBook ISBN: 978-1-80019-013-9

*For my brother Paul. Aren't you glad
I'm nothing like the sisters in this book?*

PROLOGUE

Families can be toxic.

I dare anyone to disagree.

You're forced to endure interminable gatherings and endless small talk with relatives you barely know. Faking emotion in the name of obligation.

It should be easier with siblings. Growing up together, sharing stuff, from clothes to music to excuses to get out of curfew makes the bond strong—it should be unbreakable. But sometimes it's not. Sometimes those we love the most are the ones who hurt us irrevocably and we can never go back.

Fathers are supposed to be role models. Mothers should nurture and encourage. But what if your dad doesn't set a good example and your mom doesn't care? If the family you have is in name only, patched together by the DNA that bonds you and little else?

But the worst thing about families is the secrets.

Half-truths, mysteries, and the outright lies perpetuated in the name of protection. Feelings to be considered. Sensitive souls to be sheltered from the harsh realities of life.

But that's a cop out.

I should know.

Secrets robbed me of the life I deserve.

I'm angry. Enraged.

I want what's mine.

And nobody, not even my precious family, will stand in my way.

CHAPTER ONE
BROOKE

My skin prickles as I near the outskirts of town, like a nest of ants has taken up residence under the dermis and are crawling all over me. I resist the urge to scratch because I know the feeling is psychosomatic, my body's way of saying run while you still can.

Instead, I press my foot to the accelerator and floor it past the 'Welcome to Martino Bay' sign, depicting oranges and a clifftop against an aqua background. Two hours north of LA, I'd never seen an orange grove anywhere near town. The cliffs, I'd rather forget. Rugged and terrifying, they are legendary for their beauty, and their danger.

Our house sits atop one of those towering cliffs that wend their way along the Californian coastline and growing up we knew the hazards. But as kids we found them tempting and mesmerizing. As teens we'd hang out in groups, joking about being daredevils and who'd BASE jump first. It wasn't until later I realized how menacing they could be.

I've spent the last decade running from this town and the memory of what happened eleven years ago.

The night that changed everything.

Emotion tightens my throat, regret mingling with retribution. I've lived with the guilt for so long it has become as natural to me as breathing. Returning home will make it worse, I know this, but it's time.

Freya is getting married and I wouldn't return to this hellhole for anyone other than my sister. We were close once. We shared everything. Being eleven months apart made for an unbreakable bond. Our relationship has never been easy but I love her, and the fact she reached out to me means she's as ready as I am to reconnect.

Though Freya isn't the only reason I'm back in town. My cousin Lizzie's email about Aunt Alice's deteriorating health made my ever-present guilt for staying away so long flare. I can't comprehend the strong woman who loved me like her own daughter being so ill she's confined to her room, and I have to see her. My aunt has always been there for me, and my affection for the woman who raised me has a lot to do with me gunning the engine of my beat-up Chevy as I head down the highway for another mile leading into town. I ignore the speed limit. The faster I get to Freya's the better.

The town passes in a blur, with its trendy cafés and boutiques. I bought my prom dress in one of them; Cheri's, a treasure trove of silks and chiffons, frequented by seniors and their moms alike. Eli and I had been prom king and queen, the golden couple of Martino Bay High. Everyone had loved us.

When that love turned to hate I'd had no choice but to leave. Aunt Alice had taken care of everything. She'd been there for me and now I need to return the favor. Lizzie's worried about her mom; she thinks the dementia is worsening. Aunt Alice has started to ramble about secrets and nothing's making sense. If pragmatic Lizzie is concerned, there has to be something going on.

I've been selfish, staying away for so long. But my aunt is tied up in memories of a time I'd rather forget and forgoing contact was a way to help me heal. She reminds me of what I've lost. Even now the hollow ache hasn't gone away and I'm scared seeing my aunt again will bring it all back.

I spy the crimson roadside letterbox two hundred feet ahead and my heart races. I drag in deep, calming breaths as I indicate and pull onto the dirt road beside the letterbox. Filling my lungs with air doesn't help. I'm still breathless, my pulse thundering in my ears, as I glimpse the house at the end of a twisty driveway, a single-story stucco in terracotta that looks like it has been transported direct from south of the border. I'd loved living here, loved the laid-back vibe, the coolness of the stone-tiled floors, the potted cacti Aunt Alice bought by the truckload. She'd created a real home for Freya and me, raising us as her own, alongside Lizzie.

Aunt Alice is the only mother I've ever known. She never favored Lizzie over Freya and me. We all got the same allowance, the same homemade chocolate cake for our birthdays, the same second-hand Ford for our sixteenth birthdays. She created a home filled with laughter and love. Toasted marshmallows on a small bonfire in the backyard every Sunday night, homemade pizzas if we had a bad day at school, and individual tubs of cookies 'n' cream, buttered pecan and choc-chip cookie dough ice cream, our respective favorites, in the freezer at all times.

Not overly strict, she set clear boundaries and expected us to adhere to them. She trusted us and treated us with respect, which is why I felt comfortable in approaching her when my life imploded. She'd been supportive and practical rather than judgmental and cynical. It made me love her all the more.

I definitely owe her. It's not her fault I've stayed away so long and if she's really ill, I hope I can be there for her at a time she needs me most, like she was there for me.

Three cars, two small SUVs and a monster grey van, are parked parallel near the carport. I don't recognize them. Then again, after almost eleven years, why would I? I reverse park away from the cars. It's a habit, for a quicker getaway. Not that I've done anything bad while I've been away but I don't stay long in one place. I haven't made many friends over the years and when I do those connections don't last long—there's nothing about my life I want to share.

I kill the engine but grip the steering wheel so tight my knuckles stand out. I shouldn't be this nervous. Freya loves me, despite our distance for over a decade, and she wouldn't have invited me to her wedding otherwise. Though her invitation took me by surprise. Why initiate contact now? We haven't spoken since I walked out of this house over ten years ago, never to return. I'd had to make a clean break out of necessity but a small part of me resents Freya for not reaching out sooner. Does she wonder why I cut all ties with home? Has she missed me at all? Like me, has she wanted to bridge the gap between us before now? Is that what this invitation is about, finally giving in because one of us had to make the first move to re-establish some kind of relationship?

I may not have been in the right headspace to reconnect back then but ten years is a long time to not speak to my sister. Then again, I shoulder some of the blame. I could've returned before this. Thankfully I'm stronger now and ready to face residual demons, to set the past to rest once and for all.

What seems like a lifetime later I unfurl my fingers from the steering wheel, grab my bag and open the door. I'm not surprised nobody's come out to greet me. They'll be congregated in the sunroom at the back of the house, like we always used to at this time of day. I can never taste homemade lemonade or smell oatmeal cookies without thinking of home.

I follow the flagstone path around the back, my flip-flops making a loud slapping in the eerie silence. As I round the corner of the house, I see them. Freya, her dark brown hair a stark contrast to my strawberry blonde, glowing in the waning sunlight. Her face is leaner, her cheekbones starker, and she's lost a bit of weight, but inherently she's the same. She's poring over a bridal magazine, a small smile of contentment curving her lips.

Lizzie is sitting beside her, her thumbs tapping at her cell. She's gnawing on her bottom lip, a worried frown dipping her brows. For a moment they look like sisters rather than cousins and the thought saddens me. I should've been here all these years. I'm Freya's sister, not Lizzie. I've missed out on so much.

Lizzie finishes typing and flings her cell onto the table. She glances up, sees me and her frown vanishes. Her expression is one of relief as she stands, taps Freya on the shoulder, before making her way toward me.

I smile and break into a half run, irrationally annoyed my cousin is the first to embrace me when it should be Freya. My sister seems happy enough to see me but her pace is slower as she moves toward me.

"It's good to see you, Brooke." Lizzie's hug is tight and I blink back tears as her familiar patchouli fragrance tickles my nose. I hate the smell, had teased her about it endlessly growing up. Now, a wave of nostalgia swamps me, making me cling to her until Freya draws near.

When Lizzie releases me, Freya opens her arms wide. "Long time no see, Sis."

I'm overcome for a moment as I stare into eyes as familiar as my own. We were close once and I see every emotion I've been bottling up—loss, regret, heartache—reflected in her tear-filled gaze. But she's wary too, as if she can't believe I'm here. I shouldn't be surprised she's circumspect. Like all sisters, we had our rough times. Freya had a jealous streak and she'd let me know about it sometimes. She could be moody and cunning and provoke me deliberately, but I put up with her foibles the same way she did mine.

I want to say so much. *I'm sorry for staying away so long. I'm sorry I never told you the truth about what happened. I'm sorry for being a lousy sister the last decade. I missed you.*

Instead, I manage a subdued "Yeah" as her arms envelop me and she hugs me tight. But Freya releases me quickly and I sense an undercurrent as her gaze sweeps me from head to foot, like she disapproves of my cut-off denim shorts and red tank top.

"You hungry?"

"I'm good," I say, though I'm starving. But I'm overwhelmed and would prefer to sit and take everything in than eat.

"Mom's going to be so happy you're home," Lizzie says and once again I see that flicker of disapproval in Freya's eyes. "Though she seems to be getting worse every day and may not recognize you."

I reach out and squeeze Lizzie's hand. "I'm really sorry to hear it."

"Thanks." Lizzie's smile holds a wealth of pain. "Fancy a lemonade?"

"I'd love one."

Lizzie waves us toward the outdoor table. "You two sit, I'll get it."

The moment we're left alone, Freya fixes me with a probing stare that makes me uncomfortable and for a moment I wish she'd volunteered to get the drinks. I hadn't expected Freya to be overly effusive, it's not her style, but she's acting like I'm intruding, which is bizarre considering she reached out to me.

"Everything okay?"

"Just wedding stress." Her nod is terse as she gestures at the bridal magazines on the table. "You tired?" Before I can answer, she says, "You look it."

And just like that, I feel like I'm really home. I know this Freya, with her sly passive-aggressive jibes. She's done this since we were little but I never let it bother me; not that I would show her, that is. It infuriated her when I wouldn't jibe back, my feigned indifference the best comeback.

I'd assumed we'd be past this. Almost eleven years is a long time. When I glance at her, she's smiling, but there's no joy in it. She's smug, like she's lording it over me that I've been away so long and she's the queen of the castle.

"Why did you invite me to your wedding?"

I ask the million-dollar question, the one I've lost sleep over the last few weeks while I dithered over the decision to return home. My life may have been transient for the last decade as I moved from job to job, place to place, trying to come to terms with my guilt and my grief. Volunteering with an aid organization in South

America for the last five years taught me to be self-reliant but also to read people.

And right now I can't get a read on my sister, when I once thought I knew her better than I knew myself.

"I invited you because you're family," she says, with a simple shrug. "And I've missed you."

"I've missed you too." I sling my arm across her shoulder and squeeze. "Can you believe it's been so long?"

"Whose fault is that?" She shrugs off my arm and pokes me in the ribs like she used to; we laugh. "A small part of me is still mad at you for leaving and not coming back. And I'm sorry if I acted weird a minute ago. It's just…"

"What?"

She gives a little shake of her head, as if she still can't believe I'm here. "You practically look the same and seeing you stroll in here after all this time threw me."

"It's weird, isn't it? Being apart so long, feeling like strangers almost." I wave my hand between us, wanting to ease the tension. "Remember how we used to sit here all the time in summer, giving each other manicures or trying to outdo each other in those *Cosmo* quizzes?"

For the first time since I arrived, Freya seems to relax, her stiff posture easing as she nods. "Yeah, I remember."

"Those were good times," I say, feeling like I've made a break-through when Freya smiles and blinks several times, like she's staving off tears. She always held her emotions in check better than me and I'm relieved to see this softer side to her, like she too misses what we once had.

"Anyway, there's plenty of time to take a trip down memory lane. For now, I'm happy to be home and I'm looking forward to your wedding."

"Me too." This time when she hugs me she lingers and we sniffle before easing apart.

"It's good to be home, Sis," I say, and in that moment, I mean it.

CHAPTER TWO

FREYA

Brooke is home.

Beautiful, bold Brooke.

Black sheep Brooke.

Badass Brooke.

Big sister Brooke.

I've thought of her in so many ways over the last decade. Missing her. Resenting her. Loving her. It's the love that finally won out. It's why I invited her to my wedding and to be part of the preparations. I can't deny she's part of our family, not any longer.

She'd surprised me by accepting via email. She'd given me her cell number and I could've called but I didn't want our first words to each other after all this time to be via the phone, so I'd waited.

Now she's here I don't know how to behave. I acted like an idiot earlier, too standoffish, when all I wanted to do was bundle her into my arms and cling to her for a lifetime. When she'd strolled into the backyard, all long limbs, wide eyes and strawberry blonde hair tumbling around her shoulders, my heart expanded to the point of pain, all the years we've wasted crashing over me in a sorrowful wave.

When Brooke left, I'd yearned to pick up the phone and call just so I could hear her voice. The enormity of what she'd been through made me want to hug her tight and not let go. But I blamed her too: for leaving, for our estrangement, but ultimately that was unfair. Brooke had been a victim of circumstance and we'd all dealt with the fallout in our own way.

I'd wished she'd disappear many times when we were growing up, that when it actually happened I'd felt guilty. Lost. Bereft. Wishing things could've been different. I'd been angry with her for abandoning me so I removed all trace of her from the house, hiding photos away. Like that could eradicate the memories we'd created. Stupid. Nothing could make me forget my sister.

"You okay?"

Riker lays a hand on my shoulder and it instantly calms me. I place the last of the cutlery on the table and turn, not surprised to see the concern in his blue eyes. He's intuitive and sweet despite the rugged appearance. Big, brawny, with an unruly beard and hair the color of burnt toffee skimming his shoulders. He's beautiful and most days I can't believe he's mine.

"Yeah, just nervous."

"I'm sure your sister is feeling the same way, first dinner at home and all that." His hand shifts from my shoulder to the nook of my neck, where his thumb brushes my skin and sends a shudder of longing through me. "Or are you nervous because she's meeting me for the first time?"

"Don't be ridiculous." I slide my arms around his waist. "She'll love you."

A pang of fear, a fleeting memory of the past, makes me grip him tighter. Brooke always had any guy she wanted. Eleven months older than me, she was always more noticeable, more popular, just *more*. She and Eli had been the golden couple of our high school. Everyone wanted to be them. Brooke is beautiful in a way I can never be and I hope Riker doesn't love her too much.

"I hope so," he says, before pressing his lips to mine. "But you know what your sister thinks of me is irrelevant because I'm marrying you regardless."

"I can't wait." I touch his cheek, marveling that this amazing man is mine. "By the way, it's only going to be you, me and Brooke for dinner tonight."

His eyebrows rise. "Why?"

"Because I want to reconnect with my sister, and I want her to get to know you. Time enough for her to catch up with the rest later." While I do want Brooke to like Riker, a small part of me wants to show him off too and it'll be easier with just the three of us. "She should be here any second. Can you uncork the wine, please?"

"Sure." He bends down to kiss me again and I allow myself the luxury of sinking into it.

I've never been into public displays of affection but Riker is demonstrative and I don't care who sees it when we're out. In fact, I relish the townsfolk of Martino Bay seeing me with him. They don't talk about the 'poor Stuart sisters' any longer. These days, I'm an admired and recognized member of the community: a nurse at the local nursing home, a volunteer for many causes, always willing to help out. Having Brooke back won't change that.

"I'll get the wine," Riker says and pads to the kitchen, his bare feet not making a sound on the oak boards. He's wearing faded jeans artfully torn at the knees, a black T-shirt and a camel suede vest, looking every inch the artist. He's as renowned in this town as I am, his metal sculptures sought by many.

That's how we'd met. He'd been selling his art, trying to build his business, at the local market. The animals he created out of metal had intrigued me, and I'd stopped to admire his work. We'd started chatting and there'd been something about him, something in the way he looked at me. So I'd let him wax lyrical about his art for a while and when he'd asked me out, I'd accepted. We've been a couple ever since.

"Something smells good," Brooke says from behind me and I turn.

Her smile's tentative as she pats her stomach. "I'm starving."

She's surprisingly pale, but she's showered and changed into a flowing paisley mini kaftan, and with her hair swept into a loose topknot with a few tendrils framing her face she looks like a waif.

For a moment I feel like the clumsy giant I used to be next to her: too tall, too strong, too oafish. Little wonder all the boys used to favor her over me. But then I hear a muttered curse from the kitchen and I'm empowered again. I have Riker. He chose me. I don't need to feel inferior to Brooke.

However, all that changes when Riker enters the dining room, holding an open bottle of cab sav. Because I see the exact moment he lays eyes on Brooke and his widen in recognition.

I quickly glance at Brooke and she's wearing the same shell-shocked expression he is.

My fiancé and my sister know each other.

CHAPTER THREE

ALICE

THEN

"How do I look, Sis?"

Diana twirls in front of me, the full skirt of her satin cocktail dress flaring at the hem, creating a soft swish.

I roll my eyes. "Perfect as usual."

It wouldn't matter if she wore a hessian sack, Diana will be the most beautiful girl at the party tonight. I love my sister, I really do, but having mousy-brown hair next to her reddish-blonde, brown eyes compared to her vivid blue, and a stick-thin figure alongside her curves means she gets the attention of all the boys. But it's more than that. She's vivacious and sweet, and people are naturally drawn to her, whereas I'm the introvert who fades into the background. Even our mom favors her. Not overtly, but I always get the sense I'm being compared to Diana.

Even though I finished high school a year earlier and can afford better clothes and make-up, I know my eighteen-year-old sister will dazzle tonight.

"You look great too," Diana says, her envious gaze narrowing slightly as she stares at my little black dress that had cost a week's wages. "Boring school is done so I can't wait to find a job and start working too." She smooths out the skirt of the vintage gown she picked up for twenty bucks online. "I can't wait to be able to afford better than this."

"You should be going to college."

Her nose crinkles. "Don't you start. I've already coerced Mom into letting me have a gap year, now all I have to do is work on Dad."

"Good luck with that."

Not only does Diana have the looks in the family, she got the brains too. Our folks didn't care when I finished school and started doing clerical work at a small accountancy firm because they pinned all their hopes on brilliant, gorgeous Diana bringing pride to the Shomack name as the first to attend college.

She has as much hope of ditching college in the coming year as I do of winning a beauty contest between the two of us.

"Anyone I should take particular note of at this party tonight?" Diana winks. "Any special guys in your life, Sis?"

I feel heat flush my cheeks. "I'm weighing up my options."

She laughs and pats my back. "You mumble some guy's name I can't catch in your sleep often enough that I can't wait to meet your friends."

The heat intensifies and I elbow her away. "There's a group of us that like hanging out and I'm only taking you under sufferance."

Her crimson-glossed lips pout in a way that can convince any guy to do anything. "I'm finally free, Sis. The least you can do the week after I finish high school is take me to a grown-up party."

I snort. "The fact you call it a grown-up party indicates you are nowhere near ready to come with me, but Mom and Dad made me."

"Mom and Dad made me," she mimics in a perfect imitation of my snarky tone and I can't help but laugh.

"Come on, we're already fashionably late."

The drive from our home on the outskirts of Verdant, a town that's anything but in the Nevada Desert, to Cam's house takes fifteen minutes. My palms are slick with sweat and I'm grateful for Diana's endless prattle.

Tonight's the night.

I'm going to tell Cam how I feel.

"Have you heard a word I've said?" Diana snaps her fingers in my face as I park. "I've never seen you so spaced out. This guy must be something."

"Shut up," I snap, getting out of the car and slamming the door. "And once we're in there, you're on your own."

"I can take care of myself." Diana slips the black wrap off and squares her shoulders. She fills out the midnight blue satin fifties-style dress better than any film siren from the same era. "Don't worry about me."

I won't. I have more important things to worry about, like how to get Cam alone and tell him everything.

I sat behind Cameron Stuart in every class since second grade and have crushed on him since then. He's quiet and studious and has always exuded a peace that attracted me, considering my tumultuous home life. It isn't that my parents don't care about Di and me, it's just they're so absorbed in each other their kids come a distant second.

As we grow older, Diana and I hate their overt displays of affection as much as the size of our tiny house with the paper-thin walls that allow us to hear too much. Unfortunately, their passion isn't only reserved for the bedroom and they indulge in rip-roaring fights that terrify me. Little wonder Cam's calmness draws me in.

Surprisingly, he hadn't left Verdant for college either, despite his grades. Instead, he works at his family's business, a wind farm that produces power. Because there aren't many of us who didn't escape Verdant, we hang out together a fair bit and lately I've seen something in his eyes, a glint of interest I hope means he's finally noticed me. It's given me the courage to make a move. I'm sick of waiting—and being the oldest virgin in Verdant. At this rate Diana will have sex before I do.

She's halfway up the path to Cam's door before she realizes I'm not following. She pauses and glances over her shoulder, one eyebrow raised. "Al?"

"Coming," I mutter, wishing I had half my sister's confidence.

I've been to Cam's place a few times, with a group of the old high school crew. We order pizza, drink beers, watch the latest show streaming. Low-key, friendly, but it hadn't been until the last gathering when we'd all swum in the low-frills rectangular pool out the back that I'd had any indication he might like me. He'd been friendlier than usual and it gave me hope.

I definitely have to say something tonight.

As we near the house, a contemporary two-story that would look more at home in Las Vegas, I hear voices and laughter coming from the back of the house and the booming bass of a dance track that echoes through my chest.

Diana does an excited little jig. "I'm really looking forward to this."

I would be too if my guts weren't twisted into pretzels at the thought of my impending reveal to Cam so I fake a smile and follow the stone path around the back. I'm already too tall so opt for low kitten heels while Diana's stilettos make a loud clacking alongside me. I always feel like a gangly giant next to her petite curves.

As we round the back corner of the house, my heart sinks. Cam hadn't mentioned this is a pool party and the sight of several girls in bikinis splashing daintily in the shallows adds to my nerves.

"You didn't tell me we were swimming," Diana hisses under her breath, her gaze scouring the crowd of guys gathered near the pool. "I'm overdressed."

Diana looks stunning and knows it. Besides, there are several women in dresses gathered near a buffet table so we're not completely out of place. Cam had told me to dress up so that's what I'd done. Screw everybody else.

"Want me to introduce you to a few people?"

Diana waves me away. "I'll be fine, you go have fun."

I intend to but I haven't spotted Cam yet and my rampant nerves aren't settling. "Don't drink, okay?"

Diana rolls her eyes. "Yes, Mom," she drawls, and I know my warning will have little effect. Di has always done exactly what she wants without fear of consequences. I envy her bravado.

"Behave." I nudge her before drifting away, scouring the crowd for Cam.

But before I can do a real reconnaissance, someone snags my arm. "Quick, Alice, I need your help."

It's Dave, Cam's best friend. I can't stand him because he's sleazy but I pretend to like him for Cam's sake.

I subtly shrug out of his grip. "What's up?"

"Mandy's throwing up. She says it's food poisoning but..." He shifts side to side, his face puce. "Do you think you could suss her out?" I don't understand the fear in his eyes until things slide into place: he's terrified she may be pregnant. I shouldn't get involved. It's none of my business and I don't even like him, but what if he complains to Cam that I didn't help when he asked?

So I force a smile. "Sure, where is she?"

"Upstairs bathroom." He squeezes my arm in gratitude and I grit my teeth against the urge to shake him off. "Thanks, Al, I owe you one."

Not a bad thing if he can put in a good word for me with Cam, so I head upstairs to find puking Mandy. She's in a spare bedroom, lying on the bed, staring at the ceiling, her face an unsettling greyish color.

"Hey, Mandy, you okay?"

Listless, her gaze drifts toward me. "Don't tell Dave, but I popped an E from one of the guys out there."

I bite back a laugh. I reckon Dave will be relieved.

"As long as you're okay?"

"I've been better." She presses a hand to her mouth for several moments, as if staving off another vomit, before lowering it. "I thought that stuff was meant to make you feel like partying, not puking."

I wouldn't know. I'd never touch drugs. "Want me to send Dave up? He's worried about you."

She shakes her head and winces. "I need to sleep this off. Tell him I'll be down when I can."

"Okay." I cross the bedroom to the en suite, fill a glass with water, before placing it beside her on the bedside table. "I'll pop in to check on you later."

She manages a wan smile. "Thanks, Alice, you're the best."

I don't get praised often so I'm feeling pretty pleased with myself as I head downstairs. At least checking on Mandy has served to take my mind off my upcoming revelation to Cam. I'll let Dave know his girlfriend is fine before finding Cam.

I head for the back door and scan the crowd. Dave's on the far side of the pool now, completely unconcerned about Mandy considering his head is bent close to a redhead in a skimpy black bikini. So I do a slow sweep of the crowd in search of Cam. He's tall, about six-one, with blond hair easily bleached by the Nevada sun, so should be easy to spot.

He is. I see him in the shadows to my right, behind the bar.

With his arm around Diana.

CHAPTER FOUR
BROOKE

I swear time stands still when I lay eyes on Riker again.

I'm swept back to that fateful night eleven years ago when everything changed, when my life as I knew it ended. He played a major role, not that he was aware of it.

I've deliberately blocked everything about that night from my memory because it's ruined my life. But seeing Riker again... I remember the smell of his skin, a hint of sweat blended with a light citrus body wash. I remember the wildness that swept over me when we entered the secluded shed. I remember not caring about the wrongness of being with him when it felt so right.

It had been a fleeting interlude with Riker passing through town. I never expected to see him again and I'd been glad considering the fallout from that hellish night.

So what the hell is Riker doing here now?

I school my face into a mask, hoping to hide my recognition, but it's too late. Freya is staring at me with narrow-eyed suspicion.

"Do you two know each other?"

Freya sounds wary and I'm speechless, unable to come up with a response that won't end the fragile rebuilding of our sibling bond before it's begun. Thankfully, Riker recovers quicker than me; he smiles, a wide, easy grin that catapults me back to the night I thought I was the only girl in the world he reserved those smiles for.

"Sort of," he says, and I force a laugh, adding, "We met at a party as kids years ago."

"Yeah, a lifetime ago." Riker's steely blue-eyed stare bores into me, imploring me to understand, before he blinks and refocuses on Freya. "We barely spoke."

The lie slides easily from his lips and I wonder why he covers for me, until he places the wine on the table and moves around it to slide an arm around Freya's waist.

I'm confused. "Your invitation said you're marrying a James?"

"We wanted to keep the invitations official so went with his real name, but everyone around here knows him as Riker." Freya's tone is clipped but she's looking up at Riker with open adoration and I'm thankful she's believed our lie.

"Okay," I say, though I have the distinct feeling it's not.

Freya never liked to share anything with me growing up and she coveted everything I had. If she ever finds out the truth about how Riker and I know each other she'll never forgive me. If Freya hated accepting clothing hand-me-downs from me, she'd freak if she thought Riker was sloppy seconds. Any chance I have of being assimilated back into the family I miss so much will be gone.

"Hope you're hungry," she says, slipping out of Riker's grip but not before placing a proprietorial kiss on his mouth. "I've made our favorites."

I'm touched she's remembered I loved Pad Thai noodles and a cheesy casserole bake.

"Great. Can I help?"

She shakes her head. "No, you sit, Riker will give me a hand."

I do as I'm told and take a seat at the table, trying to eavesdrop on the hushed exchange in the kitchen. I can't hear if Freya's questioning Riker but they're quiet for a few moments before re-entering the dining room, their hands laden with casserole dishes, shooting conspiratorial smiles at each other like a couple in sync, and I'm relieved the tenseness of the last few minutes has resolved.

I inhale, confused by the meaty aromas. Freya hasn't cooked *our* favorites, she's made hers—beef enchiladas, paella and fried chicken—things I never ate back then because I became a vegetarian at sixteen.

It saddens me that she's become so wrapped up in her life she's forgotten the past we shared. But as she and Riker place the dishes on the table in front of me and he pulls out her chair I glance up. Our eyes meet and my confusion increases. There's a glint in her eyes I can't fathom. Does she know she's chosen reminders of her childhood, not mine? Has she done this deliberately, a way of staking a claim on this home we once shared?

Freya's not that vindictive so when she looks at me expectantly, like she's waiting for my approval, I realize she's forgotten and I feel bad for doubting her motives. Besides, these days, I'm not vegetarian. I rarely eat meat as a health preference but I do eat it so I smile, demure and grateful, before saying, "This all looks wonderful. Thanks, Freya." My sister has welcomed me back into her life and I feel guilty for my suspicious thoughts. I hope she can hear my sincerity. "I can't wait to try everything."

"Great." Freya sticks a serving spoon into the enchiladas. "Remember that time I accidentally substituted sugar for salt in the chicken pasta?"

I laugh. "Yeah, I still can't believe Aunt Alice pretended to like the first spoonful so she wouldn't hurt your feelings."

Freya's eyes are soft with remembrance. "She's amazing."

"Will she be joining us for dinner? Lizzie?"

Freya shakes her head. "She gets too disoriented if she leaves her room so Lizzie often eats with her in there."

The thought of my vibrant aunt's deterioration saddens me, but before I can ask more questions, Freya says, "Are you dating anyone?"

I'm thrown by her abrupt change of topic, but I shake my head. "No. I've been focusing on work and not much else lately."

She's studying me with obvious curiosity, like she wants to know more, when Riker clears his throat.

"I hate to interrupt, ladies, but I'm starving and I need to eat before I faint." Freya smiles and bumps him gently with her shoulder as he pats his stomach, drawing my attention there, and a little frisson of illicit excitement shoots through me as I remember touching him, skimming my palm over his abs, lower.

My cheeks heat and I reach for the wine at the same time he does, our fingers brushing, before I jerk away.

If he notices my reaction he doesn't say, his gaze calm as he lifts the bottle. "Wine for both of you?"

"Please," I say, at the same time Freya mutters, "Yes."

I hope she doesn't think I deliberately touched her fiancé. They're about to get married in four weeks and I'd never mess with that. I may have made some monstrous mistakes in the past but living in a hut in the middle of nowhere, helping locals, gave me back some self-respect and I have no intention of reverting to the broken teen I'd been over a decade earlier.

"So how are the wedding preparations coming along and what can I do?" I ask, but before Freya can respond a young girl about ten, with freckles, a messy brown ponytail and big hazel eyes appears in the doorway, and my sister blanches.

"Mom, Lizzie sent me over to grab some sodas…" The girl trails off as she catches sight of me and another bomb detonates. First Riker, now this.

I gape, shock rendering me speechless.

Freya is a mother.

I'm an aunt.

In that moment, the reality of all I've missed out on hits home. I haven't seen my family for ten long years because I've been wrapped up in my grief, my loss, and my anger that everyone's life continued long after mine spiraled out of control. I deliberately stayed away because I didn't want reminders of a past I'd rather forget.

But I have a niece and I could've been a part of her life, I could've watched her grow and lavished her with the love of an aunt, like Alice had with me.

Why didn't Freya tell me?

CHAPTER FIVE
ALICE
THEN

I never got to tell Cam how I feel.

How could I, when he'd stared at Diana like she hung the moon for the entire party, before sneaking off with her toward the end? I wanted to hate Diana but I couldn't. With her tucked into the crook of Cam's arm, and the two of them staring at each other like they were the only people in the world, they fit. I didn't believe in love at first sight until that night. I cried more tears after the party than I ever had before.

And then Dad died.

I mourned him but I didn't miss his loud brashness and the way he dominated us. The house seemed larger without his overbearing presence. Diana didn't seem particularly affected by his death. Besides, she had Cam to comfort her. They'd started dating of sorts. Nothing overt, because that would be crass so soon after Dad's death, but I knew she snuck out some nights to meet up with him. On the few times he dropped by the house, I'd make myself scarce because it hurt too much seeing them together.

Eight weeks later when Mom stood her ground and made Diana go to college, some fancy place in Long Island that sounded more like a posh finishing school than an actual place of learning, I was relieved. I thought it would help me, not seeing Diana with Cam. But being alone in the house with Mom was even more painful.

Mom drifted around the house at night, a bourbon in one hand, a cigarette in the other. She chain-smoked all day and I hated coming home after work, the pall of smoke draping every room as bad as her moroseness.

I wanted to shake her. From the fights she'd had with Dad they'd hated each other most of the time; when they weren't all over each other, that is. I loathed their overt passion, whether it be in arguments or making up. It made me want to be the opposite, to demonstrate calm control at all costs. I was nothing like my short-tempered parents, something I was grateful for when I had to be privy to Diana's infatuation with Cam. If I'd been like my folks, I would've yelled at her, would've screamed at the injustice of her snaring the guy I loved. Instead, I'd hidden my pain beneath a veneer of indifference, lamenting that I didn't make a move sooner.

I hated Diana for abandoning me, even though I could barely look at her in the two months after the party. She'd withdrawn from me as much as I had from her, too self-absorbed with her new romance to care about anyone else. I'd been glad. I had my own sorrow to deal with.

Now, three weeks later, the only good thing to come out of Dad dying and Diana leaving is having Cam comforting me.

"Want a drink?" He holds out a chilled bottle of vodka taken straight from the freezer and I take it, gulp a generous swig, before handing it back.

"Thanks." I swipe my mouth with the back of my hand, not caring how uncouth it looks. Cam's been a good friend and despite me hoping for more he seems to be moping too, which means he's missing Diana.

He asked me about her once, where she was, and I lied. When he asked for her number, I lied again, saying Di had been heartbroken over losing Dad and wanted a clean break at college.

"Can I ask you something, Al?"

"Anything."

My stupid impressionable heart beats faster. Crazy, because he's not going to ask me any of the questions I wish he would.

"Do you ever wish you could walk away from all this?" He sweeps his arm wide, encompassing his backyard. "Leave this town? Go somewhere more exciting? Be someone different?"

I can give him the trite answer, the one he wants to hear, but I settle for the truth.

"No. I like stability."

He stares at me, his eyes wide in surprise, as if he's never contemplated anyone could be happy living in Verdant, so I feel obliged to validate my answer.

"My parents had a volatile marriage so without Dad around it's more peaceful." I shrug. "I have thought about leaving at times, but Mom's struggling and I can't abandon her."

"She's not coping?"

I shake my head. "Not at all. She drifts through the house like a zombie, chain-smoking. I've tried to make comfort meals, like mac and cheese and pot roast and tomato soup, but she barely eats. I make sure there's never silence by choosing songs from her playlist to shuffle all day, but it's like she doesn't hear them…"

I don't want to reveal too much to Cam or exactly how hard it's been caring for Mom. I don't want anyone to think less of her. She'd fed us, clothed us and supported our decisions. My parents' mutual obsession had ensured I ended up taking care of Di a lot growing up, and while I resented it I still loved Mom. With Dad gone I thought she might flourish, become her own person. Instead, she's withdrawn into herself to the point of being comatose, and I have no idea how to snap her out of it.

"Anything I can do?"

My heart melts at his generous offer. "Thanks, but I think it's going to take time. I need to be patient, help her through it."

"She's lucky to have you." His gaze is filled with admiration and I feel heat surging to my cheeks.

"So you were saying something about wanting to escape?"

"Itchy feet, I guess," he says. "I get sick of working for the family company now and then, and even though my folks gifted me this house and I'm lucky to have savings, I often wonder if there's more out there, you know?"

I do know because Diana always talked about wanting more, about leaving town and not looking back. Like everything else in her golden life, she's lucky enough to have it now, and I wonder if missing her is the reason behind Cam's sudden wanderlust.

Thoughts of my sister sour my mood and before I can second-guess my impulse, I reach out and rest my hand over Cam's, where it rests on his thigh. "There's something to be said for dependability."

I hold my breath, waiting for him to withdraw his hand, and when he doesn't I'm happy for the first time in forever.

CHAPTER SIX
FREYA

I should know better than anyone that the best laid plans go astray.

I hadn't wanted Hope and Brooke to meet until tomorrow and certainly not like the awkward run-in before dinner. Thankfully I've raised a polite, obedient kid—most of the time—and after introductions Hope had grabbed the sodas and headed back to Lizzie's.

We all live on the same property, though I'm in the main house now where Alice raised Lizzie, Brooke and me. Alice is still here, despite Lizzie insisting she should be looking after her mom full-time. But with Alice's dementia worsening almost daily, I'm the one with the training to deal with her health needs so I convinced Lizzie to let Alice stay in the main house. Riker converted a small wing with a lockable door so Alice can't wander and we all spend time with her. It's the least I can do considering I don't remember my mom and Alice has been it for me all these years.

There are two smaller bungalows on the property; Lizzie lives in one, Riker in the other. It's convenient, because I'd rather Hope didn't see Riker and me living together until we marry, but the proximity gives us all a chance to intertwine our lives as much as we want.

After Hope's appearance, dinner became a stilted affair, not that it hadn't been before. Realizing Brooke and Riker had met in the past set my teeth on edge. I'd caught her glancing at him several times, curious glances that made me anxious. It's been a long time since I've felt insecure; it's a feeling only Brooke can elicit. Besides, I'll ask Riker to give me the details of their meeting later.

"Why didn't you tell me about Hope?"

I knew this would be the first question Brooke asked as we settle on the back porch with our coffees, the wind from the cliffs at the end of the property whipping our hair off from our faces. We used to do this in the past; sit outside with hot cocoa after we'd finished our homework for the evening and chat about school and boys. I'd been envious of my sister back then; she'd had her pick of boys while most of them barely noticed me. But I loved hearing about her dating tales, even if Aunt Alice didn't know most of them. She'd been a great stand-in mom because she'd given us the freedom to make our own mistakes. Pity some of us made more than others.

I'm prepared for Brooke's curiosity but I still choose my words carefully. No point alienating her when we're trying to reconnect and that's exactly how she's going to feel if I don't give a logical explanation for why I haven't mentioned my daughter.

"I'd planned on telling you after dinner but then Hope appeared and… There's a lot you've missed out on while you've been away." I shrug, offhand, when I'm feeling anything but. I feel guilty for not reaching out to my sister earlier, for waiting over a decade. I blamed her at the start; for abandoning me, for spreading her wings when I was stuck in Martino Bay. But as the years passed and I had Hope to raise, I released the resentment consuming me and left the ball in Brooke's court.

Even now, I wonder if she would've ever returned if I hadn't invited her to my wedding. I know Lizzie told her Aunt Alice's health is worsening. Would Brooke have accepted the invitation if she hadn't learnt that too? She'd gone through a lot back then but I could never understand why she let it define her. People changed, moved on, forgot. I suppose I should be thankful we finally had this opportunity to bond again.

"It's like we're strangers," she murmurs, her gaze stricken as it fixes on mine, and a lump forms in my throat. "I can't believe I have a niece and I never knew."

I take a sip of coffee to ease the tightness in my throat. "I found out I was pregnant not long after you left and I wanted to keep the baby."

She pales and her bottom lip wobbles before she hides it by lifting her mug to her mouth. "I'm sorry. I've missed out on so much staying away."

"Yeah, you have, but we all do what we have to do." Feeling sorry for her, I reach across and squeeze her arm. "We can't change the past, Brooke, but you're back now so let's look forward, okay?"

She bites down on her bottom lip and nods, and in that moment I realize how far we've come.

"I could tell you everything about Hope but how would you like to spend some time with her tomorrow and find out what a great kid she is for yourself?"

"Sure, I'd like that," she says, but her voice is tight and a tiny groove dents her brow. "But I should see Aunt Alice in the morning first?"

I nod, knowing this confrontation was coming, wishing I could protect her from the shock. "You need to be prepared. She probably won't know you. And she rambles, a lot."

"Lizzie mentioned it." She winces, before taking a sip of her coffee. "I hate to think of her suffering."

"It's tough but I'm doing the best I can."

Brooke's eyebrows rise at my defensiveness and I sigh, pinching the bridge of my nose. "Having medical knowledge isn't always a good thing. I know how fast she's going to deteriorate, it isn't going to be pretty."

She stares at me for a long time, appraising, before she speaks. "You've done well, Sis. I never pictured you nursing or being a carer or being a young mom, yet here you are knocking it out of the park. I'm proud of you."

I don't need her praise but I accept it nonetheless. Part of me wonders if I want Brooke to feel jealous of me for once, but that's childish. Maybe more than a decade apart has been good for us and our relationship has benefited from Brooke's absence?

"Do I know Hope's father?"

"No." I drain half my coffee before continuing. "He drifted through town and I met him not long after you left. I guess I was floundering a bit, missing you a lot, so I gave him my virginity and Hope was the result. Aunt Alice badgered me to know but she stopped asking when she saw how much it upset me."

Sadness clouds Brooke's eyes. "I'm sorry you went through that and I wasn't around. Does the father know?"

I shake my head. "I didn't even know his name. He had this dumb nickname, Boots." I screw up my nose. "Besides, Hope has done fine with just me, Alice and Lizzie."

"What do you say to Hope when she asks about her dad?"

Brooke has unwittingly touched a nerve because I've hated having to lie to Hope all these years. Before Riker, my beautiful daughter used to ask me often where her dad was and I'd say I'd tried to find him but he'd vanished. The fib was better than the truth—that I didn't even know his name—but the result was always the same. Hope's disappointment made me feel like I'd failed her.

"I know you have questions, Brooke, but maybe we could leave some for tomorrow?"

She has the grace to blush. "Sorry, just catching up. It's been a long time."

"And whose fault is that?" I snap, immediately regretting my outburst. I don't want her first night home in over a decade to end with us arguing. First Riker, then Hope, nothing has gone to plan tonight. "I'm sorry too. We've been apart a long time. I guess it's going to take longer than a few hours together for us to feel comfortable in each other's company again."

She nods and I pretend not to hear her muttered, "Were we ever?"

It's the first time either of us has acknowledged out loud that our relationship hasn't always been rosy and, in a way, I'm relieved. I want things to be good between us; I don't want to revert to the way we used to be.

But it's early days. We have a lot of catching up to do. I'm sure we'll be back to normal before the wedding.

CHAPTER SEVEN
BROOKE

I expected to feel disjointed coming home but as I lie in my old bed, staring at the unchanged ceiling covered in glow stars, I can't begin to describe how utterly adrift I am.

The window above my bed is partially open and I can hear the waves crashing against the rocks at the base of the cliffs. A soothing sound as a child, but now it only serves to remind me of a past I'd rather forget.

I used to love curling up in bed, reading the latest paranormal novel and scaring myself silly. Ironic, that real life ended up being far more terrifying than any vampire in the pages of a book.

On a clear night, I could see the moon through my window if I wedged my pillow into the corner of my bed just right. I used to wonder what was out there, beyond Martino Bay. Turns out, it's not so great and coming home is what I've yearned for.

The ceiling stars aren't the only unchanged things in my room. Everything is the same, from the colorful gel pens scattered across the desk, to the glitter eye shadow stacked in tiny tubs. From the novels spilling out of the bookcase to the ancient troll doll I'd won at a fair hanging off the knob on the wonky wardrobe door that never quite closed. So many memories and my chest aches with the pressure of keeping the tears at bay.

Everything is the same yet different.

Freya seems so happy. She's a mom, a fiancée, a woman going places.

I could've handled it all—Alice's deterioration, learning Riker is her fiancé, being part of their wedding—but it's Hope that has thrown me the most.

I'm an aunt and I never knew. All these years I'd see mothers with their kids and feel that deep-seated tug. I want to be a mom too. I have so much love to lavish on a child.

Will Aunt Alice remember me when I see her tomorrow? Will she remember taking care of me when I learned the awful truth after Eli's death? Will she remember giving me the freedom to leave when I couldn't return home because I was shattered?

Will she remember any of it? For her sake I hope not. I've spent the last decade trying to forget.

I'm not afraid of running into old friends in town. Martino Bay has grown in size and isn't as insular as it once was. Back then, it felt like everyone at school blamed me for what happened to Eli. They'd stare and whisper and judge. Rumors circulated: I'd broken up with him that night and he'd leapt to his death. We'd argued and he'd jumped off the cliff right in front of me. Even the more outlandish, that we'd fought and I'd pushed him.

Nobody knew the truth and they never would.

Some things were better left unsaid.

Besides, they were partially right. What I'd confessed to Eli that night had driven him to jump, I know it. Sweet, steady, Eli. My boyfriend. My first love. My everything.

Until the party that changed our lives irrevocably.

Classmates were already talking about me and pointing fingers after his suicide, which is why Alice took me away. She'd planned it all. I would travel, work, whatever, giving the rumor mill time to settle. But the repercussions of what I'd done haunted me and I hadn't wanted to come back. Too many memories, too many ghosts. I'd drifted from job to job, town to town, glad of the monetary safety net Aunt Alice had provided me but needing her support more. I'd missed her, missed Freya, mourning the loss of the only family I'd ever known as much as the loss of Eli.

A lone tear seeps out of the corner of my eye, followed by another, and another, until I'm lying there, staring up at the ceiling, silent tears cascading down my cheeks and dripping onto the pillow. I don't cry much these days; regret and sorrow are stupid, wasted emotions. But lying in my childhood bed, I allow myself to grieve for all I lost: Eli, my home, my family, my town.

Being back here is going to be harder than I anticipated.

"I was grateful when Riker converted this wing to keep Mom safe," Lizzie says, as we sit outside the locked door to Aunt Alice's room, in a reading nook I favored as a kid. "He's been a godsend around here."

I want to quiz Lizzie on Freya's engagement but now isn't the time, not when I'm about to come face to face with the aunt I once adored for the first time in over a decade. "Freya seems happy."

"Yeah, she's much better these days." Lizzie's unable to meet my eyes and I can see I've made her uncomfortable. "When I finished college and returned home, I think she was still missing you. But she had Hope and that gorgeous girl is enough to brighten anyone's day."

I wouldn't know and once again sorrow tightens my chest for all I've missed out on.

"I can't believe Riker's only been on the scene such a short time. It feels like he's been here forever. He's good for her." Lizzie hesitates, before giving a shrug. "You better than anyone knows how Freya gets sometimes and he grounds her."

I love my sister but I know what she's implying. Growing up, Freya could be moody and irrational and prone to jealousy. I'd learned to deal with her but during those times Lizzie preferred avoidance.

"How long have they been together?"

"Six months."

My eyebrows rise. "Wow, that's a speedy engagement."

The unasked question must be obvious in my eyes because Lizzie smirks. "No pregnancy. They just clicked and I'm happy for them."

"Me too."

But I'm puzzled. Freya didn't have a boyfriend when we were growing up. She always seemed awkward around boys and preferred to hang out in groups. Having Hope so young must've put a serious dent in her dating life, so I hope she's not rushing into this marriage with Riker—he could very well be the only boyfriend she's ever had.

"Freya mentioned to me this morning that you and Riker know each other?"

I wave away my cousin's curiosity. "Ancient history. We met at a party once as kids, said hi, that was about it."

"Uh-huh," Lizzie says, and I know she's not convinced.

So I rush in with, "Sitting in this nook reminds me of our diaries and how Aunt Alice got us hooked on journaling. She did hers online and we got hard copies."

"Yeah, Mom's obsessed with keeping a diary. Has been doing it for years until recently…"

I hate the sadness clouding Lizzie's eyes, so I say, "Remember how the three of us used to hide our diaries under the cushions here?"

Shared memories soften the sorrow in her eyes. "Yeah, we used to fight over this nook. Who'd get to tuck into it with legs out, rather than having to squeeze into it together."

She chuckles. "Freya always won because we wouldn't want to precipitate one of her moods."

"I can't believe we never snuck peeks at each other's diaries. At least, I didn't."

"Me either," Lizzie echoes, but her gaze shifts, furtive.

"Liar." I laugh, and poke her in the ribs.

She smiles and holds up her hands. "Okay, you got me. But I only read Freya's because Mom asked me to."

"Why?"

"I think she was worried about her. You were popular and Mom worried Freya might be feeling second-best, and a bit resentful."

A bit? There were times I remember Freya glaring at me like she wanted to throttle me, but my sister would calm down and we'd move past it. I'd witnessed some of the fights between my friends and their siblings at school, and had been grateful the worst Freya ever did was shoot me death glares.

"Did you find anything juicy?"

Lizzie shakes her head. "Nothing. I reckon she didn't write anything in there that she didn't want us to read."

"Smart girl. Me, on the other hand? Every crush I ever had on a boy was scrawled across those pages." I wrinkle my nose.

Lizzie laughs. "Damn, I should've read yours instead."

We share a smile, happiness making me reach over and impulsively hug Lizzie. "I'm so glad I came home."

She hugs me back and I expect her to ask what kept me away, but Lizzie has always been intuitive and she settles for squeezing me extra tight before releasing me.

"I'm glad too, Cuz, we've missed you." She touches my hand. "I think you broke Mom's heart when you left. She became really insular afterwards. I didn't see it, because I wasn't around, but Freya told me. She said Mom helped with Hope a lot and never judged her for being a pregnant teen, but when I got home a few years later I could see she'd changed too."

Great, just what I need, more guilt before I see my aunt. But Lizzie isn't deliberately trying to make me feel bad. She's too warm, too genuine, for that. She's trying to fill me in on what I've missed out on, trying to make me feel a part of this family again. Little does she know it's tearing me up inside.

"Anyway, enough about the past," Lizzie says, taking my hand. "You're here now and it means the world to all of us."

"Thanks," I mumble, tears pricking my eyes. "Shall we go in? I really want to see her."

Lizzie squeezes my hand before releasing it. "Mornings are often her best time, she deteriorates as the day progresses. You sure you're ready for this?"

I'll never be ready to see the aunt I love locked in a room for her own safety, but I nod. I'd rather stay tucked into the reading nook, comforted by my favorite spot in the house. Instead, I'm close behind Lizzie as she opens the bedroom door and steps in. "Hey Mom, I've brought you a visitor."

I hear a muttered "Go away" before I follow Lizzie into the room. Pity floods me and I struggle to hide it as I catch my first glimpse of the strong, vital aunt who raised me.

She's in bed, half-propped by a stack of pillows, but her gaunt-ness stuns me. She's thin to the point of emaciated, a pretty pink nightgown hanging off her shoulders, her once shiny brown hair dull and lank, her eyes clouded with confusion.

How can this be the same vibrant woman who'd taught me how to bake apple pie, who'd spend hours in the garden tending to her veggie patch, who'd clothed and fed and loved me? Aunt Alice had always had a quiet inner strength and it hadn't surprised me she'd been practical and supportive of me when my life imploded, rather than judgmental. She'd been my rock and while I loved my sister and cousin, I'd missed her the most the last ten years.

The guilt is back, stronger than ever. Why had I stayed away so long? Why had I distanced myself from the only family I have? I'd come to grip with my nightmares over the years, yet I know the recurrent horror of what I'd been through influenced my decision to stay away. I never sought professional help. I should have. But it's too late now and I'm doing the best I can. I just hope I can be here for Aunt Alice when she needs me most, like she did for me.

I swallow my sorrow and step closer to the bed. "Hi, Aunt Alice."

When she continues to stare at me, uncomprehending, I add, "It's Brooke."

"Brooke," she repeats, her unfocused gaze roaming over my face as if searching for answers I have no hope of giving. "Bad sisters," she says, lifting a hand to wave between Lizzie and me. "Birthdays. Secrets. Silly."

Her hand falls limply to her side and she turns her head away to stare out the window. A sob wells up inside me; sensing my distress Lizzie steps closer and slides an arm around my waist.

I don't know how long we stand there but I'm reluctant to leave, because despite my aunt's catatonic state, despite her frailty, I finally feel some sense of peace in seeing her after all this time.

After I compose myself, I mouth "Thank you" at Lizzie before slipping out of her arm. I reach out and touch Aunt Alice's hand, relieved when she doesn't jerk away. She turns her head toward me and I slip my hand into hers.

"I'm home, Auntie, and I love you."

She grips my hand with a surprising firmness and her eyes clear for a moment as they bore into mine.

"I'm sorry," she murmurs, sadness down-turning her mouth. "For everything."

CHAPTER EIGHT
ALICE
THEN

I only got to spend six months with Mom before she died.

The doc said she contracted lung cancer from years of smoking but she insisted her grief over losing Dad caused it. I never understood their obsessive love that often manifested into screaming matches, but watching Mom languish in her grief made me wonder if I'd misjudged the depth of their bond. Mom's diagnosis gutted me, and caring for her as she fell further into decline broke my heart.

I sourced organic chicken and vegetables to cook her broth, the only thing she could keep down once the drugs kicked in. I fed her, I helped her bathe and when that got too hard I'd give her sponge baths in bed, making sure she turned regularly to avoid pressure sores. I read to her, inane celebrity gossip in online magazines that she once devoured. I tried to engage her in cards, as one of the few good memories I had of my parents being calm was watching them play poker together, neither blinking or giving away a winning hand. But she wasn't interested in playing poker with me and soon she took to staring at me in stoic silence. She wouldn't hear of going into palliative care so I sat by her bed when she took her final breath, when she finally reached out to clutch my hand, her gaze filled with love as she passed.

Cam stood by me through it all. He's my rock and I've fallen deeper in love with him. We're close and while our relationship hasn't taken the ultimate step yet, I'm hopeful. He'll comfort me now that Mom's gone, I'll cling to him, and he'll realize I'm alone. I need him and I'm confident he'll do the right thing and embrace me into his world.

Then Diana comes home and everything changes.

"Why are you having a memorial and not a proper funeral?" A deep frown grooves her brow as her pink-glossed lips purse in disapproval. The lipstick is inappropriate on this day of mourning, though at least she's worn black. It should make her look washed out, but somehow it doesn't.

"Because we can't afford it," I snap, hating that she's been back in Verdant five minutes and she's already judging me. Hating her for not coming home earlier to help me nurse Mom. Hating her for everything.

Her huff of exasperation riles me further, like I've disappointed her in some way.

"Are you heading back to Long Island after the service?"

Her gaze slides away, evasive, as she shakes her head. "No. I'm home for good."

Shock renders me speechless for a moment before I gather my wits. "What? Why? You've only been away seven months. You can't drop out."

She squares her shoulders, a familiar determination lighting her eyes as she refocuses on me. "I'm not going back, Sis. I'm staying. This is where I belong. With Mom gone you're the only family I have left and I don't want to waste my time being with people who don't matter to me. Life's too short."

I should be happy my sister cares enough about me to want to give up her studies to come home. But dread creeps through me. I know the bond I've built with Cam, the camaraderie I hope will develop into something more now Mom's gone, will amount to nothing.

Diana is back and I'll lose him.

I want to kill her in that moment. I want to wrap my hands around her throat and squeeze the life out of her. A rage unlike anything I've ever experienced sweeps through me and I start to tremble with it.

She must see something in my eyes because she takes a step back. "Why are you looking at me like that?"

Because I hate you.

Because I resent you for escaping and not being witness to Mom being ravaged by that awful disease.

Because you're never around when I need you.

But I say none of it. Instead, I turn my back on her and head for the door. "Let's go say goodbye to Mom."

There's a small crowd gathered around the plaque on a grassy knoll set in the back corner of the cemetery. Our family isn't particularly well known in Verdant. My parents didn't have a lot of friends. They never entertained and we didn't visit other families. Diana was my best friend and despite her being popular at school she didn't accept a lot of social invitations. I knew why; probably too ashamed to invite kids back to our place when it was her turn to reciprocate.

So I recognize most of the ten-strong crowd. Our elderly neighbors who'd babysat Di and me when we were younger, Mom's boss, and a few co-workers from the supermarket where she'd managed the deli for years, and Cam.

I see the exact moment he catches sight of Diana, the moment my heart splinters into a million pieces. His eyes light up in a way they never have for me and he's moving toward her, oblivious to everyone but her. I glance over my shoulder to see her eyes fill with tears as she presses a hand to her mouth and half runs toward him.

I want to yell at the injustice of this.

Instead, I watch the man I love embrace the woman he loves.

And it's not me.

It will never be me.

CHAPTER NINE
FREYA

I hover nearby as Brooke and Hope get acquainted. I could blame my protective maternal instincts but it's more than that.

Brooke will leave again and I'm worried I'm making a mistake in letting my daughter get close to someone who will abandon her. I'd resented Brooke when she left and didn't return. Initially, I understood. She had to get away because I watched her deteriorate after she lost Eli. Consumed by grief, she couldn't keep food down, lost weight, became pale and listless, a shadow moving through the house. She'd ignored me, when I'd been devastated by his death too. Eli had almost become part of the family; he'd been at our house so often. But Brooke hadn't seen any of that so when she went away I thought she'd come back better. Instead, she abandoned me.

A stupid, irrational thought because it wasn't her fault she had to flee Martino Bay. The kids who'd been her close friends made it unbearable for her to stay. Eli's death changed everything for her and, in turn, for me too.

They'd judged me initially when I came back to town after having Hope; a teen mom, father unknown, the sister of that bad girl whose boyfriend committed suicide after she dumped him. I'd hibernated for the first eighteen months, eschewing offers to attend a moms' group for teens or play dates organized by a social worker. I'd tried it once, with a group of young moms in the park, but I'd felt like an outsider because all those moms had been a bit older than me and had partners. While they boasted about shared parenting duties, I was up most nights tending to a grizzly, teething Hope. As they planned to give their perfect kids more siblings, I could barely cope with one child. I'd hated the pitying stares the most and that had been my first and last foray into bonding with fellow moms.

Hope had been my focus and nothing else mattered. She got me through the loneliness of losing my sister. For my twenty-first, Aunt Alice had offered to babysit so I could go out and celebrate with my friends. Friends? I didn't have any. Nobody genuine. A few people from high school used to pop in occasionally but we had nothing in common any more. While I was changing diapers and dealing with colic, they were heading off to LA for spa dates. While I could barely pull on jeans and a T-shirt in the morning, they were buying the latest fashion online to wear for glitzy Saturday night dates. We drifted apart so by the time I hit twenty-one, I had no one to celebrate with bar Aunt Alice and Lizzie, who gave me the best present ever: a day to myself, spent wandering the cliffs, a picnic lunch for one, and the latest blockbuster thriller that I read for an entire afternoon.

As Hope grew older and Brooke stayed away, townsfolk stopped casting me sly glances. Gradually, I earned their acceptance and respect by raising a polite child, completing a nursing degree, and volunteering for everything I could, more than the other moms combined. I paid my dues, but that didn't change how much I missed Brooke when she didn't come home and I fear my daughter will get too attached to a flakey aunt who will probably abscond after the wedding.

"Wow, you're good at that," Brooke says, leaning toward Hope as my daughter sketches.

Their heads almost touch, my sister's strawberry-blonde hair a stark contrast against my daughter's dark brown, but they wear the same matching expression: contentment. It's the first time I've seen Brooke appear relaxed since she got home and I'm glad. It can't be easy for her.

"Hey, you two, want some lemonade?"

They look up simultaneously and once again I'm struck by a faint similarity, more the mannerism than their actual looks. I'm interested to hear what Hope thinks of her aunt later. My child is open and affectionate and happily gravitates toward people. She's a hit at the nursing home where I work—the oldies love her—and now I can see my sister falling a little in love with her too.

I should be glad. Brooke has missed out on so much and if she wants a relationship with my daughter I should facilitate it. But my old insecurities are prompting me to wonder if my precious daughter will end up liking her vivacious aunt more than me.

"Do we get cookies too?" Hope grins and presses her palms together. "Please, Mom?"

"Sure, honey." I can never resist my daughter at her charming best. Besides, she knows I won't say no in front of Brooke. Hope's smart, knowing when she can twist me around her finger.

Brooke watches this exchange between us and I can't help but preen a little at the envy in her eyes. I'm no longer an afterthought in my family; I hold them together and I'm proud.

"Lemonade okay with you, Brooke?"

She nods and returns her attention to Hope's drawings. "Is that a rose?"

Just like that she has Hope's attention again and the two of them murmur, their smiles frequent, while I'm left feeling like an outsider. Ridiculous, when it's natural they'll bond, but having Brooke back in my life has dredged up old feelings of inadequacy I thought long conquered.

I busy myself with the snacks and when I place them on the table I get a muted "thanks" before they return to their soft chatter. Biting back a sigh, I say, "I'm popping out to see Riker, be back soon."

"Okay, Mom," Hope says, but she's still looking at Brooke like a shiny new toy she can't quite believe has dropped in her lap, while Brooke gives me a casual wave that indicates I won't be missed at all.

I leave them with a heavy heart, hating my resentment. I should be glad my daughter openly adores Brooke so quickly—my sister has a knack for making people like her, everyone adored her when we were growing up—but I'm the only one my daughter usually looks at like that. Though oddly, I don't mind when she treats Riker with blatant adoration. She loves him wholeheartedly and I know it won't be long before she asks if she can call him dad. Our courtship has been a whirlwind six months and maybe it's too soon but I'm encouraging their bond because it makes us one big happy family, something I've craved my entire life.

I know where Riker will be, in the barn behind his cottage. He practically lives in that makeshift studio, often forgetting to share meals with us. Though he's diligent when it comes to Hope and not missing any of her important stuff like helping complete a project for the science fair or preparing for a math test. I never would've picked him for a bookworm but he's devoted to reading with Hope too and it warms my heart to see the two of them together at night, Hope tucked in beneath the covers and Riker sitting on top of them, dissecting the latest chapter of the book she's reading.

I'm worrying about nothing. Brooke will never take the place of Riker in Hope's eyes even if she sticks around, and I'm her mom, Brooke can never surpass me there.

When I reach the barn and peer around the half-shut door, Riker's placing his welder back in its case before pushing up his facemask. He's sweaty, the cotton of his grey T-shirt clinging to his back in patches, rivulets of it dripping down his face. My pulse races as I watch him swipe the sweat away with the back of his hand. The initial passion of our first month together wore off quickly and these days sex is infrequent. I've got a lot on my mind with Alice, then inviting Brooke back home. I've been worried and that has exacerbated my usual post-work fatigue. Thankfully, Riker doesn't seem to mind, making me love him all the more.

On the nights I sneak into his cottage he holds me in his arms and listens to me offload, stroking my hair or cradling me tight, making me feel more connected to him than I ever have. I crave intimacy rather than intercourse and Riker is okay with that.

I enter the barn and wolf whistle. His head snaps up and for a moment I glimpse annoyance before his usual affable grin lights his face.

"Hey, gorgeous, what are you doing here?"

"Interrupting a master at work." I cross the dirt floor to clasp his face between my hands and kiss him, a long, lingering melding of lips that has him palming my ass and pressing his pelvis against mine.

"I'm all for interruptions like this," he murmurs against the corner of my mouth, grinding against me until I moan a little.

"The door's open and anyone can wander in," I say, hating to be the voice of reason when he releases me and steps away.

"Tease." But there's no venom in his voice and he winks, reaching out to swat my ass. "I'm supposed to be working. Did you need something?"

"No." I drift toward his latest creation, a life-size unicorn made from car metal scraps—Hope will go mad for it—and caress the cool metal with my palm. "Brooke's spending some time getting to know Hope so I wanted to give them space."

"That's great. It'll be good for Hope to get to know her aunt." He's surprisingly animated. "They seem a lot alike in some ways."

"What do you mean?"

The old jealousy flares in an instant. We haven't discussed how well Riker knows Brooke yet, haven't had a chance really. Brooke dismissed it as a casual meeting at a party but is there more to it? I can't bear the thought and I'm instantly on guard, wanting to delve but terrified of the answers.

"They're old souls," he says, oblivious to my inner torment. "Hope's ten going on thirty and you can see that same worldly expression in Brooke's eyes."

"And exactly how long have you spent staring into my sister's eyes?" I snap, regretting my outburst when he winces.

"Whoa." He holds up his hands. "Where did that come from?"

"Sorry." I swipe a hand over my face, knowing I'll have to give him some semblance of truth to smooth over my faux pas. "You know I've been nervous about Brooke's return, so I guess knowing you two met before has me a little on edge."

His expression softens as he approaches me and snags my hands. "We met at a party, once, when we were teenagers. I think we said hi, can't even remember if we talked, that's it. I didn't even know her name, which is why I didn't make the connection when you've talked about her before. And if I had, I would've told you." He squeezes my hands. "You have nothing to worry about. I'm not that kind of guy."

He lifts one of my hands to his mouth and presses a kiss to the back of it. "I'm marrying you. You, Hope and me are going to be a family. That's all I care about, okay?"

I nod and slip into his arms, but as he hugs me tight I'm not reassured. In fact, I can't shake the feeling I'm missing something and welcoming Brooke back into our lives may be the stupidest thing I've done in a long time.

CHAPTER TEN
BROOKE

I'm in love.

For the first time in my life I've fallen head over heels.

My niece is perfect.

I love her and I barely know her.

Crazy, but the minute we sat down and started sketching together I experienced a weird breathlessness, an expanding in my chest, a feeling of such warmth and completeness I know it has to be love. I've never had it before, being so instantly enamored, and I can't stop marveling at every little thing she does, like dotting her "i's" with little lopsided hearts, like the way her tongue pokes out when she's trying hard to draw a particularly difficult unicorn, like the way she wriggles with excitement in her seat when she finishes a drawing.

She's utterly adorable and while I love her, I'm also howling on the inside.

I could've had this.

A child to cherish, to lavish love on, to be with me so I'm not alone.

Would my son have liked art like I do or would he have preferred smashing a baseball into the outfield or scoring a touchdown? Would he have wanted to sit with me at a table lamenting the lack of real unicorns or would he have deemed me too frivolous and enjoyed sword-fighting with a nameless nemesis online? Would he have leaned against me like Hope is already doing or would he have been too tough to show affection toward his mom?

Crazy, because I was never keeping him anyway. I'd done the right thing and signed the adoption papers. But I never had the chance to say goodbye. The drugs may have helped with the labor pains but they did nothing for my broken heart when I glimpsed that bluish face wrapped in a bundle before they took him away.

My baby had died and there's no coming back from that.

A sorrow so profound, so overwhelming, makes my head spin and I grip the table.

"Auntie Brooke, what's wrong?" Hope snuggles into me instantly and I drag in a breath, another, before I can speak.

"I'm a bit sad at missing out on spending time with you all these years," I say, settling for a half-truth as emotion wells in my chest for my baby boy I never got to hold.

"It's okay, we've got plenty of time now." She slides her arms around my waist and hugs me tight, and I battle tears that are desperate to fall.

I hug her back, this openly affectionate child who still seems so innocent for her age yet worldly at the same time, and I know I have to take care not to dump all my long-buried maternal instincts onto her. I'd always been happy in my life growing up, content. I loved Freya, even if her prying eyes and passive-aggressive games got to me at times. But I never resented her, until now.

She has the one thing I wish I had.

A happy, healthy child.

When mine was cruelly ripped from me long ago and it shouldn't hurt so much now.

"Did that hug make you feel better?" Hope wriggles out of my embrace and fixes me with a solemn stare. "Riker says hugs make everything better and he's really smart."

Riker, another problem I can't deal with right now.

"I do feel better, thanks." I tap the tip of her nose. "I think you're pretty smart too, young lady."

Hope giggles, a spontaneous happy sound that warms my heart. "I can draw other stuff besides unicorns. Wanna see?"

"Sure do," I say, leaning into her as she starts sketching, subtly inhaling the sweet berry fragrance of her shampoo and struggling to quash my grief at losing my boy.

I need to move on.

Difficult to do with reminders of a past I'd rather forget around every corner.

CHAPTER ELEVEN

ALICE

THEN

It's unbearable.

Relentless agony grips me as I witness Diana and Cam fall into a whirlwind romance that results in a low-key wedding five months after she returns home, the birth of their first child Brooke six months after that and the arrival of Freya eleven months later.

My glamorous, spoilt sister should struggle with two kids under one. She doesn't. She practically glows whenever Cam glances her way and while she gets the baby blues for a while after Freya, she's soon back to her old confident self with the help of meds and a counselor.

And I'm around for it all; the loving sister, the perfect sister-in-law, the doting aunt.

While on the inside I die a little every day.

Diana didn't even hesitate to start dating Cam. She acted like it's her God-given right that he's hers, from the moment they laid eyes on each other at Mom's memorial service. I don't blame Cam. He never led me on or professed any kind of affection beyond friendship. I'd been the one to harbor secret desires that he'd eventually see me as more.

But I blame her.

I blame her to the point of wishing she had never come back.

It's been less than two years, twenty-two months to be exact, since she returned and stole the life that should've been mine.

It's hard pretending. Exhausting to the point of me being unable to eat most nights after work and falling into bed, drained and dazed. The fatigue is always worse on the days I have to see her, sitting pretty in Cam's house while he cooks dinner and kid-wrangles, clearly happy to do it for his adoring wife.

The resentment is choking me as I stride around the back of their house, shoving aside the memory of doing exactly this years earlier, filled with hope on the night I'd planned to reveal my true feelings to Cam. It feels like another lifetime ago, like I've suffered and endured more than the average person since, and I know I'm near breaking point.

Diana has summoned me tonight, a few weeks since Freya's birth, about some legal issue that can't wait. I'm sure it's nothing, something minor that could've waited until next week, but when my sister commands my presence I run because there's always a chance I'll see Cam.

I'm pathetic. Unable to date, unable to move on, stuck in some weird limbo where I'm pining for a man I can never have, a man I now have to see way too often because he's my brother-in-law.

It's Diana's fault. She's entrapped me in this awful scenario. I'll do anything to escape.

She's sitting on the back porch, sipping an iced tea, as I approach.

"Hey, Al, want a drink?"

I shake my head. "What's up?"

She glances over her shoulder, before relaxing a tad. "Cam's putting the girls to bed so we can talk. I wanted to let you know that we did our wills today and if anything happens to us, you'll be the girls' legal guardian."

I know I should say something at this apparent honor being bestowed upon me but I'm speechless, because in that moment I imagine Diana removed from her happy family scenario and me taking her place.

"If that's what you want, sure." I force a smile. "I'll love those girls like my own if anything ever happens."

Diana beams and raises her glass in a toast. "You're the best, Sis. I intend to live to a ripe old age and watch my grandchildren grow but when you have kids it pays to be prepared, you know?"

Actually, I don't, and at the rate I'm going I never will. The thought of having a husband and kids is so far out of the realms of possibility for me I don't even think about it most days.

How can I, when I still obsess over my sister's husband and the life that should've been mine?

I hear footfalls behind me and brace. I'm always like this around Cam; wanting to see him, wanting to flee, terrified he'll read every single emotion in my eyes. Diana won't; she's too self-absorbed to consider another woman might want her husband and especially not her plain Jane sister.

"Hey, Alice, did Di tell you the news?" He rests a hand on my shoulder for a moment in a friendly greeting and I grit my teeth against the urge to cover it with mine.

"Yes, and I'm honored, thanks."

He moves toward Diana to place a lingering kiss on her lips and I look away.

"We couldn't think of anyone else who'd love our girls as much as we do," he says, pulling a chair alongside Diana and sitting. "You're the best."

I manage a tight smile. "I have to go. I'll try to pop in tomorrow."

"Okay," Diana says, oblivious to my turmoil, while Cam studies me with the faintest frown lines creasing his brow. Di doesn't ask me to stay. Instead, she's done what she always does: command my presence, tell me her news, and expects me to slink away so she can continue living her perfect life.

"Thanks for dropping by." Diana smiles and I mentally will Cam to walk me out so I can have him to myself for a few scant moments.

But he merely nods and smiles too, leaving me striding away from them as fast as I can.

This is too much. Diana expects me to be grateful she's deemed to let me have her children if something were to happen to both of them. Like it's my duty. Like I don't have any say in the matter. It's presumptuous and so like my self-absorbed sister I shouldn't be surprised.

Yet I can't help but think... what if it was just Diana who was removed from this scenario?

CHAPTER TWELVE
BROOKE

I've been back a week, which means the wedding is only twenty-one days away, yet I'm still no closer to feeling a part of it, which is strange considering that's why Freya asked me to come home a few weeks before the ceremony. Freya spends all day at work and most evenings volunteering, Riker avoids me, Aunt Alice hasn't recognized me once; only Hope and Lizzie seem glad I'm around.

Tonight I have the place to myself. Lizzie has taken Hope to ballet, Riker's on an overnight delivery for one of his sculptures and Freya is volunteering with a local women's association. So I sit beside Alice's bed, reading to her from a dog-eared copy of *Pride and Prejudice*, as she'd once done to me.

One of my favorite memories growing up was being tucked into bed at night and having her read to me. Freya hadn't been much of a reader; it always made me wonder why she fought so hard to stake her place in the reading nook beside Lizzie and me. But Alice had nurtured my inner bookworm and I'd been hooked from a young age. Jane Austen had been my favorite because it had been hers. My aunt would come alive reading those romantic tales filled with sibling rivalry and brooding, handsome men. Now, as I turn the page and cast a glance her way, I hope she's deriving as much pleasure from this simple activity as I once did.

"Stop," she whispers, her voice reedy. "No more about sisters."

I've visited her every day, usually for at least thirty minutes in the morning, but she's never lucid and she always mumbles about sisters. She never hid the fact that when our mom died she gladly became our guardian but because I was so young, only just over a year old, Alice has always been my mom. When my life imploded she took care of everything. I love her and I hate seeing her like this.

"This is my favorite book, it used to be yours too." I slide a bookmark between the worn pages and lean forward to smile in reassurance. "I reckon we could both recite the thing by heart."

Her eyes fix on me, suddenly bright. "You were always a good girl. Not like my sister."

She stabs a finger at the door. Her eyes narrow and her breathing becomes rapid. "I'm going to burn in hell for what I did."

Mystified by her outburst, and hoping my reading to her hasn't confused her more, I lay a comforting hand over hers where it rests on the duvet. "Auntie, you're confused—"

"I'm not!" she yells, yanking her hand away from mine. "I have ruined so many lives. I'm a bad, bad person and she is too. Damn Diana to hell."

Drained, she slumps further into the pillows and turns her head away from me. I don't know what to say. I've agitated her somehow and wish I knew what to do in a situation like this. Freya had warned me not to stress Aunt Alice by talking about the past and Lizzie had said she chatted as normal to her mom every day, so that's what I've been doing too. So what brought on this outburst? What did my mother do that has my aunt riled all these years later, even with her advancing dementia? I want to ask but it's no use, she's already snoring softly. Besides, everything she said could be the rambling of a confused woman, as Freya and Lizzie warned me about.

Laying the book on the bedside table, I move around the room, tidying up. Alice's laptop is open at the end of her bed, the screen black. I remember her tapping at the keyboard most nights and I always wondered what she'd have to diarize. Our aunt had led a staid life but I guess we all need an outlet and keeping a diary had been hers. Lizzie said Aunt Alice had kept it up and is still obsessed with scouring the Internet, even if she doesn't understand half the things she sees. I close it before I'm tempted to pry. What if Aunt Alice kept a record of what my mother is supposed to have done? Would my knowing bring Aunt Alice some comfort if I could reassure her it's not half as bad as what she thinks?

It's wrong, justifying my urge to delve. I want to do it out of sheer curiosity because I know next to nothing about my mother. Growing up, Alice rarely mentioned Diana. Freya never seemed to care but a small part of me always wanted to know more about my parents. I have nothing of them bar a photo after Freya was born, with me in my dad's arms, Freya in Mom's, the two of them staring at each other with so much love it's like Freya and I were excluded. I still have the photo. It's one of few I carried around with me all these years, moving from town to town, job to job.

My glance drifts back to the laptop. What secrets does it contain?

Aunt Alice makes a loud sound, halfway between a snort and a groan, shifting restlessly in her sleep, and I pick up the laptop and place it on the movable table next to the bed. I back away, not wanting to disturb her.

I'll ask Lizzie if she knows anything. Discovering more about the parents I never knew will give me something to do while I wait, hoping to be reabsorbed into this family.

CHAPTER THIRTEEN
FREYA

When I get home, Brooke is curled up in the corner of the sofa, cradling a mug of steaming peppermint tea. Over the years, the smell of anything remotely resembling mint reminded me of her. She's staring into space. It's her thinking pose. She used to do it all the time as a teen. Though what did she have to think about? How to turn that A into an A+ in algebra? How to sweet-talk Eli into gifting her yet another piece of cutesy jewelry? How to wear her crown as prom queen?

What Brooke went through with losing Eli eradicated her charmed life. I'd hoped her hardship would bring us closer but she'd run away eight weeks after his death and never returned; until now. It makes me wonder why she's come home. Did she really want to attend my wedding so badly she set aside her resentment for this place and her bad memories? Or is there a deeper reason for her return?

In those eight weeks before she left home years ago, she'd already mentally checked out. She ignored me, wrapped up in her grief, drifting through the house like a ghost. I'd been helpless, unsure what to say or do, and a small part of me had been angry too. I hadn't died. I was right in front of her and she didn't care. It had almost been a relief when she'd left, until I started missing her fiercely.

I still harbor abandonment issues, which may be why I'm determined to nurse Aunt Alice at home. I want to keep her close so she won't leave me too.

"Hey, you're looking awfully pensive." I enter the lounge room, unwinding my scarf before shrugging off my jacket and sitting next to her. "What's up?"

"Nothing, really, just thinking about the past." She sips at her tea, a tiny frown appearing between her brows. "Do you know much about our parents?"

"Not really. Aunt Alice never spoke about them."

"Do you ever wonder why?"

"I figure it's too painful for her, losing her only sister when we were practically babies."

"Yeah, I guess." Brooke's frown deepens. "She never talked about Dad either."

The last thing I feel like doing after a long session helping the local women's association knit baby booties is rehashing the past. But I can see something is bugging Brooke and if this gives us an opportunity to grow closer, I'm all for it. "What's brought this on?"

She shrugs, her expression contemplative. "I guess being back here has made me feel nostalgic. I mean, I expected coming home after all this time would dredge stuff up, but the way Aunt Alice rambles about sisters and secrets makes me think there was something going on with our mom we never knew about."

The last thing I want to do is examine the past. I'm more than happy to shed it and move forward into a brighter future, but it's true that neither of us know much about our mother and father.

"What would change if we knew more about our parents?" I lay my hands out like I have nothing to hide. "Trying to force memories out of Aunt Alice can be detrimental to her health. She'll become agitated at a time when I'm trying to keep things as peaceful as possible for her."

Brooke appears suitably chastised. "You're doing an incredible job caring for her. I'm really proud of you."

Brooke's admiration means a lot because I struggle every single day, watching my once vibrant aunt deteriorate before my eyes.

She'd been amazing in the early years when I knew nothing about raising a child. She'd helped me with Hope from day one, as loving and attentive to me as she was to my daughter. The trials of motherhood made me love her all the more when I realized she'd taken on Brooke and me when she had her own daughter, at an age only five years older than when I had Hope.

"She's really been there for me all these years. It's the least I can do." I press a hand to my heart. "But it hurts to watch her fade away and there's not one damn thing I can do about it."

Brooke tilts her head, studying me. "It must be tough, dealing with dementia all day every day at your job, then coming home to do the same for Aunt Alice."

"Aunt Alice is a sweetie because she's never aggressive." I grimace. "Dementia affects different people in different ways and I've had some patients flip out."

Brooke blinks rapidly, like she's on the verge of tears. "You are something else, Sis."

She clasps my hand and we sit in silence, tears shimmering in our eyes. It's the best moment we've had since she came home.

"I'm glad you're here," I say, and mean it. I hadn't known what to expect when I invited Brooke to the wedding but I'm glad I did. I've missed this. For all our bickering as kids, and for all my mood swings as a teen, we are inherently the same. Family. Connected.

"Me too."

She releases my hand to dash it across her eyes. "Sorry for getting all maudlin on you, but seeing Aunt Alice the way she is, when I remember how vibrant she used to be, is tough."

"I get it. She's the only mom we ever knew."

Our bonding has lulled me into a false sense of security when Brooke says, "I spent some time reading to her today and she started rambling worse than usual."

I try not to show my fear. Nothing Alice says these days makes sense so I shouldn't be afraid of her spilling secrets. But I am.

Terrified, in fact. I've built a carefully constructed life. Nothing and nobody will tear it down.

"You get used to the ramblings after a while." I feign a nonchalance I don't feel.

She turns a speculative stare onto me. "You've got a lot on your plate. Have you thought about putting her into a facility, like the one you work at?"

I shake my head. "Absolutely not. Aunt Alice did everything for us growing up, the least I can do is look after her when she needs me the most." My vehemence startles her a little and I tone it down. "It's up to Lizzie, really, and if she's happy for me to be her mom's nurse, who am I to argue with that?"

Brooke nods, but she hasn't lost the inquisitive stare, like she knows I'm not telling her everything.

"You've changed, Freya," she says, with a teasing smile. "For the better. You're more patient these days, more caring."

I chuckle. "Thanks, I think."

"I guess we've all changed," she murmurs, lifting the cup to her mouth and taking another sip, her expression far away, back to ruminating.

"I'm tired." I stand and interlink my hands, stretching overhead. "I'm going to check in on Aunt Alice then go to bed."

"Goodnight," Brooke murmurs, still deep in thought, so I leave her to it.

As long as my inquisitive sister doesn't over-think things, we'll be fine.

CHAPTER FOURTEEN

ALICE

THEN

A week later, I bake a cake for Brooke's first birthday. It's a chocolate and vanilla marble covered in pink frosting and tiny marzipan farm animals. I'm not a baker generally but I take extra care with this one because my niece deserves all the good things in life, even if her mother doesn't.

Brooke is adorable, with blonde curls that cling to her scalp, big blue eyes so like her father's, and a perpetual grin. She always reaches her arms out when she sees me and I love picking her up, having her snuggle into me. She's the only good thing about visiting Diana and Cam; at four weeks, Freya is too young to know me.

The party is small, the friends that Cam and I used to hang out with, including Dave who's surprisingly still with Mandy, and Diana's best friend, Amy. Diana and Amy used to spend countless hours poring over magazines of boy bands or painting each other's nails or rollerblading in front of the football play field. I'd been jealous of their closeness and wondered if Amy suggested stuff for them to do that would exclude me. Now, Amy's hovering next to Diana, cooing over Freya, a good-looking quarterback-type with broad shoulders, lean waist, and a chiseled jaw, holding her hand.

I take care placing the cake on the main table, before lifting its plastic cover. It looks spectacular among the store-bought mini cupcakes and even though Brooke won't remember it, I will. I did this for my niece, the only person who ever seems happy to see me in this household.

Diana catches sight of me and lifts her hand in a half-hearted wave. I know she's had a relapse over the last few days and is struggling again with postnatal depression but Cam says she's doing fine with the meds and the counseling.

I make my way toward her. Pasting a smile on my face, I bend to kiss her and Freya.

"How are my girls today?"

"We're good," Diana says. "The cake looks amazing. Thanks for that."

"You're welcome."

We're always like this these days, stilted, barely able to make polite small talk.

"Where's the birthday girl? I have her gift in the car."

"Brooke's napping, but should be awake soon." Diana gestures at Amy. "You know Amy?"

"Yeah. How are you?"

"Good," Amy says, before actually turning her back on me to murmur something to her boyfriend. Her rudeness is astounding but nothing new. When Diana's around, I'm invisible to most people.

"I'll get something to drink. Do you want anything?" I ask Diana, who shakes her head.

"Cam's manning the bar. Tell him to make you something strong and fruity."

The last thing I need is to imbibe alcohol of any kind that can loosen my tongue. But I make a beeline for the makeshift bar, a row of coolers filled with ice and drinks. Cam's nowhere in sight and I'm relieved. It doesn't last long. As I select a lemon soda and straighten I feel a light touch on my arm and turn around to find Amy beside me.

"Hey." I twist the lid off my soda bottle. "Sorry, did you want a drink?"

"I'm good," she says, her gaze darting over my shoulder. "But I wanted to talk to you about Di."

"Oh?"

Why on earth would this woman, who's ignored me for the last umpteen years, want to talk to me about anything, let alone my sister?

"I'm worried about her," Amy says, sounding genuinely concerned. "I know she's getting help for her postnatal depression but I think there's more than the baby blues at play here."

"Like what?"

Amy casts another furtive glance around before leaning forward, close enough our shoulders touch. "I think having Brooke and Freya so close together hasn't made up for giving up the other one and she's struggling."

I'm lost. What the hell is she babbling about?

Giving up the other one...

"We're probably the only ones who know," she continues, oblivious to my confusion. "I don't think she's even told Cam. But I wanted to flag it with you because you see her more often than I do and I'm really worried she's pining for her firstborn."

I manage to say, "Thanks for letting me know, I'll keep an eye on her," before Amy drifts away.

Only then do I allow myself to collapse onto the nearest hay bale near the bar, a bunch of them laid around the backyard as part of the farm theme.

I'm reeling, shock making my hand shake as I raise the soda bottle to my lips. After several gulps, the sugar hit hasn't eased my trembling.

Diana hadn't gone to college.

She'd gone away to have a baby.

Cam's baby, if the timeline fit.

She left two months after the party, the night she stole him from me, and came home just over seven months later.

And Mom must've orchestrated the entire thing.

Why hadn't either of them trusted me with the truth? Even on her deathbed, Mom had kept the secret. If she'd confided in me, maybe I could've done something to help. I could've encouraged Di to come home and I could've supported her through the birth and beyond.

If I ever needed proof I didn't matter in my family, this is it. Neither of them trusted me to tell me the truth. Even Amy knew before me.

My sister has another child out there somewhere, a child she gave away.

Cam's child.

That's when the rage comes, flooding my veins, making red spots dance before my eyes. That sweet, supportive, incredible man doesn't deserve to be lied to. He's lost a baby too and he never even knew.

It's the last straw for me. Not only had Diana had sex with Cam the night she took him from me, she lied about it, then gave away her baby before waltzing back here, stealing him all over again, and having the audacity to marry him and have more kids when she'd abandoned her first.

It's wrong on so many levels.

In that moment, as I struggle to deal with the fact my sister is lying to her husband, lying to us all, my dislike for her morphs into something akin to hatred.

CHAPTER FIFTEEN
BROOKE

I run into Riker the next morning.

I heard his van pull in around dawn and interestingly, rather than slipping into the main house to be with Freya, he headed for his cottage. From what I've observed over the last week they have a weird relationship. They don't spend a lot of time together and they're rarely alone. When they hang out it's usually with Hope. Their public displays of affection are minimal, especially for a couple only dating six months. And I don't sense a strong bond between them; it's more a comfortable melding of a contented couple. They seem happy enough but there's a distinct lack of spark for two people about to get married.

Freya seems her usual pragmatic self and isn't at all dizzy over wedding cake or catering or dresses, and Riker never mentions the upcoming nuptials. I see them hold hands or gaze fondly at each other rarely, but Riker seems more enamored with Hope than his fiancée. We have that in common; she's my favorite person too.

He's offhand around me, keeping his distance, and we're never alone in the same room together, but we have to talk for no other reason than I want to gauge how much Freya knows about our past. I don't want to slip up and cause problems for them unnecessarily, so I corner him as he slips into his work studio, a giant barn behind his cottage.

"Hey, can we talk?"

He jumps and whirls around to face me. "What are you doing in here?"

"Saying hello to my soon-to-be brother-in-law," I drawl, annoyed by his bristly personality. "You've been avoiding me."

"It's better that way."

He folds his arms and glares at me, like this is my fault. It's not. There were two of us going at it that night eleven years ago and I've paid my dues. My guilt taints everything I do, but I can't help that he's engaged to my sister now.

Technically, we mean nothing to each other. A random hook-up. But what happened with Riker had devastating consequences. I came clean to Eli about my indiscretion and I'll never get over my guilt at causing Eli's death.

"What did you tell Freya about us? She hasn't asked me anything about it yet, but just in case I want to make sure our stories are the same."

"Nothing." His lips are thin, compressed, like he can't bear talking to me. "No point dredging up the past. It was a blip, a one-night stand. She'll go ballistic if she suspects anything happened between us. I told her we met at a party and barely spoke," he says, dragging a hand through his shaggy hair. I'd done the same thing the night he took me up against the wall in that shed.

"Well, you're right about one thing, we did barely speak that night."

He barks out a laugh at my droll response. "When I came back to town, you were gone."

He's given me the perfect opening to tell him.

How I told Eli what had happened.

How I broke up with him and then lost him forever.

How I'm responsible for Eli's death.

I could tell him everything but what would be the point?

"A lot happened and I always wanted to leave this place anyway."

His astute stare bores into me, coolly assessing. "Freya says you never went to college, that you hit the road and have been drifting since."

"Something like that," I say, shrugging. "Surely you can understand that whim? No ties, moving from town to town."

That's one snippet of information he'd shared with me before we'd kissed, how he'd left home at sixteen, using his art to fund his lifestyle, exploring as many towns within California as he could. Riker had intrigued me from the start and he'd fed my own subdued wanderlust with tales of adventure. It had made him irresistible and for that one hour at a party long ago, I'd lost my mind and had mind-blowing sex with a virtual stranger.

He nods slowly, almost reluctantly. "Yeah, I get it."

I lock gazes with him and something indefinable, something forbidden, shimmers between us. Must be all this talk of the past and I give myself a little shake to break the invisible bond.

"Anyway, I just wanted to make sure we're on the same page when it comes to Freya," I say, backing toward the door. "Nice work, by the way. Maybe I can stop by some other time and take a look?"

"Anytime," he says, and this time I don't imagine the warmth in his eyes, heating my skin like a physical caress.

"See you later."

I push through the barn door and bump straight into Freya.

CHAPTER SIXTEEN
BROOKE

"What were you doing in there?"

Freya's accusatory tone catapults me back to the first time I brought Eli home. He'd barely left after we shared a pizza and watched a horror film before she'd whirled on me, bristling with indignation for not telling her I had a boyfriend. I knew what was behind her outrage; I'd been caught up in the throes of a new romance and not spending as much time with my sister and she resented it. I'd felt guilty and vowed to make it up to her. She'd been placated when I spent the next weekend with her—going to the movies, rollerblading, and having a camp out in our backyard like we used to when we were kids—but I always felt like she resented my relationship with Eli because it excluded her.

Now, like then, her eyes glow with a peculiar, fanatical light and I scramble to appease her. "I haven't seen inside Riker's workshop yet so I stuck my head around the door," I say, keeping my tone light. "But he's in the middle of something, so I guess I'll take a look another time."

"He's a busy guy, you shouldn't disturb him unless he invites you in." She crosses her arms, disapproval radiating off her, and I'm relieved she hasn't overheard our conversation because this situation could've been so much worse.

"Got it. I guess I'm at a loose end and it's weird being back here."

Freya studies me, like she's still not convinced of my reason for popping in on Riker. "You've been away a long time, it's to be expected."

"Is there anything I can do to help with the wedding preparations?"

She shakes her head. "I've got it under control."

"But isn't that why you wanted me to come home earlier, to help with the wedding plans?"

She hesitates, as if searching for the right words, before shrugging. "I asked you to come back early so we could bond again. I used the wedding prep as an excuse."

I admire her honesty and want to set her mind at ease. "You never have to worry about Riker and me. We met briefly in the past, that's it."

"I know." She manages a rueful smile. "I sounded crazy jealous before, didn't I?"

I hold up my thumb and forefinger an inch apart. "Maybe a little?"

Her expression is bashful, her gaze wistful as it fixes on the barn door. "Sometimes I wonder how I got so lucky…" she mumbles.

I hear a hint of vulnerability and it gets to me. It's the first time since I've returned home that she's been completely unarmed, and it's a much nicer side to my sister. The thing is, I get where she's coming from. The night I fell for Riker's charms had been so unexpected, so intense, it left me reeling. Eli and I had walked into that party at a friend's house on top of the cliffs and everything had changed.

Technically, it wasn't the first time I laid eyes on Riker. He'd been in town a few times that summer and we'd locked eyes outside the ice-cream shop once. Corny, but true, and I'd felt his steely gaze all the way to my toes, the buzz of animal magnetism unforgettable. Riker had made me feel more alive, more aware of myself as a woman in that one scorching stare than all the times with Eli.

So when Eli started drinking heavily at the party and practically ignoring me in favor of the boys, I'd wandered off; and encountered Riker. He'd been right about one thing; we didn't speak much. I knew his name and little else bar his transient lifestyle before he bunched up my skirt, ripped off my panties and entered me.

I'd wanted him more than I'd wanted anything else in my life. The sex had been frantic, hedonistic and memorable. But the guilt after I'd run from that shed had been overwhelming. I'd vomited, twice, and known I couldn't keep a secret so monumental from my boyfriend. Telling Eli what I'd done with Riker seemed the right thing to do at the time. Breaking up with him because of my guilt had been spontaneous. I may not have pushed him off that cliff but he'd jumped because of me. No one knows my secret but Alice and considering her state of mind now, I think it's safe.

Though is that what Aunt Alice means by her constant reference to secrets? Maybe she does recognize me on some visceral level and has connected me to the past?

"Hey, where did you go?" Freya snaps her fingers in my face and I stop ruminating.

"Sorry, Sis, being back here has me reminiscing at the oddest of times," I say.

"I can understand that." She eyeballs me with respect. "Thanks for coming back. I know it must be tough, after everything you went through back then."

"I wouldn't have done it for anybody but you."

My eyes fill with tears, matching the sheen in hers, and I try to lighten the mood.

"Though if you expect me to attend your wedding wearing one of those poufy satin bubble dresses you coveted in your retro eighties phase when you were a sophomore, I'm out of here."

We laugh, one of those rare spontaneous moments of synchronicity since I got back.

"I thought my warped fashion sense is one of the many things you love about me?" She grins and I'm relieved we're back on solid footing again. "Have you had breakfast? I'm running early for work so I've got a bit of time for a coffee?"

"A coffee sounds great."

Not because I need the caffeine hit, but because I'm enjoying reconnecting with my sister in a way we never have before.

CHAPTER SEVENTEEN

ALICE

THEN

After a week of fruitless searching and ransacking the house for any clues Mom might've left lying around that might alert me to what happened to Diana's firstborn, I give up. I can't believe my mother kept old programs from a local theatre production of *My Fair Lady* that Dad took her to fifteen years ago but she kept no records of her first grandchild.

I assume the baby had been adopted out but it's difficult to access those records without knowing where to look. Privacy laws protect the mother and child, leaving me frustrated. Incredibly, I cop a break when the attorney who dealt with Mom's will contacts me out of the blue saying he discovered some old documentation regarding a safety deposit box my parents had at the bank and do I want to keep paying for it. I don't, but I'm interested in anything it may contain. As it turns out, the box has an old ruby ring I'd never seen Mom wear and the information I need.

Elizabeth Shomack was born in a private home for unwed mothers on the outskirts of LA. So much for Diana living it up on Long Island. Initially adopted by an older couple, Elizabeth is now in the custody of Child Protective Services because of domestic abuse within the family. As if my heart isn't breaking enough for my poor abandoned niece.

I understand this isn't all Diana's fault. Mom wouldn't have allowed her to return to Verdant with a baby in tow. She would've forced her. But what I can't understand is once Diana returned home and found Cam loved her enough to marry her and have more kids, why hadn't she done whatever it took to reclaim her first child?

I've always known Diana is selfish but she's my sister and I've made excuses for her vanity and attention-grabbing in the past because it's a part of her as much as her big blue eyes and we all have our faults. But this time I'm out of excuses. I can't fathom her lavishing love on Brooke and Freya while she could easily find Elizabeth if she wanted to and add her to her already perfect family.

Cam would forgive her. Diana could do anything and the man I love would stare at my sister like she could do no wrong. So why hasn't she told him? Why doesn't she find Elizabeth and bring her home?

If she won't I will.

A small part of me wants to do it for the recognition. Cam will be eternally grateful and he might look at me differently. He'll see the flaws in Diana where he only ever sees perfection. But my motivation is more altruistic; Di and I don't have any other family left and Elizabeth is a part of that family, whether my sister discarded her or not. I can't leave my poor niece with Child Protective Services, only to be given to another family and exposed to goodness knows what.

Still, I dither. I mull it for a week, the same thoughts reverberating through my head. *This is none of my business. Elizabeth could be given to a family who will love her more than my sister who gave her away in the first place and has done nothing to find her. Maybe this is for the best.*

Ultimately, it's the family ties that get to me. Elizabeth is a defenseless toddler at the mercy of the courts when she doesn't have to be. She's Diana's blood and, in turn, mine, and if my sister doesn't want her, I do.

It costs a lot of money to hire an attorney that facilitates private adoptions. But I have savings; living at home nursing Mom had its advantages. I'm too young to adopt, twenty-two, but once blood tests prove I'm a direct relation proceedings are smoother. I meet Elizabeth and she's adorable, with a sweet disposition despite her rough start to life. It makes me hate Diana all the more for abandoning her beautiful daughter and I avoid my sister as much as possible in case I let slip what I really think of her.

The day I hear I'm officially Elizabeth's mother is the day I put the rest of my plan into place.

Diana doesn't deserve one child, let alone three.

And she certainly doesn't deserve Cam.

I have a vision of Cam and me raising his three daughters. He'll see what a great mom I make, much better than Diana, and with her out of the way he'll eventually grow to love me.

How can he not?

So I head to the library, choose the furthest computer away from the counter, and research what I have to do.

CHAPTER EIGHTEEN
BROOKE

It's time I sit down with Lizzie and chat about her mom. Freya told me not to dig too deeply into Aunt Alice's condition because it upsets Lizzie and I agreed out of respect. I know nothing about the situation they've been living with regarding Aunt Alice's care and I have no right to delve. I feel like an interloper and don't want to disrupt their well-ordered lives when they seem to have everything under control. But I'm increasingly concerned about Aunt Alice's rants about my parents and Lizzie's the best person to talk to.

After Freya heads off to work, I find Lizzie in Aunt Alice's room and I knock softly when I see Aunt Alice dozing.

Lizzie beckons me in and I enter, pulling up a chair alongside hers. "How's she doing today?"

"The same," Lizzie says. "Mornings used to be her best time but she's so sleepy all the time now, like she's getting worse."

"What does Freya say?"

"That it's to be expected, that after sleeping many dementia patients wake and are totally disoriented so it adds to their feelings of panic." Lizzie pulls a face. "When I popped in here this morning after Freya had checked on her, she was worse than usual, ranting again."

I'm not sure how to introduce the topic of my parents. "Have you ever tried to access her online diary?"

Lizzie looks appalled for a moment, but I see the telltale blush creeping into her cheeks. "Yeah, I have. I know it's not right but I thought if I could read about her past I might be able to offer more comfort now somehow. Maybe even read it out loud to her, give her a sense of familiarity? A way of remembering?"

"That's exactly what I was thinking." My gaze slides to the laptop on the side table near the bed. "She gets so agitated when she starts rambling and I'd do anything to calm her. It must be disorienting not to remember the past and if something as simple as reading diary entries to her will make it easier for her, it's worth a try."

"I know. But dredging up the past may not be the wisest move either."

Lizzie's gaze slides away from mine and I know she's hiding something.

"What aren't you telling me?"

She doesn't answer for a few seconds and then takes a deep breath, as if coming to a decision. "You know when I sent you that email, asking you to come home?"

"Yeah."

"Well, she'd been focused on a particular topic for a week or so before that."

"What topic?"

Reluctantly, Lizzie drags her gaze back to mine. "Your mom."

That fit with Aunt Alice's ramblings about sisters and the bad stuff my mom had supposedly done. She might be dredging up the past in her head and getting confused. "Did she say anything specific about my mom for you to be so concerned?"

Lizzie drags in another deep breath and blows it out before she responds.

"She said she killed her."

CHAPTER NINETEEN

FREYA

When I pick up Hope from school, we don't head home immediately. I want to spend some quality time with my daughter, something that hasn't happened since Brooke returned.

Their mutual infatuation has grown over the last eight days and while I'm glad they're getting along so well I also hate the feeling of being replaced in my daughter's affections. Stupid, because Hope and I are close, but I don't know if I'll be able to cope if she starts gravitating towards Brooke rather than me.

Hope used to love baking oatmeal cookies with me once a week. It's our thing and we've done it for years. But since Brooke came back, Hope would rather make brownies with her aunt than hang around the kitchen with me. And if my daughter has a problem with her homework, she'll seek out Brooke's advice first, when I used to be her go-to person. As for their sketching together, it makes me feel like an outsider and I hate it.

"Want to grab some smoothies and head to the lookout?"

I expect Hope to beam at my suggestion. Instead, she shakes her head. "I'm pretty tired, Mom, I'd rather go home."

"Wow, you're passing up a double malt choc banana smoothie?" I press my hand to her forehead and scrunch up my eyes. "This must be serious."

She chuckles and pushes my hand away. "Mom, can I ask you something?"

"Anything, sweetie."

I know her grade is starting sex ed classes and I brace for a question that I can hopefully answer without going into too much detail.

"If Auntie Brooke has come home after being away for so long, is there a chance my dad will come home too?"

A chill sweeps over me and it takes a mighty effort to appear unfazed. "No, sweetie, your dad won't. He doesn't know about you and I already told you, I don't know where he is."

"I bet you could find him if you wanted to." Hope pouts and folds her arms. "It's not fair I don't have a dad."

My heart breaks a little but I soldier on. "You like Riker, right?"

Her nod is minuscule.

"When we get married, he'll be your dad. Won't that be cool?"

I'm talking down to her like she's five not ten but I've learned from our past conversations around this topic that keeping it simple works better than trying to lie or weave a story she'll doubt.

"Yeah, I guess."

Before I can say anything else, she says, "Why has Auntie Brooke stayed away all this time? Didn't she want to meet me? Didn't you miss your sister?" She pauses to take a quick breath. "I want a sister. Are you going to have another baby?"

Wow. I work through the questions methodically, knowing she won't settle for anything less than an answer to each. "Your aunt has traveled a lot and worked in remote countries helping other people, so it's not that she didn't want to meet you, it was hard for her to get back here."

I stick to the truth as much as possible because Hope has a way of ferreting out lies. Which reminds me, I must tell Brooke not to let slip she didn't know about Hope's existence until now. "As you can see, she's loved meeting you and I'm so glad you two are bonding."

Hope's eyes glow at this and once again I'm back to resenting Brooke and her ability to charm everybody in her sphere.

"As for missing Brooke, of course I have, but I know she's been doing important work with those less fortunate so I'm proud of her."

When I don't say anything for a few moments, Hope predictably pounces on my omission. "What about a baby sister for me?"

Riker and I discussed having kids within the first month of dating. My biological clock isn't ticking particularly loudly and he's happy to be guided by whatever decision I make; he's great like that, laid-back and amenable. So for now, expanding our family isn't in our foreseeable future but there's plenty of time.

As Hope's expression turns mutinous, I know she won't be appeased by that answer so I reach for a little fib.

"We want to get married first, sweetie, then who knows?"

I wink, as if it's some great secret between us, and after a moment she nods, apparently satisfied.

"Feel like that smoothie now?"

"Sure," she says, with an indifferent shrug. "But then I really want to go home and do some sketching with Auntie Brooke."

Biting back my disappointment, I start the engine and pull away from the school gates.

I started this, I have no right to react. It's understandable that Hope wants to get to know her aunt. But at the thought of how the evening ahead will pan out, with Brooke and Hope sitting together at the table, engrossed in their own insular world, I feel desperately lonely.

CHAPTER TWENTY

ALICE

THEN

Ever since I met Elizabeth I've been obsessing over Diana's callousness in abandoning her firstborn daughter and my hatred has grown. I want to punish her. I want to hurt her. I think of all the ways I can make that happen. But I chicken out at the last minute.

I'd planned on following the online instructions to the letter, but I have a conscience and the ramifications of what I'd been about to do as I stand next to my sister's car hit home with a vengeance and I ditch my plan. I'd been so close... running my hands over the brake lines... until I realized what I'd been contemplating and stepped back. I can't hurt my sister, no matter how much I might want to.

I feel a flicker of remorse for what I'd almost done as I knock on Diana's back door and enter. It's always unlocked. Most doors are in Verdant. Crime is low, socializing high. People help each other out here and I know how to play the pity card well once my plan works. My new plan, that is. Get Diana to tell Cam the truth, all of it, and hope he sees his wife for the woman she is, hope he finally realizes he could have so much more with dependable me.

"Di?" I call out, closing the screen door behind me.

"In the lounge room," she answers and as I cross the family room I spy her lying on a sofa, her forearm over her eyes.

"Hope I'm not disturbing you." Which is exactly what I intend on doing, in the worst possible way.

She lowers her forearm and struggles into a sitting position. She's twenty-one going on eighty by the way she moves. Maybe guilt does that to a person. "The girls are napping so I thought I'd grab a rest too."

"Cam's not around?"

I know for a fact he's not; I'd timed this perfectly for it to work. Not that it will now. Turns out I'm not as heartless as my sister and aborting my plan to harm her is a good thing. I'll have to rely on Diana telling him everything and Cam seeing sense once he knows the truth instead.

"No, he's helping the neighbors with a rain tank." She barks out a laugh. "Like we get enough rain in Verdant to make that useful."

I like living in the Nevada Desert. The dry conditions suit me. Barren, empty, like how I've felt for the last few years since my sister came home.

She glances over my shoulder at the ugly wooden cuckoo clock hanging over the mantel. It belonged to Cam's dad and I used to tease him about it during the pizza nights we shared with his friends, what seems like a lifetime ago.

"Wow, is that the time? I must've dozed off—"

"How could you do it, Di?"

She's perplexed by my question. "Do what?"

"Give your baby away."

She blanches and her mouth drops open. "What... how—"

"Save it." I hold up my hand. "I don't want to hear any more of your lies. I want you to know Elizabeth was in Child Protective Services because the couple you gave her to are abusive assholes, but thanks to me she won't be much longer."

She closes her mouth, only to open it again, but no words come out.

"I'm going to bring her home." I pause for dramatic effect. "I'm guessing Cam will be very pleased to learn he has another daughter."

Her pallor matches the wall behind her as she finally moves, swinging her legs off the sofa and pushing into a standing position. I've never been more grateful to be taller than her. I tower over her, holding all the power. At last.

"Don't you dare say a word until I tell him." It comes out an angry hiss and I laugh.

"That's what I'm counting on, you telling him everything, and Cam finally realizing what kind of woman you are."

Her eyes narrow to angry slits and her face flushes puce. "Why are you doing this?"

I can lie but what's the point? I want her to know how much I despise her.

"Because I hate you for taking what's mine."

She knows what I'm talking about; I see it in a flicker of guilt before she blinks and it's gone. "You're crazy."

"I'm guessing that's what Cam's going to say about you once he learns the truth." I tsk-tsk, waggling my finger at her. "Honestly, Di, what were you thinking?"

I know the exact moment she'll switch tactics and try to soften me up, hoping I'll pity her. Doesn't she realize I know all her tricks by now?

"I wasn't thinking, Al. I was eighteen years old and pregnant after having sex with a guy for the first time. I told Mom and she said she'd take care of it—"

"You should've told Cam," I yell, losing control for a moment. "She's his baby too. He should've had a say."

"I know, I know, but I was struggling with morning sickness and I didn't want anyone in town to know, so Mom took me to this place in LA and I—"

"Save the sob story, Di. You're a selfish bitch and always have been, getting everything you want." I pat my chest. "Now it's my turn."

Her upper lip curls in a sneer. "What do you think's going to happen? That once I tell Cam, he'll ditch me for you?" She shakes her head. "You're pathetic."

She takes a step toward me, determined to hurt me as much as I've hurt her. "He's never liked you as anything more than a friend, he told me when we first started dating. And that's not going to change despite what I've done. He loves me, we share children and he'll forgive me. And even if that's not the case, no way in hell would he turn to you."

"Let's find out, shall we?" My lips ease into a grin that's more a grimace. "Go tell him the truth."

She's wrong. When Diana tells Cam he'll be appalled by her lies and turn to someone he can trust—me—for comfort. He'll see how much I love him by the selfless adoption of his firstborn, by how far I'll go to prove my feelings.

I know a court may overturn the adoption if the biological parents state a solid case but Cam won't want a legal drama played out in this town, especially when his folks are such pillars of society. He may resent me at the start but when he sees what an amazing mother I am, how much I love his daughter compared to Diana, he'll come around. He has to.

"Go tell Cam. I'll look after the girls."

She glares at me with loathing as she snags her car keys from the side table, before sprinting out the door.

I head upstairs to check on the girls, listening for the sound of her car starting. When it does, I pause in the girls' doorway, watch them slumber, and I smile. I can afford to be smug.

I'm about to get everything I deserve and more.

CHAPTER TWENTY-ONE
BROOKE

I spend a lovely few hours with Hope at the dining table, trying our hands at watercolors, before she has to go to bed. It's early, just after eight, but I'm glad because after Lizzie's startling revelation this morning, I haven't been able to stop thinking about it. What did Aunt Alice mean when she said she'd killed my mom? I have to find out and I'm more determined than ever to find a way to access Alice's diary. Freya is at Riker's so once Hope is asleep, Lizzie brings Alice's laptop out of her room and we fire it up.

"I know the main password after watching her enter it often enough over the years," Lizzie says, her fingers tapping at the keyboard, "and I think her diary password is similar, but I've tried a stack of variations of it to gain access to it but no luck."

I grab a pencil and tear a sheet off Hope's sketchpad. "What is it?"

"BrakeMyHeartCS3. But brake spelt with an a, not what you'd expect with 'break a heart'."

I write it down and stare at it for a few seconds, deliberately blurring my eyes to allow the letters to jumble, seeing if I can come up with a similar combination. "Obviously means 'break my heart', but CS3?"

Lizzie's nose crinkles. "This may sound crazy but weren't your dad's initials CS? Cameron Stuart?"

I wrinkle my nose too. "You think my dad broke Alice's heart?"

Lizzie shrugs. "Puts all that talk about sisters and secrets into perspective, huh?"

I hesitate, hating to cause my cousin pain but eager to solve this mystery. "Do you think she muttered about killing Diana because that's what she wanted to do? If she had a secret crush on my dad it would make sense. So now her memories are muddled, she's saying stuff she would've liked to see happen but didn't?"

"Yeah, probably, but…" Lizzie trails off, pensive. "You didn't see her when she said it. She looked really tortured, like she regretted doing it."

I can't see gentle, sweet Aunt Alice hurting anyone, least of all her own sister. She's been a wonderful mother to Lizzie, and an equally generous mom to Freya and me. She'd been the best taxi mom, never complaining about driving us wherever we wanted to go. She'd been courtside at every one of our basketball games and would shout the team to hotdogs afterward. She'd been generous with her time and money and I can't imagine her doing anything nefarious to her sister.

"Does she talk about your father at all?"

Lizzie shakes her head. "Never. She was nineteen when she had me, practically a kid herself, and said he didn't want to be a dad so took off."

"Do you know who he is?"

"No." She gnaws on her bottom lip, sadness clouding her eyes. "I pestered her a lot growing up but it always made her shut down and I felt bad for giving her grief after a while so I stopped."

"Speaking of fathers, does Freya ever talk about Hope's?"

"Uh-uh. All I know is she left not long after you did. I was away at college and when I came home for summer break, she was here with her baby."

"And Aunt Alice never talked about it?"

"She forbade me from asking Freya anything to do with Hope's paternity because it upset her too much." She rolls her eyes. "I know how that felt already. If Mom wouldn't tell me about my own dad, what hope did I have of getting anything out of her about Freya?"

"This is making my head hurt." I press my fingers to my temples and rub a little, before refocusing on the password. "Let me jot down a few variations of this and we'll see if we can crack her diary password."

Lizzie watches as I doodle, shifting letters around, transposing the 3 into variations between words. When I'm done I have a list of about twenty different passwords. I turn the paper around so Lizzie can see it.

"I've tried at least half of those, let me try the rest."

She opens up the diary software and starts typing. I hold my breath each time she hits the 'enter' key, disappointed whenever we get the 'denied access' message box.

When she tries the last one and we get more of the same, I huff in exasperation. "It was always a long shot."

She nods. "I've also tried obvious stuff, like our birth dates, 1234, along with variations of 'secrets' and 'birthday' to no avail."

"Have you tried asking your mom for the password? I mean, she's confused and she probably won't know why you're asking." I wince. "I know it's low trying to access her personal stuff like this but if we can give her some peace, set her mind at ease, it's worth it?"

Lizzie blushes. "I've already tried. The week before you came back, when I chatted to her about Freya's wedding and you coming home, she got really agitated and her rambling became worse. That's why I emailed you…" She trails off and offers a wan smile. "I've always been closer to you than Freya and I wanted you to come home. I thought her invitation might not be enough so I sent that email practically begging."

"I'm glad you did." I squeeze her hand. "We're more like sisters than cousins and I've missed you."

She hesitates, as if unsure what to say. "Why did you cut off all contact with us? One minute you were here, the next you were gone and you never came back. You changed your number, had limited access to email, then eleven years later here you are."

It's a legitimate question but I have no intention of revealing any of my secrets. Better off focusing on Alice's.

"I went through a lot when Eli died and I didn't handle it well. Getting away from here, cutting all ties, was something I had to do to heal."

Confusion creases her brow. "But you just said we were like sisters. Why would you think I wouldn't support you? I mean, I know I wasn't around at the time, but later, when I came back from college, I would've been here for you."

"I wasn't thinking about anything or anyone, Lizzie, and that's the truth. I was eighteen, I'd gone through a horrendous experience that everyone blamed me for and I had to get away. Plus the guilt…" Emotion clogs my throat, a breath-stealing sorrow after all this time. "Breaking up with Eli in the state he was in was stupid. I should've waited until the next day but I didn't and he died because of me." I shrug, like the constant guilt means little when it's shaped my life. "I had to stay away for my sanity."

"Is that why you haven't been into town since you got back? Afraid to run into people you know?"

"Partly. I know Martino Bay's bigger now and a lot of time has passed, but I haven't left the house yet because I'm actually savoring being back here." I clear my throat to ease the tightness. "I've moved around a lot over the last decade and I'm finally home."

"I get it." She envelops me in an impulsive hug before easing away. "It's why I've never left." She grimaces. "And why I still technically live at home, even if it is in a separate cottage. Not having a father has made me appreciate the family I have more and I like being close to Mom and Hope." She winks. "Freya at times too."

We laugh and I'm glad we've had this chance to talk. But we're still no closer to cracking Alice's diary password and gut instinct tells me it's imperative we do.

CHAPTER TWENTY-TWO

FREYA

I'm up at five every morning. It gives me time to tend to Aunt Alice before Hope wakes and our busy day starts. I work the seven to three shift at the nursing home, which suits me perfectly, allowing me to pick up Hope from school and be a present mom rather than an absentee one.

I often wonder what type of mother Diana would've been. I was six weeks old when she died and Aunt Alice is the only mom I've ever known. I liked how she treated Brooke and me the same as Lizzie, never favoring her biological daughter over us. Though a small part of me always thought she liked me better than Brooke. I'd catch her staring at me sometimes with this soft, faraway look in her eyes. At first I thought it was pity but on closer analysis the emotion resembled more… empathy, like she knew how I felt being second best to my gorgeous, smart sister and wanted to shield me from it.

Later, with Hope's arrival, she virtually proved it. From the moment I held that squalling bundle of joy in my arms Aunt Alice was there, helping me, nurturing me, urging me to be the best mother I could be. We've become close over the last decade. She helped me through Hope's teething, potty training and beyond. When I fell apart on Hope's first day of school, Aunt Alice brought me home, plied me with nachos and diet cola—my favorites—and watched reality TV with me all day, something she hates. We'd sit together most evenings after Hope had gone to bed, reading in comfortable silence or chatting about the latest instant pot recipe online.

Aunt Alice spent a lot of time scouring the Internet for recipes and I loved recreating them with her. We had a system in the kitchen: I'd prep, she'd cook, and we'd enjoy a crisp white wine while we did it. We perfected our latest favorite recipes—fettuccini carbonara for her, honey soy chicken for me—and would try to outdo each other in the flavor stakes. As Hope grew older, she'd perch on a stool at the island bench and assist with prepping, her smiles as she watched our competitive antics making me appreciate my aunt even more.

We didn't talk about the past and we never mentioned Brooke. It was an unspoken agreement between us and I'm not sure if we avoided talking about my sister because we missed her so much or we were furious at her for turning her back on us.

Whatever Brooke's motivation for cutting all ties, I stopped mulling after a while. I liked having Aunt Alice all to myself. Even when Lizzie came home from college, I never felt our bond waver.

Aunt Alice has been my rock for so long, which makes watching her deteriorate all the harder.

I brace myself for the draining morning routine and unlock her door, slipping inside before locking it behind me again.

"Good morning, Aunt Alice, it's going to be a beautiful day." I draw the curtains a fraction, enough to let the pale dawn light filter in, and switch on a lamp. "Ready for your medication?"

She's drowsy, her eyes unfocused as I perch on the side of the bed and reach for her hand. "Just need to check your pulse."

Her hand is limp and cold, but her eyes remain trained on me. She has the odd moment of lucidity before I administer her meds and I watch for any signs of clarity. But today is not one of her better days and she remains confused, staring at me like she can't quite figure out who I am.

"Your heart's all good," I say, releasing her hand to unlock the medicinal cabinet beside her bed. "And taking your pills will make you feel better."

I dispense the usual cocktail from a variety of bottles into a small white cup and re-lock the cabinet. Thankfully, she takes her meds without fuss every morning and the occasional top up at night on a particularly bad day. She's been having more of those lately and I keep her dosage high.

I hand her each pill individually and watch her wash them down with a sip of water. Six in all, some double strength.

"Well done." I pat her shoulder, startled when her hand shoots out to grip my arm so hard I wince.

"You. Are. Bad."

Her eyes glitter with malice and I recoil, shrugging off her grasp.

"It's okay, Aunt Alice, you'll feel better once the meds kick in."

I don't know for certain that's true but I can hope.

CHAPTER TWENTY-THREE

ALICE

THEN

It's dusk when I hear a loud knocking on the front door. The girls are settled. Thankfully Diana isn't breastfeeding Freya so I've given her a bottle and fed Brooke some pre-prepared toddler veggies. The girls seem happy enough, with Brooke watching TV and Freya lying on her back under a play mobile contraption.

They're happy, while I churn with dread. Diana has been gone for hours and I'm worried. I want to break up her marriage but I'm wondering if she's talked her way out of this with Cam like she has her entire life. Nobody can spin a story like my sister. Though a small part of me hopes she hasn't done something stupid and rather than tell Cam the truth, she's harmed herself. I want her marriage to fall apart, not to physically hurt my sister, and I'm annoyed I haven't thought of this outcome before now.

I'd counted on Diana's selfishness in wanting to tell Cam the truth herself, to cajole and appease him in the way only she can. But what if she couldn't face him? Is she hiding out somewhere like a child, hoping this will blow over?

I doubt it. Diana is selfish but she wouldn't leave her children, surely? Then again, she's done it before; poor Elizabeth is proof of that.

I open the door and my trepidation morphs into panic when I see two police officers. They radiate grimness; wearing matching deep frowns and compressed lips, but couldn't be more different. The taller one is young and clean-shaven, the shorter one is a veteran by the weary slump to his shoulders and beady eyes that have seen too much.

"Are you Alice Shomack?" the short officer asks and when I nod, he says, "Can we come in?"

"Is everything all right?"

It can't be, considering their ominous presence, and my hands shake as I wave them inside. Has Diana done something foolish? Has she hurt herself because of what I've put into motion? Cam is her world and if he ends their marriage… I'm overcome with guilt I may have caused this and I drag in several deep breaths before closing the door.

"We need to talk to you, ma'am." The younger one takes off his hat a fraction after the shorter one. "I'm Officer Burdette and this is Officer Cowley."

I lead them into the lounge room and we stand in an odd circular threesome. "What can I do for you, officers? I'm minding my nieces who are in the family room, so if we can make this quick—"

"I'm sorry to say we have some bad news." Officer Cowley has been doing this a long time and he's not going to stand around making chitchat. "There's been a car accident."

I feel the blood drain from my face. No. It can't be. I didn't tamper with those brakes, no matter how much I wanted to. I'd thought about it, at length. I'd watched the video how to do it three times, memorizing the steps. But when I had my hands on the relevant parts, I couldn't do it. Had I dislodged something inadvertently? Am I responsible for my sister being injured?

"You're awfully, pale, miss." Officer Cowley gestures to a chair. "Why don't you take a seat—"

"I'm okay. You were saying something about a car accident?"

He nods, increasingly grave. "I'm sorry, there were fatalities."

Shock renders me speechless as I focus on that one word. Fatalities.

I scream on the inside. I didn't want to hurt anybody. I didn't do this. But I can't get out of my head how close I'd been to actually fiddling with Diana's brakes. I didn't, but what if I messed with them just the same? I'm horrified that somehow this is my fault and not only have I killed my sister, but some poor helpless third party has become unwittingly caught up in our sibling rivalry.

"Your sister skidded off the road and hit a tree about five miles from here, and both she and her passenger died on impact." Officer Crowley moves toward me as I sway, an icy chill rendering me immobile.

I'm woozy, disoriented, gasping for air.

Passenger?

"Neither her husband nor your sister suffered," Officer Burdette adds, thinking his inane comment is helping, as I let out a blood-curdling wail and crumple to the floor.

CHAPTER TWENTY-FOUR
BROOKE

I have the house to myself the next day. Someone always has to be around for Aunt Alice, considering her door is kept locked to avoid her wandering, and we can't leave her alone in case of fire.

Lizzie works from home usually, running an online company that sells baby paraphernalia including strollers, clothes, toys and anything else expectant and new mothers might need, but today she's out checking an incorrect delivery. Riker took off in his van to scrounge for scrap metal early this morning, and with Freya at work and Hope at school, I'm left to check in on Aunt Alice and do my own thing.

I'm planning a surprise bridal shower for Freya. She hates surprises but it's something I want to do after being away for so long. Lizzie's in on the secret and thinks it's a great idea. I want it to be a low-key affair at home, in the backyard, where we spent so much of our time growing up. She loved the colorful fairy lights Aunt Alice used to string up on special occasions, like birthdays and Christmases, so I'll pretty up the garden with plenty of those, maybe some lanterns and sheer chiffon draped from tree to tree. Freya also loved fancy finger food, so I'll get a catering company to assist with menu planning, and maybe do a special cocktail. Freya has loads of friends apparently, courtesy of her job and volunteering for various causes, so Lizzie's taking care of the guest list while I do everything else. I'm good at taking care of practicalities.

My tenacity got me top grades at school; I wouldn't leave any question unanswered. Teachers lauded me for it, friends were slightly jealous and Freya thought I was a kiss-ass. She hated when teachers compared her to me and being only a year behind it happened often.

I'd been tolerant of her growing up because of the eleven-month gap between us but eventually our closeness became an issue. Any boy I liked, she liked. I wanted to be a cheerleader; she did too. I joined gaming club, she had to follow, despite thinking online games were pointless. I'd whine to Aunt Alice occasionally but she always took Freya's side, encouraging me to be nicer to my sister because she idolized me and that's why she wanted to be like me. But I found it suffocating at times and I wanted to find out who I was, make my own friends, my own life, which only made her hound me more. I'd hoped a boy would start dating Freya and that would distract her but unfortunately, despite a few offers, she never showed interest in any of the guys at school.

When I started going steady with Eli in our senior year, she had no choice but to back off. He was nice to her—Eli was nice to everybody—but I wanted him to myself and tired quickly of having Freya pop up when we least expected it. He'd laugh about it but I didn't find it so funny.

Eli...

It's painful to think of him, even now. Any time I hear the ocean I think of the night we fought, the waves crashing over our ankles at the beach, the ugliness of it all as I confessed and he went berserk. He'd said some awful things, called me terrible names, and I'd lost it too. I'd dumped him, he'd stormed off and I'd let him.

Freya had been distraught over Eli's death and I felt bad for all those times I'd tried to ditch her when I'd been with him. She didn't know the truth, of course, that my confession must've caused his suicide, but she knew how much he meant to me and she was shattered almost as much as I was.

Thinking about the past makes me more determined than ever to discover more about my parents. Aunt Alice is obviously suffering and I'll do anything to set her mind at ease. Since last night I've been mulling Aunt Alice's password and something Lizzie said, about her having a secret crush on my father.

I know next to nothing about my parents. Whenever I asked Aunt Alice as a kid, she'd clam up and become visibly upset—her face would flush, her hands would shake, her eyes would get this weird wild glint—so I soon gave up. Losing her only sister in a car accident must've been awful, and to have her brother-in-law killed in the same accident, leaving her in sole charge of Freya and me, would've been traumatic.

She'd been so young at the time, only twenty-three, with a toddler of her own. Having to raise three girls under three must've curtailed her social life and left her with little free time. I never realized it as a kid but me badgering her for information about my parents must've been awful, dredging up memories of a time she'd rather forget.

With no answers forthcoming from my aunt, I'd done some online research when I hit my teens but learned little. Two local newspapers in Nevada, where my mom and aunt are from, had articles on a car accident that killed Diana and Cameron Stuart. Speed, erratic driving and brake failure were deemed the causes of the crash, one of countless tragedies that occurred on our roads every day.

Back then, those articles had assuaged my curiosity but now I want to know more. Precisely, I want to know about my mom, my dad, and what kind of relationship my aunt had with them both. Alice never married and growing up I can remember her going on a few dates but never having a relationship with any guy.

I have no idea if that changed over the last decade but neither Lizzie nor Freya has mentioned anyone special in her life and no guy has come visiting since I've been home. Being struck down with early onset dementia at fifty would send any guy running.

Before I delve deeper I fire off a quick text to Lizzie.

Did your mom date anyone special since I've been away? Wondering who else CS could be?

I stare at my cell, willing Lizzie's response to come quickly and thankfully it does.

No. She saw a few guys, locals I know. No CS.

After answering with a *Thx. Checking a few things, will let U know later* I open up a fresh search engine.

I need to know more and starting with my dad seems as good a place as any.

I type CAMERON STUART into the search bar. I get millions of hits. Annoyingly I don't even know his date of birth but I know the town where I was born.

I add VERDANT, NEVADA into the search and it narrows considerably. No one had social media accounts back then—I checked during my first search as a teen—but it looks like one of their friends had a blog back then, some woman named Amy Cresswell. She posted a few pictures, most of them involving young people drinking by a pool, and one of those has my dad's name under it. I see Mom's name too and my heart beats a little faster.

Aunt Alice has been a great mother and I had a good life until I screwed up at that party, but how different would my life have been if my parents were alive? Would I have more siblings? Would we still be in Nevada, not California?

Silly to lament a past I never had, I scan the photo. I recognize Mom and Dad from the old picture I have, but this one is more revealing. Dad has his arm slung around Mom's shoulders and is staring at her in open adoration, while Mom's looking up at him and laughing. Their friend Amy is nearby, raising a beer in their direction and behind her, blurred and almost indistinct, is my aunt.

Glaring at the cozy group with stark longing.

If Amy Cresswell knew my parents she'd be the best person to contact. It's about all I've got at the moment.

She's on several social media sites so I join the one where she has the most friends and send her a message offline. I tell her I'm Diana and Cam's daughter, and I'd like to chat with her about my parents. Simple. Truthful.

I see she's online by a tiny purple star next to her name and her response comes quickly.

Hi Brooke,

Nice to hear from you.

Last time I saw you was at your first birthday party, can't believe twenty-eight years have passed since then. I'm old!

Anyway, I'm happy to chat about your folks anytime. Your mom was my best friend and I adored her.

I still live in Verdant, with a family of my own. Do you want to come visit or shall we chat on the phone? Either is fine with me.

Thanks for reaching out.

Chat soon,
Amy x

Talking on the phone would be easier and I'd get my answers faster but I know from experience it's easier to get honest responses face to face. Maybe Lizzie will come with me, so I fire back a quick reply.

Thanks for getting back to me so quickly, Amy.

I'd love to come visit. I'm not working at the moment so any time is fine.

Let me know when's convenient.

Look forward to meeting you.

I hit send and once again Amy answers quickly, giving me her address and a range of days and times. It should take about four hours each way to get to Verdant from here, a long trip for a potential let-down, but I have to do this.

So I choose Saturday, two days from now, at midday, and once she confirms I thank her and log off. I don't know if I'm doing the right thing. In fact, I have serious doubts that delving into Aunt Alice's past will provide answers to help bring her peace now.

But I have to try.

Aunt Alice was my rock for so long; it's time I repaid the favor.

CHAPTER TWENTY-FIVE
ALICE
THEN

Losing my father had been hard at the time. Not because I missed him so much as how his death affected Mom. Her crippling grief distracted me, and in the end I didn't mourn him that long. When Mom died I was almost relieved. Seeing her suffer those last few weeks as the lung cancer ravaged her had not been pretty: her anger at the injustice of dying too young, her humiliation when she became incontinent and had to rely on me for everything. Her antipathy had increased exponentially with her deterioration until she'd been unrecognizable at the end, a shell of the woman I'd once loved.

But I never knew real grief until Cam died.

Each day blends into the next, an all-pervasive numbness that makes the simplest of tasks impossible. But I have to function, the girls are depending on me, and no way in hell I'll lose them.

They're the only part of Cam I have left.

He was supposed to be alive, raising his girls with me. A tight-knit family bound by our mutual disbelief Diana could give away their child so callously, Di left out, me being stoic and gentle so he couldn't help but love me eventually. The good sister. The dependable sister.

But Diana screwed me over yet again. I've pieced together what must've happened from the neighbor Cam had been helping. Apparently he got a call that had him running across the field, where he got into the car with Diana by the gate. Diana had been distraught, yelling and screaming, and they'd driven off in a squeal of tires. The neighbor had been concerned because the car had been swerving until out of sight, but had attributed it to a tiff between husband and wife.

Though I hadn't tampered with those brakes, Diana's erratic driving had been because of me regardless. I was responsible. I'd made my sister so distraught she couldn't drive properly and she'd ended up killing them both.

I did this. I've lost the love of my life because of it.

It makes me want to protect his children even more.

Lizzie is with me now too, formally adopted. She's a sweet two-and-a-half-year-old, the image of her father, and I'm instantly drawn to her. I expected trouble from the relevant agencies because of my age and being sole guardian of Brooke and Freya, but the attorney had somehow wangled it so that worked in my favor, a loving aunt providing a stable home environment for Di and Cam's three girls.

Not that Lizzie will ever know she's theirs. I hate the thought of her growing up and learning her mother dumped her, so I have a plan and this time it will be foolproof.

I have already put both houses on the market, Cam's and mine. They both belong to me now and courtesy of Cam's life insurance policy his daughters will never want for anything. Once the houses sell we will move, leaving Verdant and its haunting memories behind.

A new start in a new town far from here, where I can claim Lizzie as mine, and no one will be the wiser. I must protect her from the truth and that means telling a little white lie.

I will be her mother, and a stand-in mom to Brooke and Freya as their aunt. They're all too young to remember otherwise and after much searching I find the perfect place.

A sprawling Spanish-style stucco on top of a clifftop, with smaller bungalows on the property. It's beautiful and I instantly fall in love. Martino Bay channels the beauty of nearby Monterey but appears more unspoilt.

I like its hint of wildness, of promise.

It's the perfect place to raise my family, leaving secrets that can destroy us far behind.

CHAPTER TWENTY-SIX

FREYA

Brooke's distracted when I get home from work. She's her usual bubbly self around Hope and after we eat the simple mac and cheese Brooke cooked for dinner, the three of us play several games of checkers. Lizzie's reading to her mom and Riker is locked away in his studio trying to finish a commission for the mayor's office, and I'm glad it's just the three of us.

Does Brooke remember she taught me how to play checkers on this very board over twenty years ago? How our games usually ended in tears—mine, not hers—because I hated losing to her in anything.

She never understood my competitive streak, how everything I did was to beat her. Aunt Alice got it though. It made me wonder if she ever felt second best to our mom, even though Alice was the older sister. It would make sense because she would always console me and while she never overtly made Brooke feel bad I could tell she liked me best.

"Mom, you're toast." Hope jumps my last three checkers and whoops, as I huff in faux exasperation.

"Who taught you how to play like that?" I pretend to pout and she laughs.

"Auntie Brooke, she's a killer with board games."

Don't I know it and my mood instantly sours.

"Time for bed, young lady," I say, and Hope groans.

"Can't I stay up a little longer?"

"Going to bed means you get more time with that amazing new paranormal novel I got you," Brooke says, laying a hand on Hope's shoulder and my daughter practically glows.

"Off to bed now," I say sharply, and two sets of accusatory eyes focus on me. "Sorry, I'm a tad tired."

"Or a sore loser." Brooke winks, referring to my tantrums in the past, and I want to throttle her.

"Will you say goodnight later?" Hope asks and to my chagrin she's looking at Brooke.

"Sure, munchkin." Brooke gives her a brief hug and I busy myself packing away the checkers so she can't see my dour expression. "I'll be in later."

Hope barely gives me a second glance as she heads off to her room and I wait until my angst is under control before glancing up to find Brooke staring at me.

"You sure you're just tired?"

"Yeah." I fake a yawn. "We've got a lot of deteriorating dementia patients at work at the moment and some days are a lot worse than others."

"Speaking of dementia patients, how bad is Alice, in your professional opinion?"

"What do you mean?"

"On a scale of one to ten, how bad is she now and is there any hope of improvement?"

"Why do you want to know?"

"Because I love her and I'm concerned," Brooke snaps, immediately swiping a hand over her face. "Sorry, I know we've already discussed this but I want to know more about our parents and Alice is so out of it all the time, I guess I wondered if there was a chance she'd ever be lucid."

This, I can handle, giving a trite medical answer she has no hope of analyzing and finding it lacking in any way.

"She's about an eight at the moment."

While I hate seeing Aunt Alice so non-compos, I'm thankful she is. Not that I like seeing her deteriorate so quickly; it guts me, watching the once vibrant woman who loved me become a blathering mess. But with our aunt's increasing incoherency, I'm terrified she'll let my secret slip. Aunt Alice and I have managed to keep the past where it belongs for so long and no good could come of dredging it up now.

What would my sister think if she knew about Eli and me?

"And she's probably going to get worse. Early onset dementia often has a swifter progression."

Brooke's face falls. "So there's no hope?"

"There's always hope but I've seen too many patients go through this." I shake my head, dutifully sad. "If it's any consolation it's always harder on the family than the patient."

She nods, thoughtful. "How's she been since I left? Has she led a full life?"

"She's been fine before the dementia started four months ago. She's dated occasionally, but she's mostly helped me raise Hope and hung out with Lizzie a lot."

Brooke doesn't say anything and I probe. "Where's all this coming from?"

Brooke lets out a little sigh. "She never spoke about our parents and now it's too late to find out anything."

That prickle of unease is back, rippling down my spine. I can't have Aunt Alice letting the truth slip about Eli and me. It will ruin everything.

"Why do you want to dig into the past? What good can come of it?"

I aim for blasé, like it doesn't matter how much probing Brooke does into the past. But I know my sister. She doesn't give up easily and if she gets a hint of a mystery, she'll delve until she discovers the truth.

It doesn't bode well for me.

"I want answers," Brooke says, and I recognize her mutinous expression. It's one I've seen countless times as a kid. What Brooke wants she gets.

"Leave it alone, Brooke. What's the point of looking back when you're finally home and it's time to move forward?"

I hope she'll agree with me but I know better.

Brooke won't let this go.

CHAPTER TWENTY-SEVEN

ALICE

THEN

I fall in love with Martino Bay and the house perched upon a cliff at first sight.

Falling in love with my girls is harder.

Raising three girls on my own is a far cry from doing it with their father in the picture and I struggle on a daily basis. The tasks are endless: changing diapers, heating up formula, puréeing organic vegetables, mothering a bewildered Lizzie who's had more upheaval in her short life than any toddler should have to deal with. The girls are clingy, which is understandable considering they've lost their parents, but I never get a moment to myself. Going to the toilet is a feat, usually punctuated with the door opening unexpectedly or a loud wail demanding attention. As for showering, I skip it most days, when I used to love a long, leisurely shower first thing in the morning and another at night.

Showering every third or fourth day means my skin's pasty, my hair's lank, and I haven't slept properly since Di and Cam's deaths, so when I almost run over a woman at the park with my overflowing stroller, she takes one look at my stricken face and introduces herself as Marie, a forty-something mom who had twins in her early twenties and is looking to earn some extra money. I hire her on the spot to help out. She's a godsend. She cooks healthy meals for Brooke and Lizzie, prepares formula for Freya, bathes them and generally calms them down when I'm so frazzled I could scream.

She also allows me to have some semblance of a life. I don't realize how ostracized I've been until I've been in town six months and I get to do a grocery shop at the supermarket on my own. I'm so giddy at not having kids hanging off me I literally bump into a guy with my cart.

"Hey, watch it…" The chastisement dies on my lips as I stare at the tall, blond guy. With his lanky frame and big blue eyes, he reminds me of Cam and I press a hand to my chest to stem the hurt.

"Are you okay?" He stares at my hand, one eyebrow rising. "Or have I had such a profound effect on you that you're in danger of having a heart attack?"

An unexpected laugh bursts from my lips and I lower my hand, holding it out toward him instead. "I'm Alice."

"Toby."

He shakes my hand; his fingers are long and warm and comforting as they wrap around mine. When he releases it, he gestures at my trolley. "Are you a big eater, Alice?"

He's teasing; I love the twinkle in his eyes. Cam used to tease me sometimes—usually about being too straitlaced, unfortunately—and he'd get that same look in his eyes, as if I amused him and he liked it.

As I glance at my cart I see what Toby sees: six cartons of milk, several loaves of bread, bags of fruit and veg, two boxes of cereal. Lucky I did a diaper run yesterday; the sight of those would've sent him running instantly.

"I have kids to feed," I say, but rather than his expression closing off as I expect he appears genuinely interested, so I continue. "My sister and her husband died in a car accident so I'm guardian for their two girls, and I have one of my own."

His eyes widen in surprise. "But you're what, twenty?"

"Twenty-three."

"Good for you," he says, eyeing me with respect. "I'm assuming you don't get out much?"

"This is about as wild as it gets for me." I gesture at the supermarket. "I'm living the dream."

My droll response earns another laugh. "I take it you have someone looking after the kids now?"

"Yeah. It's my first time shopping without them and I'm going a little crazy with the freedom."

"My sisters are the same. They have three kids each too, and escaping the house for half an hour is a luxury."

"I can relate," I say, slightly breathless as he stares at me with blatant interest. I'm not used to the attention and it makes me lightheaded, like I used to feel in the early days when I first fell for Cam. How many sleepless nights had I wished Cam would look at me like this? Too many, and with Toby's vague resemblance to the love of my life, I can't help but feel overwhelmed and excited at the same time.

He leans in close and lowers his voice. "How about we do something really radical like ditch our carts and go for a coffee?"

I shouldn't. Nothing can come of this. I don't have the time to date, let alone allow a guy I don't know near the girls. But Marie instructed me to take my time with the shopping, had even encouraged me to stop for a coffee on the way, so why can't I share that coffee with Toby?

Besides, it's the first time in my sheltered life a man has ever looked at me this way and I want to whoop with joy. Is this how Diana felt when guys fawned over her, proud and desired and beautiful? One coffee with Toby can't hurt and for this short interlude, I want to savor this experience and not think about responsibilities or kids or how mundane my life has become. I want to feel like a woman capable of having a handsome guy interested in her. And for the next thirty minutes or so, I can pretend it is

Cam I'm having coffee with, Cam who's staring at me like I'm the most gorgeous girl in the world.

I find myself nodding. "I'll pay for my groceries, and meet you out front?"

"I like the sound of that."

He touches my shoulder, the briefest glance of his fingertips, yet it sends a shiver of longing through me the likes of which I've never had from any guy but Cam. "See you soon, Alice."

I watch him lope toward the checkout, long, easy strides that channel Cam perfectly.

This is silly, because no man will ever replace the love of my life, but what harm can having one coffee do?

CHAPTER TWENTY-EIGHT

BROOKE

I reach Verdant around eleven-thirty on Saturday morning, after leaving at seven. It takes me longer than expected because I got halfway and had a mini panic attack. Not literally, but I did pull over at a roadhouse and imbibe two strong coffees while second-guessing the wisdom of this trip before hitting the highway again.

Lizzie had to stay behind to watch Aunt Alice. We lied to Freya; I said I had to travel to San Fran for a wedding surprise so she couldn't ask me anything else. She believed me. Thankfully, Freya only has weekends off and she'd already promised to take Hope dress shopping so she didn't badger me. I don't like lying to my sister, not when we're re-establishing a bond, but she'd been so edgy when I'd questioned her about our parents and Aunt Alice's care at home that I don't want to rock the boat. If I discover anything relevant I'll come clean and share it with her. Besides, a small part of me is hurt she didn't think to include me in her outing with Hope. I would've loved to go dress shopping for the wedding with my sweet niece, but Freya made a point of telling me it was just the two of them, so in a fit of pique I'd lied about my plans for today.

As for Riker, he spends more time holed away in his workshop than he does with his bride-to-be and I still can't figure them out. They are the least lovey-dovey couple I've ever seen. Not that I've spent a lot of time with couples. I avoided them over the years because they always try to fix up the single person in their friendship group and I didn't want that. Not that I have friends either. Friendship breeds confidences and I don't want to tell anyone my story. I'm a loner and prefer it that way. As for my track record with guys, I'm no expert. For all I know Freya and Riker could be cool in public, passionate behind closed doors.

An unexpected pang at the thought of them together surprises me and I push it down deep where it belongs, before pulling into the first gas station I see and refueling. Once I meet with Amy and hopefully get some answers, I don't want to dilly-dally. Besides, if I get the right responses it might give me some clues on how to crack Alice's diary and I'll want to get back to the coast in a hurry.

Whoever named this town Verdant had a good sense of humor because the dry, barren town is anything but. There's no greenery but lots of dust, with desert as far as the eye can see in all directions. Vegas is about two hours away and I wonder if Aunt Alice and my mom ever took trips there for girly weekends. Then again, considering they both had kids in their teens, that was highly doubtful.

Amy has invited me to her home to meet and while I would've preferred the informality of a café I agreed because she may have photos of my parents in albums somewhere. Even after filling my car I'm still fifteen minutes early but I follow directions on the navigational display regardless and am parked out the front of her house a few minutes later.

She must be looking out for me because the front door opens and she steps out, elegant in beige capris and a turquoise silk T-shirt, her blonde bob sleek. She waves and I get out of the car, feeling like an intruder on a fool's errand.

This is crazy, chasing ghosts from the past. But I'm here and I want to give Aunt Alice some peace if I can, so I'm doing this.

As I get closer to the front step, Amy's eyes widen. "Wow, you look a lot like your dad." She blinks several times rapidly and I hope she's not going to cry. "You have his eyes."

My throat tightens with emotion. I've only seen the one picture of my parents, the one I've kept all these years. When Aunt Alice first showed me, she'd wanted to keep it hidden away because she didn't want Freya and me to feel sad over what we'd lost. I'd thought it odd at the time but had demanded I have the photo. She wouldn't give it to me, not until much later, and I'd been seven at the time, grateful to have a mom like Alice, and terrified something would happen to her too and we'd be left alone.

"Thanks for meeting me." I hold out my hand and she shakes it, before clasping it between both of hers, her welcoming smile making me relax.

"Come in. Hubby has taken the boys to the baseball so we've got the place to ourselves."

"How many children do you have?"

"Two boys, eleven and fifteen." She grimaces. "I started very late, not like your mom."

Hearing Amy mention my mom makes my chest ache, like I'm stifling a sob. In that moment, standing in the hallway with my mom's best friend, I feel a tenuous connection to the mother I never knew and I'm happy.

"I can't wait to hear all about her."

"Well, I'm not sure I'll be able to tell you anything you won't already know."

"I don't know much, to be honest."

Amy's eyebrows rise. "Doesn't Alice talk about her?"

"Not much," I admit, hating how that might make Aunt Alice sound and feeling obliged to defend her. "I haven't been around for the last eleven years and before that we didn't reminisce because I didn't want to remind her of everything she lost."

Amy nods but I see an odd expression cross her face. "Your aunt always was a strange one."

Before I can ask what she means, she ushers me into a sunroom. "Herbal tea? Coffee? Wine?"

I'm still hyped from my earlier coffees so I settle for herbal tea. Amy asks about my drive and how long I'm in town for and whether I have any food allergies, before placing a plate of peanut butter brownies in front of us alongside a steaming pot of peppermint tea.

I wait until she pours us both a cup before launching into my spiel. "Returning home after so long has got me thinking about my past, how much I've missed out on, that kind of thing, and I realized I barely know anything about my parents. Aunt Alice did an amazing job raising us but she has early onset dementia now so I can't ask her and—"

"That's awful." Amy places her teacup carefully in its saucer, the brew forgotten. "Is she okay?"

"Not really and her prognosis isn't good. She's rambling a lot, and it's repetitive, and she becomes quite distressed so that's why I'm here. I'm hoping you can shed some light on my parents, particularly my mom, as she seems like the focus of Alice's anxiety and I want to reassure her."

"You're a good person for wanting to do that but I'll be honest, you may not like what you hear."

Foreboding grips my gut and twists. "What do you mean?"

"Your mom and Alice were close in age, but that's where the similarities ended. Everyone adored Diana and your mom loved Alice but she was wary, because your aunt tended to be jealous."

"Of?"

The tension bracketing Amy's mouth softened. "Your mom was stunning in every way. Bold and vivacious and the life of every party. All the boys were after her, but the moment she met your dad they only had eyes for each other." Amy smiled. "Love at first sight with those two."

"So was Aunt Alice jealous because Mom had a boyfriend and she didn't?"

Amy hesitates for a second, a worried frown denting her brows, before she nods. "Alice was envious because she wanted everything Diana had, and I think that included her husband."

CHAPTER TWENTY-NINE

FREYA

Brooke lied to me.

I don't know what she's up to today but she's certainly not going to San Francisco. Even when we were kids I could spot her lies a mile off. Not that she lied often but when she did I could tell. Small fibs usually, like telling me she'd be studying in the library when she'd be sneaking off with her friends to the mall. Or saying she had an extra study period after school when she was loitering around the gym locker room waiting for the jocks to flirt with. Or insisting I couldn't accompany her to a school fair because one of her friends had five younger siblings and didn't want siblings tagging along, when I knew Brooke was the one who wanted to ditch me.

She'd lied to me the night Eli died too. We were at the party and she told me she was organizing a surprise for him and if he came looking for her to keep him busy. But, like late last night when she told me about her San Fran trip, she couldn't look me in the eyes and a tiny vein pulsed near her temple.

The thing was, I couldn't find Eli that night until much later and by then Brooke had broken up with him, so I never had to lie for her. She may have been comfortable with hiding the truth, but it never sits well with me.

A lot has happened since that night and I've strived hard to build the life I want. Having my sister back shouldn't disrupt that but

I can't shake the feeling she's up to something and I don't like it. She's probably off on a wild goose chase searching for information about our parents. What that will prove I have no idea. But she's been asking me a lot of questions about Aunt Alice and thankfully my aunt can't answer any of them.

I don't want to disappoint Hope otherwise I would've called off our shopping adventure and tried to distract Brooke. The wedding is only a few weeks away though and while it's low-key, Hope does need a special dress.

"Mom, how do I look?"

I turn as Hope emerges from behind a plush purple curtain shielding the dressing room in Martino Bay's sole bridal boutique and my breath catches.

"Oh, sweetie, you look incredible." I cross the room to take her hand and lift it overhead. "Do a twirl so I can see the full effect."

Hope obliges, doing several spins so the silk flares and shows a peep of tulle petticoat underneath. "I feel like a princess," she says, squealing in delight when I tickle her with my free hand.

"You look like one." I release her hand to squat so we're eye level. "You are the most beautiful girl in the world."

"I love you, Mom." She flings herself at me and as I slide my arms around her and cuddle her close, I know everything I've done is worth it.

I blink back tears but as we disengage Hope spots my shiny eyes. "Are you crying?"

"I'm happy, sweetheart, so it's all good."

She studies me a moment longer before nodding and turning to face the floor-to-ceiling mirror across one wall. "I love this dress." She gives a giggle and a little bow. "Princess Hope."

I smile, glad such a simple thing can bring her so much joy. I've never been a girly girl so don't take Hope shopping very often. When I do it's for practicality rather than frivolity. I should rectify that. Besides, as she hits the tween years and beyond, the closer

I keep our bond the better. Can't have her getting into the same kind of trouble her aunt and I did.

Having children young has its advantages but it takes its toll too. When I could've been out partying I was changing diapers and waking up for night feeds. When classmates in my year at school were at college I was stuck at home reading up on the terrible twos before I was twenty. Aunt Alice helped but she made it clear early on that Hope was my child and I had to be a present parent, not fobbing off duties onto her because we lived together.

I've been a good mom and as I see my daughter doing another proud twirl in her pale apricot silk dress with a cream satin sash tied at her waist, I know all the sacrifices have been worth it.

"What about you, Mom? Where's your dress?"

"I want it to be a surprise."

And it will be, particularly for Brooke. I wonder if she'll recognize the style and the significance? It's a replica of the one she wore the night of the party but longer, and ivory, rather than midnight blue. It's a statement dress. One I'd coveted but Brooke had seen it first online so of course she'd got it.

But since then, I've never forgotten what that dress represents to me: not being second best ever again.

I've had the dress designed to my specifications and the dressmaker has done a superb job replicating what I want. It's a beautiful boho style, with ivory chiffon draped over a rose satin slip underneath. The neckline is scalloped with fine lace, the bodice is fitted and the skirt brushes the floor with a gentle swish. It's modern and graceful and I feel amazing in it.

I can't wait for Riker to see me walk down the aisle.

I can't wait to see Brooke's reaction.

I love my sister but for once, in the dress I should've had first time around, marrying an amazing guy, I'm going to be the Stuart sister people take notice of.

CHAPTER THIRTY

ALICE

THEN

I'm never impulsive, unlike Diana. I've weighed decisions carefully my whole life. Choosing to stay in Verdant after I finished school. Saving every cent from the first day I started working. Mentally rehearsing what I'd say to Cam when I revealed my feelings. It's the latter thought that makes me want to do something rash and extend my coffee date with Toby. I'm having fun for the first time in years. I like feeling this carefree and I want to make it last, so I call Marie.

"Can you watch the girls a little longer?" I murmur into my cell, watching the restroom door so I know when Toby reappears.

"Sorry, Alice, I can't. I need to leave in an hour at the latest because I have book club tonight."

Disappointment makes my shoulders sag. I've never asked Marie to stay longer with the kids and because she'd been so encouraging when I'd called earlier to tell her I was catching up with a friend for coffee after grocery shopping, I thought she might be accommodating. But she leads a busy life, with a host of hobbies since her girls left for college, and I can't begrudge her.

"Okay, I'll be home by then." I hang up, resentment at the girls simmering. But that's unfair. I took on the burden. I need to live with my decision. But being on my own, even for a short time, is liberating and I want to prolong it.

Besides, being with Toby for the last forty-five minutes makes me wonder if this is what it would've been like if I'd ever been out with Cam. Having him really look at me while listening, the intensity of his stare like there's nowhere else he'd rather be, the slight upturning at the corners of his mouth hinting at a smile. Having Toby solely focused on me, the ever-present pressure in my chest since those two police officers delivered their devastating news has eased.

I watch him wend his way between the tables. His loping stride is reminiscent of Cam. Or maybe I'm projecting onto Toby because he's the first guy who's ever shown any real interest in me? Physically, he only bears a vague resemblance to Cam and perhaps I'm seeing things in his mannerisms that aren't there, a case of wishful thinking?

When he reaches me, Toby touches my shoulder and a sizzle shoots through my body at the warmth of his touch. "Hey, what's wrong?"

I can't answer honestly—I'm so pathetic I'm still pining for my first love and besotted by a stranger who loosely reminds me of him—so I settle for, "My sitter can't stay so I have to head home."

"That's okay. We can catch up another time."

My heart sinks. I know how this plays out. Another time means never. Once our coffee date finishes he'll have time to ruminate all the reasons why he shouldn't date a woman with three kids and that'll be the end of it.

Logically, it makes sense. What do I envisage happening? I have the girls to take care of and I can't flit around on dates like other women my age. I should thank him and walk away. But I can't. Because for the first time in forever I feel… free, like a woman who can command the attention of a cute guy, like a woman who is unencumbered, like a woman paying attention to her own needs rather than those of others.

I'd cared for my mother, I cared for my sister's kids, why can't I be impulsive for once? I've never been bold in my life and look where it's got me. Nowhere.

"You could come back to my place and I'll cook you dinner?"

His eyebrows rise and I instantly second-guess my forward invitation.

"I mean, only if you want to. It's going to be noisy and messy, because I'll need to feed the girls and put them to bed and it's chaotic—"

"I don't mind. I'm used to my nieces and nephews running wild when I visit my sisters. Kids are great."

He leans over and places his lips on mine, a gentle, tender kiss that has me sighing. He pulls away too soon, which is just as well considering we're in a café and I'm the oldest virgin in California and would probably jump him if he kissed me properly. The type of long, hot, open-mouthed kiss I crave. The type of kiss I imagined having with Cam and never did.

"Okay, let's have dinner at my place," I murmur against the corner of his mouth and I sense his smile.

We ease apart and I see my excitement reflected in his eyes.

"Let's go." He takes hold of my hand, and as I glance at our joined hands, a sliver of unease pierces my euphoria.

What am I doing, inviting a stranger into my home? I'm not this woman, ready to throw caution away for the sake of a cute guy. And I shouldn't have let him kiss me, no matter how much I wanted it. This is insane.

Sensing my prevarication, he squeezes my hand. "It's only dinner, and I'm fine if you want to do it another time."

I still hesitate, second-guessing the wisdom of having a guy I barely know around my girls. It's my duty to protect them. It's what Cam would've wanted.

It's the thought of Cam that settles it. Hanging back in the past got me nowhere and resulted in Diana stealing my man.

This time I won't make the same mistake.

"It's okay, come over and have dinner tonight."

I want to spend more time with Toby.

Starting now.

CHAPTER THIRTY-ONE
BROOKE

I'm stunned as Amy reveals more about Aunt Alice and my father. How Amy spotted Aunt Alice staring longingly across a room at him sometimes, how Aunt Alice never dated, how she'd seek out my dad to chat at every opportunity. It sounds like a crush to me. My aunt was single. Who knows, she may have felt out of place with my parents being so insular in their relationship and besotted with each other? Maybe Aunt Alice had just been lonely?

"Do you think Alice was in love with my father?"

"It was obvious to everyone." Amy smiles. "Then again, most girls were back then. Your dad had this way about him, of commanding attention yet being approachable. He was nice to everybody." She taps her temple. "Smart too. He could've been anything if he left town to attend college, but he chose to stay." Amy's expression softens. "I think that had a lot to do with your mom. He was smitten from the minute he laid eyes on her and even when she went away to have the baby he didn't date anyone else. Then when she came back, they picked up where they left off. She got pregnant again, they married and you probably know the rest."

I don't but I'm still trying to process why Diana would go away to have me?

But before I can ask Amy continues. "As for Alice, she tried to be Cam's friend when Di went away. She was always hanging around him, usually in a group, but there nonetheless. I was on the fringes as they were older than me but I saw what went on." She grimaces. "I felt sorry for her. She hung around Cam like a puppy grateful for whatever scraps of attention he threw her way. To his credit, he remained loyal to Di and only ever saw Alice as a friend, though I often wonder if he had any clue how obsessed she was with him."

I'm more confused than ever. Did my parents break up after Diana fell pregnant with me, only to reunite and have Freya?

"You've said how great Alice has been raising you and I'm happy to hear it, because when your parents died some of us had our concerns." She glances out the window, lost in thought. "Alice took the news of their deaths hard, really hard, but only those closest to Di, like me, knew she mourned the loss of Cam more than her sister. And she didn't stay around long. She put Cam's house and hers on the market, sold quickly, and moved away. No one knew where."

If anyone understands the need for a fresh start I do but learning about this obsessive side to my aunt is unsettling. She's never been anything other than devoted to me, Freya and Lizzie and I'm not sure having confirmation of her crush on my dad has solved anything.

"I have to say, taking on three kids at her age was admirable." Amy shakes her head. "I couldn't do it."

I nod. "Yeah, being responsible for Freya and me along with her own daughter must've been tough."

Confusion clouds Amy's eyes. "What are you talking about? Alice never had a child."

"But… yes, she did. Lizzie is my cousin."

Shock makes Amy gape for a moment before she shakes her head. "Only Alice and me knew when Di went away, it was to have a baby and give it up for adoption. After your parents died, Alice gained custody."

Realization hits me like a kick to the guts as Amy says, "Lizzie isn't your cousin. She's your sister."

CHAPTER THIRTY-TWO

FREYA

When Hope and I get home from dress shopping, Lizzie is waiting for me in the kitchen and she doesn't look happy.

I send Hope off in search of Riker in his workshop and watch out the window as she knocks and waits as she's been taught to do. If he's welding he doesn't like to be disturbed and we all know it. When the barn door opens, I see his face light up and a breath I'm unaware I'm holding whooshes out. Hope says something, he beams, takes hold of her hand, and leads her inside. I love him even more for how he loves Hope.

Only then do I turn to Lizzie, who's pacing the kitchen. "What's up?"

She stops and fixes me with a no-nonsense stare. "I'm worried about Mom. I think she's getting worse."

We've had this conversation before, usually when Lizzie has to spend alone time with Alice and can't take a break. She thinks it's time we move Alice to a nursing home. She hates having Alice locked in her room, and wants her free to be able to roam around where there's more space.

"Lizzie, we've talked about this. I work in the place where you want to put your mom so I know what it's like. While the level of care is excellent, we're understaffed and overworked. Patients don't get the same level of care we can give Alice here. And patients with this kind of dementia can present as weak but can have bursts of strength combined with aggressiveness, so I'd rather manage that here at home than have some stranger who doesn't really know Alice do it."

"But she's so confined here." Anguish darkens her eyes. "I hate seeing her locked up. She never wants to leave the room even though she can walk."

That's news to me. We've been using the wheelchair whenever we take her to the bathroom.

"She's walking?"

Lizzie gives me an odd look. "Of course, I make sure of it. I get her out of bed every day and we do laps of the room. She's frail and shuffling but is getting better."

"That's great." I sound too perky and immediately tone it down. "If I had more time I would do it with her too. The more active she stays the better."

"She's so out of it most days I don't think she realizes what she's doing." Lizzie nibbles on her bottom lip, worry evident in her rigid shoulders. "I thought if she's surrounded by more people all day she might be more inclined to focus and at least try to remember who we are. Brooke and I have been discussing it and she's worried too."

Brooke. Of course. I should've known she'd try to take over like she always did.

It annoys me that Lizzie has been happy to go along with my opinion regarding Aunt Alice before now, but the moment Brooke pokes her nose into our business, Lizzie sides with her.

Their closeness had always got under my skin and I'd often felt like a third wheel growing up alongside them. Brooke has been AWOL for over a decade. How dare she waltz back into our lives and profess to know what's best for Aunt Alice, better than I know myself?

But I can't let my resentment toward Brooke show. Lizzie can be stubborn and she'll dig her heels in if she thinks I'm pushing to keep Aunt Alice at home because Brooke wants the opposite.

"Lizzie, I know this is heartbreaking." I cross the kitchen and pull her into my arms for a brief hug before I release her. "Let's consider it, okay? See how she goes over the next few weeks? It will be nice to have her here for the wedding and then we can re-evaluate?"

Lizzie appears satisfied when she nods and some of the tension holding her rigid eases. "Don't get me wrong, I'm indebted to you for all you do for Mom, but I want what's best for her."

"We all do," I say, unable to shake my annoyance that Brooke is interfering when she has no right to.

CHAPTER THIRTY-THREE

ALICE

THEN

I don't have the heart to tell Toby I rarely drink when he says he'll pick up some wine on the way to my place so will be about ten minutes behind me. Still high on my uncharacteristic forward behavior, I don't want anything to spoil tonight, and as I thank Marie and pay her for the last week's nanny duties, I try not to rush her out the door.

She'll judge me for inviting a man I barely know over for dinner and I harbor enough doubts without her adding to them. I shouldn't have done it and as Freya wails in hunger, and Brooke and Lizzie argue over who gets to use the red crayon first, I'm tempted to call Toby and tell him not to come.

If I had his number.

"Idiot," I mutter, stomping around the kitchen to prepare the girls' dinner, grateful to Marie yet again for her cooking skills in whipping up meals and portioning them into small containers and freezing them. She also makes lasagnas and casseroles for me, so I pop one of the lasagnas into the oven to heat; I'll make a salad when my guest arrives.

Cam will be here any moment… I stop dead in the middle of the kitchen and press my hands to my cheeks. I mean Toby. This is wrong. I am projecting onto him and it's not fair. I may not know

Toby well but it's not right to use him as some kind of warped stand-in for Cam because I'm still yearning for the love of my life.

Obsessing over Cam isn't healthy.

Cam is dead.

Because of me.

And no amount of sobbing into my pillow at night or rallying against a god I don't believe in will change it.

Maybe I need this dinner with Toby as a distraction? I'm too young to feel this jaded. I need a dash of excitement in my life, something just for me that has nothing to do with caring for three young girls.

Twenty minutes later the girls are fed and Toby still hasn't arrived. I don't know whether to be relieved or annoyed. The girls are lined up in front of the TV, even Freya, who's kicking her chubby legs in time to the music of some educational program for toddlers. Brooke and Lizzie are engrossed so I whip around the kitchen, cleaning up, wondering what Toby and I will talk about over dinner and wishing I had time for a shower.

I hear a car pull up and my pulse goes into overdrive as I peek through the blinds and see him get out of the car, all long, loose limbs. He walks around to the passenger door, opens it and grabs a few bags off the seat, before kicking it shut and loping toward the house.

I'm beyond nervous, completely out of my depth. I've never dated. What will I say? All I can converse about is the girls: the best educational programs and books, the healthiest meals. Not exactly riveting dinner conversation for a young guy, even if he has got nieces and nephews. At the café he'd done all the talking, telling me about himself: Toby Lundgren, twenty-five, graphic designer, traveling the west coast in search of a place to put down roots. My wishful thinking wonders if he'd like to stick around Martino Bay for a while.

My palms grow clammy and I swipe them down the sides of my dress. I changed after Marie left into a simple black shift, the only decent dress I own, with a pink cardigan over it—and head for the door.

Toby knocks and Brooke and Lizzie's heads swivel toward the door. "Who's that?"

"A friend of mine," I say softly. "So I need you to behave."

"You don't have any friends," Lizzie says, with a disapproving frown, "and they never visit."

"Well, this one does." It hurts when I realize she's right. Marie is the only person in this town I can class as a friend and even then, would she be if I wasn't paying her? "Be good, okay?"

The girls ignore me and turn back to the TV so I take a deep breath and let it out before opening the door.

"Hey," Toby says, and I wonder how one small syllable can make me so nervous. I stand there like a silent dummy, until he clears his throat.

"Come in," I mutter, and hold the door open.

"I brought something for the girls along with the wine." He brandishes a large paper bag. "Is it too forward if I greet you with a kiss?"

Before I can respond, Lizzie yells, "Yuck," and embarrassment flushes my cheeks.

Toby laughs. "Guess it's time for me to meet your girls."

I'm impressed, as most guys wouldn't want to hang out with a single mom of three, let alone want to meet the rug rats. Then again, he sounded like he enjoys his uncle duties earlier and it's a relief that he's used to kids.

"Let's take that bag into the kitchen then I'll introduce you."

"Sure."

He follows me into the kitchen and when he places the bag on the kitchen bench, I sneak a peek. He's brought a bottle of red, a store-bought carrot cake, and a packet of chocolate farm animals Lizzie and Brooke will love.

Touched by his thoughtfulness, I say, "Come meet my girls."

"My nieces think I'm the best uncle ever so hopefully your girls will be equally impressed."

However, as we squat next to the girls and Freya spots Toby, her face crumples into an expression I know well: she's about to yell the house down.

As if sensing an incoming meltdown, Toby averts his gaze to Brooke and leans in close. "Hey there. You must be Brooke. Your Aunt Alice has told me about you and—"

"Don't you touch my cousin!" Lizzie screams and we jump. "Get away from her! We don't know you."

I'm mortified but Toby takes Lizzie's animosity in his stride, easing away with his hands held up.

"Lizzie, it's okay," I say, kneeling to give her a kiss, mouthing, "Sorry," to Toby.

"No, it's not okay." Lizzie's face is red and she's jabbing her finger at Toby. "We don't want him here."

"Toby's a friend—"

"No, he's not. He's a stranger." She glares at him. "Stranger danger, Mommy, you taught me that."

She's right and in that moment I know I've made a mistake. What was I thinking, inviting a man I barely know into my house? Am I that needy, that desperate, I fall for a sweet-talking guy who reminds me of Cam on my first outing alone without the girls?

I press a kiss to Lizzie's forehead to calm her. "You're right, sweetie, I did teach you that, and I'm proud of you for remembering."

Mollified, Lizzie casts one last malevolent glare at Toby before turning her back on him to refocus on the TV.

I risk a glance at Toby and he's bemused. I don't blame him. I gesture at the door. "Perhaps we can do this another time?"

"Sure," he says, but I know it's a lie.

I can't do this; pretend like I'm a woman who can date and invite guys back to my place without a thought of the consequences.

I chose to care for these girls and that's what I have to do. Their needs must come first. That's what Cam would want.

I walk Toby to the door and open it. He pauses, his smile rueful. "Kids are unpredictable and, for what it's worth, I think it's great you've taught them about stranger danger. It's stuff they need to know. So don't feel bad, okay? We can have dinner some other time—"

"I shouldn't have invited you. I'm sorry." My gaze flicks to the girls, who are angelic now, of course. "Those kids are my world and right now, I don't have room for anyone else in it."

He's surprised by my curtness, but nods. "Okay."

His easy-going response reminds me of Cam and I fight back tears. I'm so conflicted. I want a man to love me, to make me feel like a woman. My identity has become so wrapped up in the girls I don't know who I am anymore. I'm twenty-three going on forty. I don't have fun. Then again, did I ever? I'm staid and responsible and I brought this on myself. I want to raise Cam's girls the way he would've wanted me to. Their needs come first.

Toby reaches out and touches my arm, a fleeting brush of his fingertips that makes me feel worse because I know it won't happen again. "If you change your mind—"

"I won't." I shake my head, needing him to leave before I break down completely.

"For what it's worth, Alice, you need to have a life too."

With a funny little salute, he's gone, loping back to his car. I wait until he reverses out of the drive before closing the door, leaning my forehead on it, and willing the sobs simmering in my chest to dissipate.

I can't cry in front of the girls. So I do something I've been thinking about for a while, a coping strategy I read about online, a way to pour my frustrations out.

I need to offload for my mental health and, without any friends or family to talk to, maybe journaling is it?

I march to the dining table, flip open my laptop and open a program I downloaded last week. After registering, and entering a password I'll never forget, I start typing.

CHAPTER THIRTY-FOUR
BROOKE

"You're wrong, Lizzie is not my sister."

My response to Amy's outrageous claim is quick and instinctive. She has to be wrong. Because if her supposition is right and Lizzie is my sister, not my cousin, everything I ever believed about my aunt is a lie.

Amy shifts in her seat, uncomfortable with my outrage. "All I know is, Di got pregnant to Cam the first night they met and her mother arranged for her to go away for the duration of her pregnancy, then have the baby adopted. Di told everyone she was going to college in Long Island but only I knew the truth." She presses a hand to her chest. "She trusted me like a sister. We were closer than her and Alice ever were."

I can't comprehend the enormity of this. "But why would Aunt Alice lie?"

"Why would Alice do half the things she did?" Amy rolls her eyes. "Look, it's no secret I never liked your aunt but I'm not making this up. There'll be birth records, certificates, stuff you can look up for confirmation."

I press my fingers to my temples. I came here in search of answers that could hopefully bring peace to my aunt. Instead, I've stirred up trouble and I'm left doubting if I know Aunt Alice at all. As for Lizzie... what will this mean for her? How will she feel? What a mess.

I have so many questions, but I'm not sure I want answers anymore.

"If my mom came back to town and got back together with my dad again, why wouldn't she reclaim her child?"

"Your mom wasn't the same when she returned to Verdant." Amy gives a little shake of her head. "She confided in me how devastating it was to give away her child, how conflicted she'd been right up until labor, but her mother insisted she couldn't bring a baby home."

Amy tapped her temple. "It messed with Di's head. She wasn't the same vibrant, bubbly girl any longer. She'd drift off at the oddest of times and she smiled infrequently. And she didn't want your dad knowing what she'd done because she feared it would tear them apart."

If anyone understands the devastation of losing a child, I can, and this tenuous connection to my mom bonds us in a way I never anticipated.

"I'm surprised she didn't confide in my dad if they loved each other so much?"

Amy shrugs. "I don't think she expected to hook up with Cam again, to have him pursue her so relentlessly. They really only ever had eyes for each other, couldn't keep their hands off each other either, which is why she fell pregnant again with you so soon."

"Contraception was still popular back then," I say, but Amy doesn't acknowledge my dry response.

"Have you ever been so in love with someone that nothing else matters? Like nothing exists around you and you don't care about anyone else? That's what it was like for Di and Cam, and when they found each other again I don't think she wanted to ruin it."

My head is spinning but I need to know more.

"How did Aunt Alice end up adopting Lizzie if my mom already gave the baby away for adoption years earlier?"

"That, I don't know, you'd have to ask Alice."

I would if I had any hope of getting a straight answer and I realize now more than ever how imperative it is I gain access to that diary. Regardless of what I've discovered, Aunt Alice raised me, loved me, supported me. I'm honor bound to defend her.

"Whatever my aunt did, she took on three young kids that weren't her own. She must've done it out of love."

Amy quirks an eyebrow, as if she can't believe I'm so naïve.

"Or she hated your mother so much she did it to spite her."

I must look incredulous because Amy laughs, a harsh sound devoid of amusement.

"Alice's way of giving your mother the finger from beyond the grave. A 'look what I've got and you don't' kind of thing."

"That's harsh," I say, appalled by Amy's supposition.

"You don't know Alice the way I did and from what I saw back then, she was so jealous of your mother she was capable of anything."

CHAPTER THIRTY-FIVE

FREYA

I hear Brooke pull up just before midnight. Riker's snoring softly beside me and I slip out of bed trying not to wake him. I pull on a dressing gown and leave his cottage, flicking the lock and pulling the door shut behind me. It feels illicit, naughty, visiting each other in the dead of night, and I hope we never lose this sense of fun. I don't have enough of it in my life.

I've always been the staid one, the sensible one; everyone said so when Brooke and I were growing up. In fact, people who didn't know us often mistook Lizzie and Brooke for sisters with their similar coloring, and I was the odd one out. I hated that.

When Brooke left I envisaged Lizzie and me becoming closer but it never happened. She didn't come home for the main holidays like Thanksgiving and Christmas, and when she finally returned from college, she fell in love with Hope, but our bond didn't change. Sure, we went to the occasional movie together, shopped in LA for Aunt Alice's birthday, that kind of thing, but we were never as close as the relationship she'd shared with Brooke. Living on the same property meant the three of us often shared meals occasionally, but Aunt Alice and Lizzie were in the main house and I felt like an outsider in the cottage Riker now occupies. I'd liked my independence when it was just Aunt Alice, Hope and me, the privacy of having my own place. But after Lizzie returned, I wished I'd been in the main house too.

Me moving into the main house to look after Alice felt like coming home and I took a strange satisfaction in relegating Lizzie to the other cottage, while Hope took her old room. Lizzie didn't seem to mind as I've got the expertise to look after her mother, but it didn't do me any favors in trying to get closer to her. Then again, if it hadn't happened over the last eleven years, what difference would five months make?

The wind picks up as I make my way across the yard. It's often blustery at night, when the waves crashing against the rocks at the base of the cliffs are particularly loud. There's a full moon tonight and it bathes the house in an ethereal glow, as bright as if a light switch has been flicked, so I see Brooke let herself into the main house through the back door. Where has she been and why is she getting in so late?

I don't like not knowing things and my sister has secrets I want to be privy to. I hated being left out when we were growing up too, and used to read her diary. Not that there was ever anything juicy; just endless pages about which boy said what to her, who she liked, who she didn't. Boring, mundane stuff, with the occasional revelation to shake things up, like when she wanted to lose her virginity. I'd never been that stupid to write anything personal in mine but I had liked those journaling sessions when I'd sit with Brooke and Lizzie in the reading nook and we'd scribble in relative silence.

Brooke is sipping water from a glass as I let myself in and she jumps when she hears the door snick.

"What are you doing sneaking around at this time of night?" She places the empty glass on the sink, before a slow smile creeps across her face. "Actually, don't answer that. You've got booty call written all over you."

To my annoyance a blush surges to my cheeks. "I'm engaged. What of it?"

"Hey, I'm kidding." She holds up her hands and they shake slightly, like she's nervous. "What you two get up to after dark is none of my business."

Something in her tone rankles; I hate being teased. "Speaking of business, you're back awfully late for a trip to San Fran."

"I had a few things to take care of." Her gaze slides away from mine, deliberately evasive, and she's gnawing on her bottom lip. She's upset about something and I'm worried. It's not like Brooke to be this cagey.

"Like what?"

"What's with the interrogation?" She crosses her arms, her jaw jutting because she's clenching her teeth so hard. "I've got a private life just like you."

My eyebrows shoot up and I try to placate her. "Where's that coming from?"

Indignation radiates off her before she gives a little shake of her head and unfolds her arms to rest her hands behind her, bracing against the sink. "I'm tired of this family and its secrets."

My heart skips a beat. "What are you talking about?"

Her shoulders slump, like she's shouldering a giant invisible weight, and when her gaze locks on mine, her concern is clear. "Before Aunt Alice got sick, did she ever confide in you about stuff she's done in her past?"

I freeze. Surely she can't know…

"I think Alice was in love with our dad."

I exhale in relief. "What?"

"Yeah, and it doesn't stop there…" She trails off, shaking her head again, and I'm gripped by panic again. Surely she can't know the rest?

"You know you can confide in me, right?"

She nods, but she hasn't lost the defeated posture. "I need to process it all before I tell you."

Tell me what? I'm increasingly worried she's stumbled onto the truth but if that's the case, she would've confronted me already. This is something else and I'll have to give her time rather than badger.

"That's fine, Sis, I'm here for you whenever you're ready to talk."

She manages a tight smile in gratitude and turns away, so I barely hear her murmured, "You're in for one hell of a surprise."

I hope not.

Brooke and I have that in common. We don't like surprises.

I've had enough to last me a lifetime.

CHAPTER THIRTY-SIX
BROOKE

The next morning, Lizzie is curious to discover what I found in Verdant and as much as I want to tell her everything I don't want to turn her world upside down until I have facts.

But to dig further I need to start with the basics and that means getting hold of Lizzie's birth certificate.

"Hey, I'm doing a digital family album for Freya's wedding and was wondering where all the birth certificates, old school grading cards, that kind of thing, are stored these days?"

I keep my tone blasé and thankfully Lizzie doesn't suspect a thing. "They used to be in that monstrous cookie tin next to the fireplace but Mom put them into a filing cabinet in the den years ago."

Damn, I'd already checked there and, while the folders for Freya and me are bulging with documentation, Lizzie's isn't and only starts around school age.

"Thanks, I've already had a look through that. Anywhere else she would've stored stuff?"

"Not that I know of."

I try another tactic. "Have you traveled at all over the last decade? I was hoping to make a collage of pics too."

My heart sinks when she shakes her head. To get a passport she would've needed a birth certificate and this is my roundabout way of asking if she has it.

"I'm a homebody, always have been." She shrugs. "Guess I get that from Mom. She never traveled either."

I know Lizzie's date of birth so I have a place to start searching. But to get a copy of her birth certificate she'll need to apply and who knows how long it will take? I could expedite the entire process by asking her for it but she's not stupid, she'll want to know why and I'm plum out of excuses. So I try one last time.

"Do you have your birth certificate? I can't find Freya's either and I really want to get this family album done."

"Sorry, I have no idea where they could be. To be honest, I've never seen any of them."

Her astute gaze focuses on me and I know she's figured out I'm not being entirely truthful.

"What's this really about, Brooke?"

I don't want to hurt her. Discovering Alice lied to us is hard enough. But Lizzie will find out her mom is her aunt, that our mom gave her up but kept us. It could be devastating. I don't want to tell her but I see by the determination in her blue eyes so like my own she's not going to let this go.

"Okay, I'll tell you, but this information could be wrong so don't freak out."

A dent grooves her brows. "You being evasive is freaking me out."

I take a deep breath and let it out, steeling myself. This is what comes of delving into the past and I of all people should know secrets are best left hidden.

"You know I caught up with Mom's best friend Amy Cresswell when I went to Verdant yesterday."

"Yeah, and you still haven't told me what you discovered."

"Amy told me a lot about Aunt Alice. According to Amy, she was in love with my dad and was jealous of Diana."

Lizzie gives a little shake of her head. "She's always been a great mom, I can't imagine her being jealous of anyone."

"That's not all."

Lizzie leans forward, waiting for me to continue, and I swallow the trepidation clogging my throat.

"Amy said Diana slept with Cameron the first night they met. She got pregnant and went away to have the baby."

Lizzie's eyebrows shoot up. "Why would she do that? You and Freya are only eleven months apart so if something bad happened between her and your father they must've made up pretty quick."

"As far as Amy's aware I wasn't the baby she went away to have in secret." I eyeball Lizzie, silently imploring her to understand. "You are."

Lizzie's reaction isn't what I expect. She laughs, slightly hysterical, until tears seep from her eyes.

"That's crazy." She uses her pinkies to wipe away the tears. "Why would my mom lie about something like this?"

"That's what I'm trying to find out."

The seriousness in my tone sobers her up and her amused smirk fades.

"You really think there's something to this?"

I nod. "Amy has no reason to lie. She was Mom's best friend and I saw a stack of photos that showed how happy our parents were, with Aunt Alice always left out, hovering in the background, staring at them with longing. And Amy had a lot to say about Aunt Alice. Apparently nobody knew about Diana going away to have a baby apart from her and Alice." I hesitate, knowing what I say next will hurt her but needing to tell her all of it. "She said Diana gave you up for adoption, then came home and ended up rekindling things with our dad again, and having me and Freya pretty quickly."

Pain, raw and real, contorts Lizzie's face for a moment. "But if I was adopted, how did Alice get hold of me?"

I note she's switched from calling my aunt "Mom" to "Alice" and it breaks my heart I'm tearing her world apart.

"I don't know. I guess we have to do some more digging."

She frowns and swipes a hand over her face before leaping to her feet. "This is ridiculous. Why would she lie for all these years?"

"Probably to protect you." I stand and go to her. I envelop her in my arms and she tolerates my hug, stiff and unyielding, before shrugging me off.

"Protect me from discovering my real mom gave me away while keeping her other two better kids?"

Her bitterness is audible and I wish I could hug her again.

"We don't know what happened back then, Lizzie. Don't forget Diana would've been eighteen when she had you and probably freaking out over being pregnant in a small town." I shrug. "From what I saw Verdant is tiny and stuck in the middle of nowhere. Everyone would know everyone else's business and, while I never knew our grandmother, Amy said she pushed Diana into 'taking care of things'." I make inverted comma signs with my fingers. "Amy also said Diana changed after she gave you up, that she came back a different person and was really cut up about it. I know we can't make assumptions, but whatever Aunt Alice did, I'm sure she did it out of love."

"I could've handled the truth." Lizzie lashes out and kicks the nearest thing, the back of the sofa, her face flushed with fury. "She could've told me at any time but she chose not to and now I can't bloody ask her."

Her anger is understandably focused on Aunt Alice but I want to distract her, to make this easier for her if possible.

"I guess it explains why I've always felt close to you," I say, with a wry grin. "You're my big sister and I think that's pretty damn wonderful."

The tension bracketing her mouth softens. "I've always loved you like a sister anyway."

This time she moves toward me and we hug tight, sniffling into each other's shoulders.

But I can't ignore the niggle of worry; what will Freya make of this? She'd resented my closeness with Lizzie growing up.

Will this shatter the bond we've re-formed?

CHAPTER THIRTY-SEVEN

ALICE

THEN

It's true what people say, that when you have kids time flies. I've lived in Martino Bay for over a decade, pretending I'm content with my life.

I'm luckier than most. I have a great house in a picturesque spot, I have three gorgeous girls who adore me and I have enough money to live comfortably.

But I can't keep the memories at bay and some nights I wake drenched in sweat, gulping in lungfuls of air, seeing Diana's lifeless eyes staring at me and Cam walking toward me with open arms. When I wake from this nightmare I never know what upsets me most: the fact I may have inadvertently killed my sister or that Cam died with her.

I never should've contemplated tampering with Di's brakes, shouldn't have touched them even if I didn't do anything. I was young, stupid and insanely jealous, determined to take back what's mine. But technically Cam never was mine. I let her have him the night they met and I didn't put up a fight. I should've ranted and raved and clawed her eyes out for making a play for my man. I should've staked my claim. Di may have snagged Cam but the blame lies with me for being passive, and I'd lost him.

But I have his girls. I'm older and wiser now, and the guilt I may have contributed to Di and Cam's deaths has grown exponentially over the last ten years. It will consume me if I let it so I focus on being the best mother I can be, trying to make amends for robbing them of their parents.

The girls are fine overall. Lizzie is lovely: sweet, unassuming, unaware of her beauty. She's a nurturer, enjoying nothing better than taking care of her younger siblings. Not that they know it. Brooke and Freya idolize their cousin and I'm glad they're close.

Brooke is a beauty, able to charm anyone and everyone. She's an extrovert, her vivacity as captivating as her big blue eyes and sunny smile. She and Lizzie are a lot alike and they gravitate toward each other.

Freya is the one I worry about. She reminds me of me, always hanging off Brooke, wanting to be like her, wanting what she has. I need to watch her because I don't want her making the same mistakes I did.

Today, I'm particularly worried. Lizzie is taking Brooke to a friend's party at a local fair but because Freya is under twelve and won't be allowed on some of the rides she can't go. She doesn't like being excluded from anything and I know a storm is brewing.

I drop Lizzie and Brooke at the fairground and greet the parent in charge, a woman who's only recently moved to town. But the girls know everyone there and are quickly absorbed into a group of fifteen giggly, chattering girls.

I glance in the rearview mirror and Freya's face is contorted with resentment as she glares at the happy group. I quickly pull away from the curb and say, "How about we grab your favorite ice cream then head to the movies?"

She doesn't answer for a moment and I can almost see her trying to get her breathing under control.

After thirty seconds she finally mutters, "I want to go home."

She sounds disappointed, and I want to distract her. "Perhaps we can watch a movie and have ice cream at home?"

"Whatever," she murmurs, her petulance audible, and she's sullenly silent until I pull the car into the drive and switch off the engine. When I turn to face her, she's still sulking, arms folded, shoulders rigid with tension, frowning.

"Freya, you can't always accompany your sister—"

"Leave me alone!" she yells, before flinging open the door and bolting, running across the lawn toward the backyard.

I should go after her but I'm weary, thirty-four going on fifty. These girls consume my life and I don't do much beyond parenting. After the Toby saga I avoided men for an entire year. I eventually lost my virginity at the ripe old age of twenty-four to a single dad I met at a toddlers' playgroup, but I didn't like him enough to pursue anything. Since then I've had a fling with an artist passing through town and a substitute teacher at the girls' grade school, but I ended up feeling guilty for abandoning them to extra hours with Marie so I walked away from both those relationships.

I keep telling myself I don't need a man. I'm content, happy even, but when that familiar nightmare comes and I see Cam walking toward me I know I would give anything to have that happen for real. I'm doing right by him, raising his girls, loving them as he would've wanted them to be loved. But I miss him, even after all these years, and I feel stupid pining for a ghost.

I'm lost in my musings and realize I've been sitting in the car for five minutes. As I get out, I hear a sob coming from the makeshift cubby house the girls built in the backyard many years ago. They don't use it anymore but as that sound comes again I know where to head.

The cubby house has a mirror inside it, an old one taken off the back of my bedroom door. The girls loved having it in the cubby house so they could do fashion parades in front of it, dressing up in oversized old clothes, prancing around in wobbly high heels.

When I round the back corner of the house Freya's in front of the mirror, tears streaming down her face, a pair of scissors in one hand, Brooke's favorite jacket in the other. It's bright pink with diamanté edging at the collar and cuffs. I think it's gaudy but Brooke fell in love with it the moment she saw it in an online catalogue and pestered me to order it. Predictably, Freya wanted one just like it but it had been a sample, a one-off, and I know she's coveted it ever since.

Now, the jacket hangs in tatters. I watch as Freya slashes at the jacket over and over, stabbing with a ferocity that makes my heart ache. I should stop her. I should do something to ease her pain. But I know from personal experience nothing I say will help so I let her take her fury out on a piece of material.

Better that than her sister.

CHAPTER THIRTY-EIGHT

FREYA

When I get home from work the next day, Brooke and Lizzie are waiting for me. Tension radiates off them but their expressions are shuttered and I can't get a read. They want to talk to me and I agree to meet them by the back of the property near the cliffs once I get Hope settled.

I'm edgy as I listen to my daughter prattle on about the circulatory system she started learning about in school today, between demolishing a banana muffin and a glass of milk. She barely takes a breath between mouthfuls, her excitement palpable. She's exceptionally bright and I'm proud but all I want to do is rush out of the house and head for the cliffs.

When she eventually winds down and takes out her homework, I press a kiss to the top of her head. "You make a start on that while I go chat to your aunts, okay?"

"Sure thing, Mom." She waves me away, already engrossed in the various chambers of the heart and how oxygenated blood is pumped around the body.

I quickly check in on Aunt Alice—she barely registers I'm in the room—before locking her door and slipping out of the house. Riker's van isn't parked in its usual spot and I have no clue where he is. He knows I don't like getting texts or calls while I'm at work so he'll check in later.

Trepidation wars with eagerness as I make my way along the worn dirt pathway toward the back of the property, the roar of the ocean crashing against the rocks at the bottom of the cliffs becoming louder with every step. Hope knows never to come down here unless supervised and I avoid the place.

As I stumble over a small rock, it reminds me of another day I stubbed my toe heading down here. Lizzie and Brooke had told Aunt Alice they were taking a picnic to the cliffs. We were sixteen, fifteen and fourteen respectively and I hated how close those two had become, always whispering about boys. While I'd been stuck inside finishing algebra homework because it always took me longer, they'd gone off on their own.

After I finished I'd been eager to find them and had been half-jogging when I tripped over a rock, bruising my big toe in the process. I'd hopped around for a moment, irrationally blaming them, before continuing along the path. When I reached the highest peak I saw them sitting on a picnic blanket, their heads bent close as they studied something on one of their cells. They looked so alike with their shiny blonde hair hanging halfway down their backs, their slim torsos, their perfect postures, and I never felt more alienated than I did in that moment.

I'd heeded what Aunt Alice had told me several years earlier on the day I ripped Brooke's favorite jacket to shreds and kept my antipathy at bay. I love my sister, I don't hate her, but it's times like this when I feel ostracized and completely alone that it becomes difficult to hide my resentment.

Now, I blink several times to eradicate memories of the past and glance down to kick away the offending rock. I'm older, wiser, but as I reach the top of the path and see Brooke and Lizzie huddled together, murmuring something in low voices, I'm struck anew by how much of an outsider I am in my own family.

"Hey," I call out, and they glance up wearing matching guilty expressions. "You two look like you're up to something."

"Not really," Brooke says, while Lizzie appears strangely nervous. She's tugging on the ends of her sleeves and shifting her weight from side to side like she's about to bolt. "But we want to talk to you."

"About what?" A gust of wind blows me back a little. "And why the hell are we meeting in this godforsaken spot?"

They know what I mean. Eli died about two hundred meters from here, on the boundary of our property with our faraway neighbors. Hope likes the view so I bring her on occasion but we never stay long and we never picnic like I used to with these two so many years ago.

"Actually, now I think about it, maybe it's not the best spot," Lizzie says, screwing up her nose. "Then again, I'm the one most likely of the three of us to jump off a cliff at this news, you should be safe."

Trepidation tiptoes through me. What have they discovered?

"Don't be so dramatic." Brooke pokes her in the arm and Lizzie smiles. "Tell her."

"You discovered it, you tell her—"

"Will one of you idiots tell me what the hell is going on?"

Startled by my outburst they stare at me, wary, and I temper my question with a calmer, "All this hedging around isn't helping so why don't one of you spill?"

They exchange brief glances before Brooke nods. "You know I said I was in San Fran the other day and you didn't believe me?"

My heart starts to pound, roaring in my ears along with the wind blowing a gale. "Yeah?"

"You were right. I wasn't there. I was in Verdant, meeting with an old friend of Mom's."

The tightness in my chest eases a little. This can't have anything to do with me. "Why would you do that?"

"Already told you, I'm curious about our parents." She's not telling me everything but I won't push for answers now. I want to hear this great secret they're keeping. "But I found out something that shocked me."

"Shocked us," Lizzie adds, her fingers continuing to pluck at her sleeves. "Me most of all."

My head swivels between them and I'm increasingly nervous.

Brooke fixes me with an odd stare. "Lizzie isn't our cousin. She's our sister," she blurts in a rush, reaching out to clasp Lizzie's hand, as I stand rooted to the spot, shock and something else rendering me speechless.

That something is rage.

The fury expands through my chest, making me breathless. I gasp, craving air, as it spreads into my arms, my legs. I'm numb. Can't move. Can't compute.

"I know it's a shock, Freya—"

"You don't know anything!" I yell and they both take a step back. "This is crazy. It's bad enough having one sister, now you're telling me I have another?"

I bark out a sharp laugh devoid of amusement. "How can Lizzie be my sister? It's ridiculous. I don't need another bloody Stuart sister to feel inferior to. As for you." I jab a finger in Brooke's direction. She's staring at me in open-mouthed disbelief. "Stop poking your nose into other people's business because it will only end badly."

I pause, chest heaving, out of control, and despising myself because of it.

I turn and run, stumbling down the path, desperate to get back to the house. My house, my home, where I have a daughter and a fiancé and a carefully constructed life I will not have disrupted by anyone.

But as I near the backyard my steps falter. Hope can't see me like this. I'm distraught, a mess. My anger fades, replaced by mortification. I wanted Brooke to come home. I wanted to reconnect with my sister. And my over-the-top reaction to the news I have another sister is not going to endear me to either of them.

It all makes sense now, that constant feeling of alienation growing up: of being excluded from their cozy twosome, of looking different to them, my dark features to their light, of not quite measuring up to their perfection.

I always thought Aunt Alice was on my side. She championed me, she defended me, she *understood* me.

But she's lied to me about this too and I'll never forgive her. I feel so betrayed.

I glance toward the barn, wishing Riker was here. He'd comfort me. He'd know what to do to smooth this over. But he's not and I know I'm the only one who can fix this mess. I created it; I need to deal with it. And I will, but I can't stop the images flashing through my head like a horror movie.

Brooke and Lizzie swapping clothes as teens.

Brooke and Lizzie going to parties together without me because I was deemed too young.

Brooke and Lizzie moving forward now, re-establishing that closeness, ostracizing me further, making me feel like the third wheel I've always been.

The fury rises again but this time I push it back down.

I'm about to marry a wonderful guy and complete my happy family scenario.

I can't let anything derail that, least of all my jealousy.

CHAPTER THIRTY-NINE

ALICE

THEN

I move towards Freya, taking slow steps so she won't startle. She's still holding the scissors and by the erratic behavior I'd just witnessed, I don't want to scare her. She hears me coming because she turns, her eyes blurred by tears, her expression so desolate it's something I will never forget.

I wait, knowing that feeling of almost being out of one's body while lashing out. In my case I'd reined it in before I could tamper with those brakes, but the guilt I'd got so close still lingers. Freya will experience the same regret. She'll calm down, see what she's done and feel guilt-ridden she let her resentment overwhelm her.

My heart aches for Freya. It takes a few moments before she blinks and her face softens into the girl I know and love. She stares at the tattered jacket in her hand, the scissors in the other, and lets them fall from her fingers.

"I don't know why I did that," she says, her voice soft, broken, and only then do I step forward and bundle her into my arms.

She cries, gut-wrenching sobs, drenching my top with her tears. I hold her tight, waiting until the sobbing peters out before easing away to look her in the eyes.

"It's okay, sweetie. We all do stuff we're not proud of at times."

She hiccups. "Even you?"

"Especially me." I wipe away a tear about to drip off her jaw. "Nobody's perfect, Freya."

"Brooke is," she mutters. "Little Miss Perfect, getting everything she wants, loved by everyone."

Bitterness laces her words and I can totally identify, though for me it had been Diana.

"Go inside, wash your face." I press a kiss to her forehead. "I'll take care of this then come in and we can talk."

Her gaze is drawn to the shredded jacket lying on the lawn. "What are you going to tell her?"

"Nothing. I'll say she must've misplaced it, left it somewhere."

Freya's eyes widen. "You're going to lie?"

It won't be the first time.

"I don't condone it but in this case, yes." I cup her cheek, hoping to convey how much I understand. "You love your sister, right?"

She hesitates before nodding.

"Then this will only hurt her and drive a wedge between you. It's easier if we do it my way."

"Okay," she says, but she's still eyeing me suspiciously, like she can't figure why I'm taking her side.

"Go inside, I'll be in shortly."

She trudges toward the house, dragging her feet, shoulders slumped. She's the picture of misery and I empathize with this poor child so similar to me.

I fetch two plastic bags, stuff the macerated jacket into one before double bagging it so it's not visible. I push it down to the bottom of the trash outside and rearrange garbage bags over it. Only then do I pick up the scissors and head inside to find Freya sitting at the kitchen table staring into space. She hasn't washed her face, dried tear streaks tracking along her cheeks, and she looks so small, so forlorn, tears well in my eyes.

I blink them away, put the scissors back in the utility drawer alongside a plethora of ice cream scoops, vegetable peelers, hair ties, pens and notebooks, and pull up a seat next to her.

"I know why you did it."

Her eyes meet mine but she doesn't speak, so I continue. "Your mom was the prettiest, smartest, nicest girl I knew. Everyone loved her. I did too, but sometimes it made me feel invisible."

I have her attention now and she inadvertently leans toward me.

"I was the big sister, so I found it really tough that everyone paid her all the attention. And while we're always meant to love our siblings, there were times when I almost hated her."

A hate that drove me to end her life, no matter how inadvertently, and that will eat away at my conscience until the day I die.

"That's how I feel about Brooke sometimes too," she murmurs, so softly I have to lean closer to hear. "She's only eleven months older than me but it feels like she's this bright star and I'm an invisible speck of meteor dust."

I bite back a smile. Freya's learning about outer space at school at the moment and she's become obsessed with the cosmos.

"You're not invisible." I take her hand. "You're an intelligent, beautiful girl and I want you to stop comparing yourself to your sister, okay?"

She gives a slight nod and I squeeze her hand.

"You're unique and as you grow older you'll come to recognize it's a good thing being different from her."

I did, way too late. Diana may have been smarter and prettier than me but I'm a better mother than she ever was. She gave away one child and practically ignored the other two. Admittedly she struggled with postnatal depression and the medications were helping, but deep down I know I'm more caring, more nurturing, than she ever would've been.

Cam would've made up for it though. He'd adored his girls from the moment they were born. A hands-on dad, he'd changed diapers and made up bottles and paced until they fell asleep in his arms. Guilt may be eroding me day by day for what I did but it's Cam I still mourn with every fiber of my being.

"How did you feel when Mom died?"

The insightful question startles me and in that moment I fear Freya is more like me than I think.

"Definitely sad," I say, the lie burning my gullet. "It's not good to wish ill on anyone, Freya, because karma will always come back to bite you."

I don't like the shifting emotions in Freya's eyes so I release her hand and tip her chin up so I can eyeball her.

"Promise me you won't ever do anything to hurt your sister. That you'll come to me if you ever feel like this again?"

She doesn't answer and I give her chin a little pinch.

"Promise me."

Eventually, she shrugs, and mutters, "I promise."

I really hope she keeps it.

CHAPTER FORTY

BROOKE

"That went well," Lizzie says, her drollness finally breaking through my shock.

I shake my head as I try to assimilate Freya's reaction after she disappears from sight. "I should go to her—"

"Leave her." Lizzie lays a hand on my arm. "She'll need to process and when she does I'm pretty sure she's going to be embarrassed by her outburst. Give her some time."

Lizzie's right and I clamp down on the urge to run after Freya. What did she mean by saying it's bad enough having one sister? We were close growing up. Sure, she annoyed me by trying to mimic my clothes and take my stuff and hang around when I wanted to be alone with my friends, but all siblings go through that. We still had each other's backs, always.

So to witness her vitriol a few minutes ago, to see the hatred blazing from her eyes… I'm shocked to my core. I thought Lizzie would be most affected by Aunt Alice's lie, I never anticipated Freya would be this rattled. It makes me feel guilty, that despite the time we've spent together since I returned home, I've been away too long and can't get a proper read on my sister.

It also makes me wonder: if Freya had this extreme reaction to learning the truth about Lizzie being our sister, how would she react if she discovered my secret about Riker and how well we really know each other?

"She snapped." Lizzie guides me to the ground where we sit, the wind howling around us. "She's been under a lot of pressure, what with Alice's deterioration and the wedding and you coming home, it's probably bound to happen."

I agree with some of what Lizzie says, but not all. "How does my coming home make her stressed?"

An odd expression crosses Lizzie's face. She hesitates, as if doubting the wisdom of telling me something, before saying, "Freya's always been in your shadow and I think having you home might've made her nervous it would happen again."

"What's she nervous about?" I immediately think of Riker, deliberately ignoring the memory of his hands all over me, his tongue in my mouth, the ecstasy of it all.

Lizzie shakes her head. "Hang-ups like that don't fade away completely and by that crazy outburst we witnessed, she still feels second best."

"But I've done nothing to make her feel that way."

I shared most of my clothes with her, except my favorite jacket, which I still lament to this day. I took her places and introduced her to my friends, and didn't mind when she stole my make-up. I included her. I loved her. She's my sister.

"This has everything to do with her and not you," Lizzie says. "When we were younger, I saw the way she looked at me whenever we went out together, she was jealous and I put it down to sisterly possessiveness." She rubs her chin, absentmindedly. "But after today, I wonder if she was jealous of you, not only me."

I want to dismiss Lizzie's supposition as ridiculous because Freya and I have had good conversations since I've been home in our efforts to re-establish a bond. We're adults now and I left my hang-ups in the past when I returned, to start afresh, But now I feel like I've been kidding myself. Is Freya still obsessing about the past?

I remember the day I confronted her about my jacket. She'd coveted it from the second I saw it online and was furious when Aunt Alice told her there was only one. Every time I wore it, and I wore it a lot because I adored it, she'd get this mutinous expression and would barely talk to me.

Then I'd come home from a party at the fairgrounds, high on adrenalin from the rides and sugar from too much cotton candy, to find it gone. I'd virtually torn the house apart looking for my jacket and had been distraught when I couldn't find it. Aunt Alice had placated me, saying I must've misplaced it and we'd go search in all the places I'd been over the last week. Freya had merely shrugged like it meant nothing, but I'd seen a glint in her eyes that made me think she'd taken it.

I'd waited until she was in the shower that night to go through her room, checking in every nook and cranny, but I hadn't found the jacket and I'd felt bad for suspecting her of stealing it. And despite Aunt Alice taking me to the library, the pool, and the games arcade, all places I'd been in the last week, I never found it.

"Jealousy between sisters is natural," I say, but knowing I've never been envious of Freya. "And in her defense, you and I spent more time together as we got older and she felt left out."

Lizzie frowns and clasps her hands together, shooting me several glances, before I finally say, "There's obviously something on your mind, so tell me."

"I think Freya wished she could be exactly like you and if she couldn't, she wanted what you had."

Lizzie's proclamation echoes what I've been thinking about that old jacket and I wait for her to continue.

"Did you know she had a thing for Eli?"

My mouth drops open for the second time in the last ten minutes. "No."

Lizzie nods. "You two started dating when? Around seventeen?"

"Yeah."

"I didn't notice it at first, but every time he came around Freya would make a point to be there, never leaving you alone. She hung on his every word and lit up when he so much as greeted her."

Considering how much I adored Eli I would've barely noticed if Freya danced naked in front of him. He'd been the center of my world for a year, until I ruined everything.

"I didn't know."

The concern pinching Lizzie's mouth softens. "I didn't think you did, you were smitten with him."

"He was the best," I murmur, my chest aching over how much I hurt him, how I drove him to do something so horrific.

Eli hadn't been like other guys. He didn't care about being cool in front of the boys. He didn't jostle and boast and try to outdo the jocks. He wanted to be with me and would spend all his free time hanging out wherever I chose: the library, the park, the beach. He didn't muck around in class and valued his grades as much as I did. And while he loved making out as much as I did, he never pushed me to take the next step until I was ready. He respected me, had made me feel special in a way I haven't had since, and I hate that my revelation pushed him to end his life.

"Eli was one of the good guys," Lizzie says. "Did he know about Freya's crush?"

"If he did he never said anything to me."

Lizzie's pensive, staring at the ocean. "I remember how awful it was the day after his suicide, how distraught you were."

I don't want to remember. I've quashed the memory of that devastating day because I never want to relive that kind of pain, ever. For too long afterward, every time I closed my eyes I could see the exact moment my world fell apart in excruciating detail.

Eli's father on our doorstep, eyes bloodshot, wearing a flannel shirt, dress pants and white sneakers. His odd mismatched outfit and swollen eyes hadn't alerted me to something being wrong as much as his expression.

He looked like his world had been ripped apart.

Aunt Alice had answered the door the morning after I broke up with Eli. When I saw Roger, his dad, I hovered in the background, unseen, listening in. So I heard the words that tore my heart in two. *"Eli's dead."*

I'd staggered, clutching at the wall, as Eli's dad continued, "I came to tell you in person because I didn't want Brooke finding out any other way. Can you tell her for me?"

Aunt Alice had said, "Oh my God, Roger, I'm so sorry…" and stepped forward, her arms outstretched, but he'd backed away.

"I can't do this right now. But I wanted you to know before the police come to ask Brooke questions…" His face crumpled and tears welled in his eyes. "I have no idea why my beautiful boy jumped to his death but when we're over the shock it would be good if we can talk to Brooke, find out what she knows."

"Of course." Aunt Alice nodded, while I struggled to breathe, my lungs constricting with the knowledge of why Eli had jumped and my overwhelming grief that I'm responsible for my boyfriend's death.

"I will never, ever, understand this." Roger had tears streaming down his face as he turned and stumbled back toward his car.

That moment is the reason why I never returned to Martino Bay after I fled. I could've dealt with the innuendo, the finger-pointing, but having to face Eli's parents knowing what I'd done… his parents had lost him so my family had lost me. I didn't deserve their comfort. I didn't deserve happiness. And the only reason why I've finally come home is because Aunt Alice needs my support in the same way she'd once supported me.

"I also remember Freya's reaction to Eli's suicide…" Lizzie turns to look at me. "I've never seen anyone fall apart like that, like someone had carved out her heart. At first I thought it was because you were in so much pain, but it was more than that. I think she genuinely liked him and losing him gutted her as much as it did you."

I'm stunned by Lizzie's revelations. "Why didn't you ever say anything?"

She shrugs. "What's the point? Your grief was overwhelming and I wanted to support you as best I could. Learning Freya was as devastated would've made things worse and served no purpose."

"So why are you telling me now?"

She jerks a thumb over her shoulder. "Because from what I just saw, Freya hasn't changed a bit and it's probably wise to tread carefully around her."

"What do you mean?"

Lizzie takes hold of my hands and they're as freezing as mine. "Because I see a hint of something on your face every time Riker enters a room, like you're hiding something, and if Freya reacted badly to hearing I'm a sibling, I'd hate to think how she'll freak if she discovers whatever secrets you're concealing."

CHAPTER FORTY-ONE

ALICE

THEN

Freya keeps her promise to me for six years.

She doesn't hurt Brooke and she doesn't touch her sister's belongings again. Brooke is generous with her sister, offering to lend her clothes and make-up, and I see Freya come alive under her sister's attention. I'm relieved, because the closer the girls are, the less likelihood Freya will revert to the all-consuming jealousy of that awful day when she destroyed Brooke's favorite possession. Brooke includes Freya in her busy social life too and they're closer than I could've hoped for. Maybe Freya has her sibling envy under control?

Then Brooke brings Eli home.

I'm cooking dinner, the kitchen warm from the oven and filled with the tantalizing aromas of roasted tomatoes, onions and garlic from the homemade pizzas that the girls love, when the back door opens.

"Hey, Aunt Alice, I'd like you to meet someone." Brooke steps inside, holding hands with a striking young man she's already told me about. "This is Eli."

I like that Eli looks me straight in the eye; I can't abide kids who appear shifty. And his smile is instant, warm, genuine, whereas some young men can be awkward meeting their girlfriend's parents.

"Pleased to meet you, Eli." I dust flour off my hands and hold one out.

"Likewise, Miss Shomack." He shakes my hand with a firm grip I respect. "Brooke talks about you a lot."

"Please, call me Alice. You're staying for dinner?"

"I'd love to, thanks," he says, his impeccable manners as impressive as the rest of him.

He's tall, about six feet, with dark curly hair and chocolate-brown eyes. Brooke showed me a photo of him on her cell but he's more remarkable in person. More than his looks and his manners, it's his open expression I admire, like he's got nothing to hide. For someone living with secrets every day of my life, that's a quality I'm envious of. I'm happy for Brooke. He's the first boy she's ever brought home and he's lovely. They make a stunning couple.

"Why don't you two lay the table while I finish off this last pizza?" I point at the toppings laid out on individual plates. "Are you happy with all these, Eli, or do you have allergies?"

"No allergies, but I'd prefer no peppers on mine, please."

"Sure," I say, pushing that plate aside. "One pepperoni, tomato, mushroom, onion and garlic combo coming up."

I snap my fingers and Brooke groans. "Please ignore my aunt, she's putting on a show for you."

He laughs, revealing straight white teeth that are as perfect as the rest of him. Freya enters the kitchen at that moment and the atmosphere instantly changes. It's like a cloud has passed over the sun and my skin pebbles.

"Oh, it's you two," Freya says, as she crosses the kitchen toward me. "Need a hand, Aunt Alice?"

Her dismissive greeting of Eli and Brooke and her sour expression captures my attention. Usually she's better at hiding her jealousy of her sister, and while Brooke rarely notices Freya's subtle animosity, that greeting seems overt even for her.

"No, I'm good." I lay a comforting hand on Freya's arm, trying to convey I understand but she needs to cool it. "Why don't you help Brooke and Eli set the table?"

"I'm sure they've got it covered." She shrugs off my hand and studiously avoids looking their way. "I'll get the drinks sorted."

She's already heading for the fridge, her gait stiff and stilted, like she's uncomfortable and trying to hide it.

"Thanks," I say, seeing Brooke roll her eyes at Eli over Freya's shoulder.

Brooke told me they've been dating for about a month already, Freya's met him, and everybody's happy for her.

As I catch Freya's sulky pout, maybe not everybody.

"I'll have sparkling water and Eli will have a lemon soda, please, Freya," Brooke says, gazing up at Eli with the adoration only a teen girl can muster. "We'll get started on setting the table."

Only I hear Freya's muttered, "Whatever" as her hand grips the fridge door so tight her knuckles appear white through the skin. Her back is rigid, the muscles in her neck standing out with tension.

But her recalcitrance doesn't bother me as much as the look she casts at Eli's retreating back as he heads for the dining room, holding Brooke's hand.

It's proprietary, covetous, and the same way Freya had once looked at Brooke's gaudy pink jacket.

Before she slashed it to pieces.

CHAPTER FORTY-TWO

FREYA

I have to apologize to Brooke and Lizzie. They obviously give me time to calm down because it's thirty minutes before they come back to the house. I'm waiting for them in the backyard, with homemade lemonade and an upside-down pineapple cake I'd been saving for supper.

They eye me suspiciously as they approach, as if they expect me to upend the cake on their heads and fling the lemonade in their faces. I don't blame them.

"A peace offering," I say, holding my palms up over the table. "The least I can do after flipping out. I reacted badly earlier and I apologize for everything I said. Neither of you will understand this, but I sometimes felt hideous growing up next to you two. You were beautiful and I was the plain baby of the family. And you were close, so I felt left out…" I shrug. "I guess I let my old jealousy flare."

Lizzie's the first to move forward and take a seat at the table opposite me. "Shock makes us do crazy things sometimes." She points at the cake. "Considering this is my favorite, you're forgiven."

Brooke is more circumspect, approaching the table cautiously before sitting next to me, staring so intently I struggle not to squirm. She has this odd expression on her face, like she's seeing me for the first time, and I don't like it.

An awkward silence descends and I know I have to say something to show them I'm okay now. "How do you feel about everything, Lizzie? I mean, you just found out your mom is actually your aunt?"

I glimpse a flicker of pain in Lizzie's eyes before she blinks. "Honestly? I was mad when Brooke first told me but I'm calmer now. Alice mothered us all in the same way. She always did what was best for us and she raised us right, like any mother would. What does it matter if a DNA test says otherwise?"

I'm impressed by Lizzie's magnanimity. If I found out my mother had lied to me all these years, I'd want to throttle her. "So you've done one?"

Lizzie and Brooke share a conspiratorial glance that makes me feel left out again. "Yeah, once I heard the truth from Amy, Mom's friend in Verdant, and we couldn't find Lizzie's birth certificate, we got an expedited DNA test done and it confirmed it. But Lizzie's right, Aunt Alice loved us equally and has been a great mom. And the fact we're all sisters? Mind-blowing but great."

"It is mind-blowing." I nod. "We've always been sisters in a way and this confirms it."

Lizzie's blinking back tears and Brooke's wary expression softens.

"Let's have some cake," I say, before we dissolve into tears. I'm ashamed of my earlier outburst, of allowing my latent jealousy to get the better of me, and I want to make amends.

Lizzie smiles at me, but Brooke is still giving me side-eye. She's slower to forgive, considering the harsh things I said, and I don't blame her. If she'd told me "It's bad enough having one sister" I would've been pretty pissed off too.

As Lizzie cuts the cake, I lean closer to Brooke and give her a gentle nudge. "You know I didn't mean that stuff I said, right? You've been a great sister. I was just shocked." She glances at me and I see she's still hurting.

"I never made you feel inferior."

I sigh, unwilling to have this conversation but needing to give her something for us to move on. "Not intentionally, but you were so perfect, with your grades and your friends and your popularity, I couldn't help but feel second best."

"But that's on you," she says, accusatory, and I bite back my annoyance.

"It is, and that's why I'm apologizing for my crazy outburst before."

She eyeballs me for several seconds before finally nodding. "Okay. But Lizzie's the one we should be focusing on now. She's taken the news exceptionally well but she must be freaking out on the inside."

"I'm right here, ladies." Lizzie waves and we smile.

"You're seriously okay?" I ask.

"I am. As long as you two are." Lizzie's gaze swings between us like she's watching a riveting tennis final and I'm struck anew by the likeness between her and Brooke. I put it down to them being cousins but now I know they're sisters the similarities are more pronounced. The same slight uptilt at the end of their noses, the same tiny green flecks in their blue eyes, the same shape of their earlobes.

How many hours did I waste staring into the mirror growing up, wishing my brown eyes were blue, hoping my dull brown hair would lighten to blonde if I spent enough time in the sun? Countless, and I never expected to feel like the ugly stepsister all these years later.

"I'm okay," Brooke says.

"I am too." If I inject enough sincerity into my voice they'll believe me. They have in the past.

My candor garners a breakthrough when Brooke reaches out and lays a hand over mine where it rests in my lap. "I didn't know you felt that way. Apology accepted."

Lizzie smirks and points to the cake again. "Like I said, you had my forgiveness with this."

She breaks the ice and we chuckle. I serve cake and pour lemonade and this time the silence between us is comfortable.

I pick up my glass and raise it. "To the Stuart sisters."

Brooke and Lizzie echo my toast and as we clink glasses I know I'll have to be more careful in future.

CHAPTER FORTY-THREE
BROOKE

Lizzie's warning regarding Freya has kept me up the last few nights. I would've dismissed it as meaning nothing if I hadn't seen her reaction to Lizzie being our sibling firsthand.

She'd looked like a different person standing on that cliff, someone I didn't recognize. Lizzie is right. I need to be extra careful to keep my link to Riker secret from Freya. Has he seen that side to her? Or worse, has Hope? Freya's been nothing but a doting, loving mother whenever I've seen them interact but who knows what's gone on the last decade?

If only I could ask Aunt Alice. She always looked out for me growing up and I trust her. Then again, I don't need to ask her anything. With Hope living under the same roof, she would've cared for her great-niece the same.

I'd never tell Freya this but I missed Aunt Alice the most when I left. My aunt always exuded calmness. She never rushed headlong into a decision; she weighed up the pros and cons, then made an informed choice. I wonder how she felt, having to adopt the three of us after our parents died. She wouldn't have had much time to consider that decision; it would've been thrust upon her and I love her all the more for taking on what must've been a massive responsibility at her age.

It also makes me think about my mom and how she gave up Lizzie. Considering I was prepared to do the same thing if my baby boy hadn't died, I can empathize. Had my mom felt the same emptiness I had, the same desperation to forget the past? Had she wanted to make a fresh start away from the town she grew up in? Had she felt like her heart had ripped in two when she saw the nurse take her baby away?

Aunt Alice finding Lizzie and reuniting her with us is something I'll be thankful for every day. It's been five days since we learned the truth about Lizzie and have finally unearthed a birth certificate via the adoption agency. We've also discovered how Alice got custody of Lizzie, after her adoptive parents ended up in a domestic violence situation and Child Protective Services took over.

The timing is strange though. Alice didn't take custody of Lizzie until after my parents died, yet CPS would've contacted them earlier. Yet another reason to gain access to Aunt Alice's online diary. Both Lizzie and I have tried various combinations but nothing works. Looks like we were right about CS being Cameron Stuart and the 3 obviously meant three girls.

Lizzie is still calling Aunt Alice mom because she doesn't want to confuse her any more than she already is, but I see the way she looks at her now. She's wary, disappointed at being lied to for so many years. It doesn't make sense why Aunt Alice would lie to us all. Did she want a child of her own so badly she claimed one of Diana and Cameron's as hers? Did she want to protect Lizzie from knowing she'd been adopted out? That seems the most likely scenario but why not come clean now we're all in our late twenties?

Freya isn't interested in discussing this; Lizzie and I have tried. She treats Lizzie the same and shows no interest in getting to the bottom of why Aunt Alice perpetuated the lie. That leaves only one person left to talk to who knew Aunt Alice before she started losing her mind: Riker. Lizzie mentioned Aunt Alice would spend time in his workshop every day. They shared a love of strong espresso and when Freya went to work, Aunt Alice would take him a coffee and they'd spend an hour chatting.

He's been dating Freya for over six months now, meaning he knew lucid Alice. I doubt she would've revealed any deep, dark family secrets to him but he might be able to give me some insight into the aunt I haven't seen in over a decade. It's often easier to talk to a stranger about issues and with a little luck Aunt Alice might have told him something during their daily coffee chats.

He's in the barn as usual so I knock and stick my head around the door. He's polishing a wave sculpture. It's stunning in its simplicity, the cool steel mimicking a stormy ocean.

"Come in," he says, not looking up from his work, and I slip through the door and close it behind me. "What brings you by?"

"I want to chat about Aunt Alice, but first… wow." I point at the wave. "This is incredible."

"Thanks. The new surf shop in town commissioned it."

"They're going to love it."

The last time I was in here I didn't have a chance to look around but now I do a slow three-sixty, taking in the magnitude of his talent. Riker has constructed pieces out of various metals—copper, wrought iron, steel—creating art from simple fruit bowls to elaborate furniture sets. He's extremely talented and for a moment I wonder why he's happy to be stuck in Martino Bay and not traveling the world finding inspiration. He must really love Freya, and I'm glad she's found happiness.

"What do you think?" He sweeps his arms wide at his creations, that lazy grin I'd fallen for so many years ago making my heart beat faster when it shouldn't.

"You're incredibly talented."

"And you thought I was some lay-about dude cruising through town, huh?"

"In my defense, that's a long time ago and it's all I knew you as."

"Over a decade is a long time," he says, the intensity of his stare surprising me. "To be honest, I don't do a lot of reminiscing, but when you walked into dinner that night and I recognized you…"

He shrugs, oddly bashful. "It brought back how I thought you were the prettiest girl I'd ever seen, and then when we hooked up at that party… you dazzled me."

Heat flushes my cheeks. We shouldn't be talking about this. Nothing good can come of it. But I'm curious.

"You mentioned coming back to town after that?"

What I'm really asking is "Did you come back to town looking for me?" I don't know why I want to know but I do. Not that I would've known if he had back then. After Eli's death I'd holed up in the house because the few times I ventured into town I got heckled or glared at by people who blamed me for it.

To this day I don't know who witnessed our big blow-up that night. No one had been around when we argued and broke up. I'd run home, heartbroken, and he'd been stalking into the darkness last time I'd seen him. The next morning when news broke of his suicide, I'd shut down: mentally, emotionally.

"The gang I was with left the morning after the party. We headed up the coast as far as Seattle so I didn't get back to Martino Bay for about three months." He rubs the stubble along his jaw, pensive. "I came looking for you but your family had gone."

"Did you know Freya was my sister when you two got together?"

"No." He grimaces. "That's plain wrong."

And would play right into Freya's paranoia about being second best from her recent revelations.

I need to get this conversation back on track.

"As much as I've enjoyed our stroll down memory lane, I want to ask you about Aunt Alice."

Rather than appearing relieved to change the subject, he's staring at me with something I could almost label as regret. I have no idea why. We would've never worked even if our one-night stand had evolved into something more. I was too broken after Eli's death and never would've dated the guy who precipitated it even if he didn't know it.

"Before the dementia set in, did Alice ever mention anything about the past to you? About our family back then?"

The corners of his eyes crinkle as he thinks. "Not a lot. She thought I might be drawn to Freya initially because my folks are dead too, so it's only my sister and me, but she never really said much about her family."

"I'm sorry about your parents."

He shrugs. "It's okay, they died within a year of each other when Kel and I were in our twenties."

Freya hasn't mentioned his sister; then again, she's had enough to deal with discovering another of her own. "Is Kel local? Will she be coming to the wedding?"

A shadow passes over his face as he half turns away. "She's on the east coast so no, she won't be coming to the wedding."

There's a story there but it's not mine to delve into. "So Aunt Alice didn't mention my folks or us moving here or anything like that?"

He shakes his head. "No. I got to spend some time with your aunt when I moved in here." He smiles and my heart does that weird little flip it shouldn't. "She brought me coffee every morning and would hang out here, sometimes chatting, other times checking out my latest work. We got on well and I was shocked when she went downhill so fast."

"What do you mean?"

Lizzie has mentioned Alice's rapid deterioration but why would it shock Riker?

"To me, it seemed like one minute she was okay, forgetting normal stuff like we all do, misplacing keys, losing bills to pay, that kind of thing, the next she was being locked in a room for her safety, dosed up on meds."

I'm no dementia expert but for someone so young that sounds like a fast decline.

"Does she ever seem lucid to you?"

"Not really." He tears his gaze from mine but it's too late, I glimpse a flicker of unease. He knows something and he's not telling me. "To be honest, I don't spend a lot of time with her anymore. Seeing her like that, lying around and listless, is awful, and I prefer to remember her the way she used to be in here, joking around or poking fun at my 'little hobby' as she used to call it." He spreads his hands wide. "But she's in the best care, with Freya a nurse for patients like Alice."

"Yeah, I guess so."

I've learned nothing and tears of frustration burn the back of my eyes. But I can't cry in front of him because I don't want him asking questions I can't answer so I make a dash for the door.

"Thanks, I'll see you later," I murmur, my throat tight with emotion, and I make it out the door when his hand lands on my shoulder.

"You okay?"

I blink rapidly, willing the tears away, before turning to face him. "I'm really worried about Aunt Alice," I say, as a tear spills over and trickles down my cheek.

"Hey, your aunt's a fighter." He hauls me into his arms before I know what's happening, and hugs me tight. "It'll be okay."

My face is buried against his chest and I can't help but inhale the earthy blend of hay and sweat mingled with his musky deodorant. It's intoxicating and for an illicit second I give myself over to the pleasure of being in his strong arms again.

It's a comforting hug, nothing more, and when he releases me I smile my gratitude. "I better let you get back to work."

He nods before heading back inside to resume polishing the wave sculpture. So he doesn't see what I glimpse when I walk away.

The curtain in the kitchen moves, too late to hide the shadow behind it.

Someone is watching me.

CHAPTER FORTY-FOUR

FREYA

I've had a terrible day.

One of my favorite patients at work died, a seventy-year-old grocer who used to undercharge me for oranges when Hope was younger because they were her favorite fruit. I used to shop at Bruce's rather than the supermarket because I loved his ready smiles and the knock-knock jokes he'd tell Hope. He'd been just as happy since being admitted to the nursing home a year ago and it had broken my heart that I'd been the one to find him dead in his bed this morning. The only comfort was the myocardial infarct claimed him quickly and he didn't suffer. That didn't make it easier when I had to comfort the grieving family, his only daughter and her husband, while struggling to hold myself together.

Then I got halfway home before remembering I'd forgotten to have Alice's scripts filled at the pharmacy, so had to turn back and wait another thirty minutes for her medication due to the after-work rush. The delay meant Hope was late for ballet class and I had to deal with a grumpy ten-year-old the entire way home.

Now this.

When I grab a glass of water before heading to my fiancé's workshop to debrief after the day I've had, I don't expect to see him with his arms around my sister.

I freeze, my blood turning to ice. My vision blurs and I clutch at the sink. It's probably nothing. He could be hugging her for any number of reasons. But I'm catapulted back to the first night Brooke returned home when the two of them saw each other and how awful I felt they'd already met.

I have no reason to doubt Riker. He's never given me any reason to. He's dependable, big-hearted, and a straight shooter. So when he said they barely spoke at that party so long ago I believed him. But seeing the two of them locked in an embrace makes my old doubts rise to the surface, along with a long-suppressed antipathy toward my sister.

Memories flood in. Brooke, a year ahead of me at school, getting straight A's, gaining awards, winning over teachers. The same teachers who, twelve months later, would try to hide their disappointment at my average C's, some going as far as to say I was nothing like my sister. Brooke, sitting in the redbrick quadrangle at lunchtimes, surrounded by the popular kids, graciously accepting an apple or a chocolate bar from friends. Brooke, being able to wear anything she wanted and look good, while I often got her hand-me-downs that looked dowdy on me.

And more. Brooke being the first to kiss a boy at the lookout point, the first to get to second base, and as it turned out, the first to lose her virginity. She'd always had a superior air; not from trying, it came naturally to her, and that was part of her charm. People were drawn to Brooke from the time she could walk and a small part of me had been glad when she'd virtually been driven out of town by her friends' derision.

So what if Brooke's gotten everything she wants her entire life? She won't be getting Riker.

I gulp the water and slam the glass down, hating that I've allowed my latent insecurities to flare. I should be past this. My relationship with Brooke is different now. I'm happy with my life and I won't allow my frustrations at letting old feelings bubble to the surface mess with that.

I nudge the curtain aside to get a better look, in time to see them disentangle. There's nothing furtive in their body language and Riker heads back into his studio without a backward glance. Brooke dabs at her eyes like she's been crying and I realize Riker was probably comforting her.

Am I curious as to why she's been crying? Absolutely. And as much as I want to believe in my fiancé, a small part of me hopes Brooke isn't crying over some shared secret from their past.

Damn it, once the thought insinuates its way into my head I can't dislodge it. I should confront Brooke and ask, but I'm self-aware enough to know it will take longer for my jealousy to subside.

I back away from the window before Brooke sees me but it's too late. She's staring directly at the window and her step falters. I should pull the curtain back again and wave, make light of it.

But I don't. Let her worry. I need her off guard. She's not the only one who harbors secrets from the past and mine has the potential to tear apart her world all over again. Not that I will ever tell her. What good would it do? She's already paid her dues regarding Eli's death and nothing I reveal will change that.

Besides, she's done enough damage poking her nose into Aunt Alice's business; I can't risk her discovering anything more.

CHAPTER FORTY-FIVE

ALICE

THEN

I'm missing Lizzie. She's been at college for two months and the house seems empty without her. The night before she left I was in her room watching her pack, and I've never been closer to telling her the truth.

When we'd first moved from Verdant to Martino Bay I'd given her a tiny stuffed toy cactus. I thought it signified our past perfectly: dry, arid, prickly. Leaving Verdant was the best thing I ever did, giving my girls a fresh start on the Californian coast far from the sins of their parents.

That night she'd packed the last of her clothes and I'd spied the cactus on the top shelf of her closet. She must've seen me looking at it because she reached up and grabbed it, pressing it into the nook of her neck between her cheek and shoulder.

"I can't believe you still have that old thing," I said, nostalgia making my throat tighten. "It must stink."

"Yeah, but it smells like you so I better take it," she said, blinking as she stuffed it down the side of her suitcase between underwear and jeans. "For luck, right?"

"You don't need it, kid, you're going to kill it at college." My voice sounded tight, squeaky and I cleared my throat. "You're a good girl, Lizzie, and I'm proud of you."

"Aww, Mom, cut it out." She flung herself at me and we had a good cry together, tangled on the bed in a tight hug.

That was the moment I should've told her the truth. The words hovered on my lips. *"I love you like my own daughter, Lizzie girl, but you're actually Diana and Cam's firstborn."*

I opened my mouth to speak but then she released me and scooted away, a grown-up again, and as I stared into her guileless blue eyes, so like her dad's, I knew I couldn't do it.

Telling her before she left for college would disarm her and I didn't want her leaving home hating me. So I kept my mouth shut and the next morning she was gone.

That was eight weeks ago and I wish she'd never left. For purely selfish reasons: without Lizzie here to deflect some of Freya's attention, it's focused solely on Brooke, and not in a healthy way.

Eli has become a permanent fixture in our household and I like hearing his deep voice and the rumble of his laughter. But Freya likes it too, a bit too much, and I'm constantly on guard, watching her watch Eli.

I wonder if he knows. Brooke remains completely oblivious because she's in the throes of first love and she only has eyes for Eli. But I'm concerned as I see Freya's obsession grow. She's lost weight, picking at her food at mealtimes, and she spends a lot of time in her room listening to music. Her grades have suffered too; not that they were outstanding to begin with. Brooke is the brains in the family, which almost seems unfair alongside her beauty.

To make matters worse, Brooke loves her sister and doesn't want her to feel left out, especially with Lizzie out of the picture, so she often invites her to tag along with her and Eli. I see Freya's eyes light up when this happens and on those evenings when she accompanies the happy couple, to the movies or the skating rink or for ice cream, she comes back practically glowing.

It's not healthy and I need to put a stop to it. But how to do it without hurting both my girls? I must try because I fear Brooke is unwittingly fostering Freya's unhealthy crush and if Freya is bottling everything inside I'm scared of what might happen…

My opportunity comes one evening when the girls are waiting in the lounge room for Eli to arrive. They're going to an outdoor concert in the park where a new high school band is making its debut. Brooke is wearing dark denim slashed at the knees and a sparkly black tank top. Freya has tried to copy her, but her denim is faded and her top is purple velvet.

They're sitting side by side on the sofa and in profile they both channel Cam. Strange, how I never see Diana in any of her girls, apart from the blonde hair Lizzie and Brooke have. Then again, maybe I don't want to remember anything about my sister.

Some half-hearted argument about who's dating the lead singer drifts toward me and I smile. At times like this I can almost imagine they're like other normal siblings, but I know better.

My smile fades as Brooke's cell buzzes because I see Freya's expression of joy; she must know that individual message tone belongs to Eli too.

"Eli's not coming," Brooke says, her thumbs flying over the screen to respond. "His mom's got vertigo and he needs to drive her to the doctor."

I see Brooke's disappointment in the slump of her shoulders but Freya's expression is a scary mixture of anger and disdain. I rush into the room. "Hey, girls, ready to go?"

"Eli's not coming, his mom's sick," Brooke says, with a grimace. "But that's okay, I can drive us—"

"I'm not feeling great either," Freya says, clutching at her stomach. "You go, I'll stay here."

Brooke shoots her sister a concerned glance. "You sure? Because I can stay and hang out with you if you want—"

"No, you go." Freya fakes a small moan. "Probably some viral thing that'll pass if I rest."

"Okay." Brooke squeezes Freya's shoulder before standing and turning to me. "I won't be late, Aunt Alice."

I nod. "Have a good time."

Brooke casts one last concerned glance at her sister before heading out the door, leaving me with the perfect opportunity to have a discussion with Freya. I wait until I hear the car start and pull out of the driveway before fixing Freya with a no-nonsense glare.

"Why didn't you want to go with your sister?"

To her credit, she doesn't try to convince me of her sudden fake illness. "Because I know what tonight will be like. We'll get to the park, everyone will fawn over Brooke and I'll be ignored as usual."

I have to broach the awkwardness of her crush, now. "Yet you were looking forward to it when Eli was going?"

An angry flush stains her cheeks crimson and her lips compress.

"Freya, it's okay to like Eli, he's a good guy, but he's your sister's boyfriend."

She rolls her eyes. "Like I need reminding. Perfect Brooke, with her perfect boyfriend. Do you know they're going to be crowned prom queen and king?"

"No, I didn't know. Aren't you happy for them?"

I will her to say yes. I want her to say she loves her sister and she'd never do anything to hurt her. But her brown eyes are glowing caramel, lit from within with a familiar resentment, and I'm worried all over again that this will boil over in a way I won't like.

"Why does she always have to be the best? The prettiest, the smartest, the one with the great boyfriend…" Her voice is tight with anger and her fingers are curled into fists. "And she's so damn nice all the time."

"If you let this consume you, it *will* make you unhappy," I say, not making the mistake of reaching out to touch her. She won't welcome it. I hadn't way back when my mom had given me a similar lecture when I'd broken down one night and admitted how I felt about Diana. My mom had let me rant, to get my vitriol out of my system, and only then had she hugged me.

The way Freya's eyes are blazing, she harbors a lot more resentment than I ever did.

Yet look what you did to your sister.

I ignore my conscience and focus on Freya. "If you can't talk to me, I think you should see someone—"

"I don't need a shrink!" She leaps off the sofa like I've prodded her. "I'm fine."

I beg to differ but I've pushed enough for one evening. Besides, I hope that sowing the seed of seeking help will take root and she'll consider it. I have to do something to help.

CHAPTER FORTY-SIX

BROOKE

I assume Freya saw Riker hugging me in the barn doorway and had been the one spying on me from the kitchen, because she's tightlipped for the rest of the evening. I wish she'd bring it up so I can set her mind at ease. I tried twice but she changed the subject. It reminds me of our childhood when she'd avoid me during one of her 'moods'. Back then, she'd be happy to hang out with me, then something would set her off and she'd be in a huff but trying desperately to pretend nothing was wrong. She's doing the same thing tonight and it's disappointing, considering how far we've come since I returned.

Luckily, we've got Hope to defuse the tension and my gorgeous niece has no idea her mom's upset. I've enlisted her help with the surprise bridal shower I'm throwing Freya, which is in two days' time. It can't come quick enough if it gets her out of this mood.

Hope and I are in her room, sitting on the floor, scrolling through her laptop looking at teeny-tiny canapés from a local supplier. Freya thinks I'm helping Hope with her homework and while I don't like encouraging kids to lie, I want this to be a fun surprise for Freya.

"Mom loves shrimp," Hope says, pointing to a dainty shrimp and lox combo.

Confused, I stare at the picture. "Really?"

As I remember it, Freya had been allergic to shrimp. She'd had a major meltdown one day at the beach when she'd tagged along yet again with Eli and me and a bunch of our friends. One minute everyone had been having fun, the next she'd begun coughing and spluttering after eating a shrimp roll, saying her throat was closing up.

Eli had helped some kid up the beach earlier who'd had a similar reaction to peanuts, so he lay her down, checked her airways and fussed over her. She'd popped an antihistamine someone had in their first aid kit and she'd recovered quickly. Strange, to learn she now loved the thing she professed to be allergic to. Had she been attention-seeking? Yet more proof she might've liked Eli as more than a friend. It makes me feel sorry for her. She'd never had a boyfriend when we were teens and having a secret crush on mine must've been tough. I thought her grief when he'd died had been because of her sympathy for me; it never crossed my mind she had deeper feelings for him too and that's why she'd been devastated.

"What's wrong, Auntie Brooke?"

Hope is staring at me in consternation and I carefully blank my expression. "What other foods does your mom like?"

"Practically everything."

I laugh at Hope's blunt response. "In that case we better start choosing some for the party, huh?"

As we pore over the online offerings, I resist the urge to cuddle her. She's the sweetest child and not precocious for her age. Soon she'll be entering the tween years and I'm sure Freya will have her hands full, but for now I'm glad I came back home so I can spend time with her.

"Why is it called a bridal shower?" Hope asks after we finish choosing the food and email our order to the catering company.

"Probably because we have to shower the bride with gifts."

"Oh man, we have to get Mom a gift too?"

I chuckle and this time I sling my arm around her shoulder and squeeze. "Yeah, we do. Got any ideas?"

Hope's brow furrows as she thinks, before she straightens and snaps her fingers. "I know. What about one of those pill dispenser thingies?"

It's a bizarre choice and totally from left field. "Uh, what would your mom need one of those for?"

"Because I saw her once in Aunt Alice's room and she had a lot of bottles filled with pills, and she looked really worried trying to sort through them so I thought something like that might help?"

I'm surprised. As far as I know Aunt Alice is healthy apart from the dementia. Why would she need a lot of pills? Then again I know nothing about her medication schedule; Freya's the expert.

"That sounds like a great idea, sweetie, and very thoughtful, but perhaps something more fun?"

Her shoulders slump in disappointment. "I thought it would be good so she wouldn't get mad at me again."

"What do you mean?"

"Apparently I wasn't supposed to go in there when she was giving Aunt Alice her pills. But I needed her to sign a permission slip so I could go on a field trip and when I went in the room, Mom flipped out." She bites down on her bottom lip. "She yelled at me really loudly and said it's important Aunt Alice gets the right medication and I'm never to go in there again when she's taking her pills."

When Hope raises her eyes to mine, I see genuine fear. "She really freaked out. She's never yelled at me like that before so that's why I thought the dispenser might be a good gift."

I'm annoyed Freya overreacted and if it's anything like the way she behaved when she learned the truth about Lizzie, no kid deserves that. But Hope's her daughter and I have no right to interfere, even though I hate the thought of this precious girl being yelled at.

"You have bad moods sometimes, yeah?"

Hope nods.

"Adults do too and your mom's probably really sad to see Aunt Alice the way she is. So maybe when you interrupted her doing something important for Aunt Alice she yelled?"

"Yeah, I guess." Hope shrugs and her expression clears. "And you're right, a fun present might be better." She angles the screen toward me. "Let's do a search for 'fun bridal shower' gifts."

"Now why didn't I think of that?"

We share a conspiratorial smile but as Hope starts typing I can't help but wonder why Freya blew up like that at her own daughter.

Maybe it's time I start doing a few online searches of my own, namely how early onset dementia is treated.

CHAPTER FORTY-SEVEN
FREYA

While Brooke is helping Hope with her homework I go in search of Riker. He hasn't been at many family dinners lately and, while I know his work is all-consuming when he's creating a commission, I miss him. I've tried to excuse his frequent absences from mealtimes since Brooke got back because I know if I start to dwell on his rationale I'll drive myself crazy with paranoia. It's a worry though, how he rarely leaves his studio these days and when he does it's to deliver his latest masterpiece. Even Hope has noticed he hasn't been around much and while I make excuses for my fiancé, those same excuses that are whirring inside my head are wearing thin.

He works hard. I'm used to not having him around all the time. But it feels different now, as if something has shifted since Brooke came home and I don't like it. Even at his busiest, Riker would pop into the kitchen for his first coffee when Aunt Alice got too ill to have it with him in the barn. I'd be in a hurry, getting ready for work and hurrying Hope along for school, but seeing him for those brief five minutes brought a smile to my face.

He's stopped doing that now and I wonder if it's because he doesn't want to run into Brooke.

I can relate, because I used to do the same thing after Brooke started dating Eli, preferring to stay in my room than run into the happy couple. It had been a combination of jealousy and fear that had kept me away; I'd been insanely envious of Brooke dating the guy I had a crush on, and fear they'd see right through me.

Is this why Riker's avoiding the house? The thought makes my stomach cramp and I press a hand to it. This is crazy. I've seen nothing that suggests he's into my sister and while Brooke had tried several times earlier to broach the subject, I hadn't wanted to discuss it with her because I knew I'd end up feeling bad; like I'm overreacting, like I'm imagining things. Brooke would've explained what I'd seen as meaning nothing and made me feel worse than I already do.

Which only leaves me with one option. Confront Riker and discover why he was comforting Brooke.

When I slip into the barn he's sitting on an overturned crate, a sketchpad resting on his knee and a piece of charcoal in his right hand. He rarely draws his pieces before he starts sculpting but if he gets stuck he resorts to this medium to get the creative juices flowing.

His brows are drawn together and he's glaring at the paper like he wants it to spontaneously combust. I'm loath to interrupt when he's like this but breaking his concentration is a small price to pay if I can sleep tonight, and I know I won't if I don't put my fears to rest.

He's so deep into his work he doesn't hear me approach. When I'm two feet away and my shadow falls across the page he looks up. For a second I glimpse annoyance before his mouth eases into the familiar grin that makes everything right with the world.

"Hey, beautiful, sorry for missing dinner." He brandishes the sketchpad. "I'm having trouble with this latest design and wanted to get some new ideas down."

"You know it's no problem." I bend to place a lingering kiss on his lips before pulling up a crate alongside his. "I'm used to the trials and tribulations of being engaged to a creative genius."

"Tell me more about the genius bit," he says, swooping in for another kiss that makes my toes curl. Deep, open-mouthed, incredibly hot and I sway toward him, giving myself over to the pleasure of my man.

I pretend to swat his chest when he releases me. "As much as I love that, you keep going and I'll be distracting you in the best possible way."

He laughs. "Hold that thought for later." He wiggles his eyebrows suggestively. "Then you can distract me all you want."

"Deal."

I should leave. What's the point of dredging up what I saw earlier? Riker has never given me any reason to doubt him and we're in a good place, why spoil it? It's not long until the wedding and after that, I'll look back on this time and realize how silly I'm being. But I know myself. I'll dwell over what I saw, not because of him. I trust Riker. I don't trust Brooke.

"When I got home from work I saw Brooke was here," I say, keeping my tone light. "She looked pretty upset."

I watch for the slightest flicker of guilt and exhale in relief when his gaze is as guileless as ever. "She was talking about Alice and got a bit teary. In fact, one minute we were talking about Alice, the next Brooke was running out the door. I went after her." A slight frown dents his brow. "I barely see her and I don't know her that well, but I think she's struggling."

Riker's insight surprises me. "With what?"

"Being back here. Seeing Alice the way she is." He shrugs. "I mean, she must be pretty tough to stay away from her family for so long, yet every time I see her she seems upset?"

Guilt floods me. I've doubted Brooke, wrongly accusing her of making moves on my fiancé, albeit in my head, and maybe she's turned to Riker because I haven't been around enough for her? It's often easier to offload to a stranger and perhaps that's why she's been discussing her worries with Riker?

"You could be right," I say, determined to make more of an effort with my sister.

Riker's solemn as he eyes me. "You looked ready for battle when you marched in here. You weren't jealous that I gave her a hug, were you?"

I roll my eyes, hating how close to the mark he is. "Like I'd be jealous."

"I think you are." He tickles me and I wriggle, playfully slapping him away. "You saw me hugging your sister and got all crazy."

"I did not."

My response is uncharacteristically sharp as I jerk away. Being labeled crazy is a trigger for me. Another guy had made that mistake in the past and it hadn't ended well.

Riker's eyebrows shoot up in surprise. "I'm kidding, babe." He grasps my chin and I let him, needing to smooth things over. "You know that, right?"

"Of course." I bridge the inches between us to press a concilia-tory kiss against his lips. "I'm just crabby after a bad day at work, then I missed you at dinner. It's not a big deal."

"I hope not, because we're getting hitched in a few weeks and don't you forget it."

The tension drains from my body at the thought of this amazing guy being all mine. And though I believe Riker was just comforting Brooke, it makes me uncomfortable. I want to be the one he reassures.

"I can't wait." I snuggle into him, letting his heat infuse me, calm me.

"Speaking of our wedding, I want to talk to you about something."

There's an underlying thread of nervousness in his voice and my tension returns, bunching the muscles on the back of my neck so hard I want to rub them.

I ease away and search his face for some clue as to what this is about. "What?"

"I want to instigate proceedings to formally adopt Hope," he says in a rush, the words tumbling over themselves. "I want us to be a real family and with us tying the knot I don't want her to feel left out."

I'm stunned. We've never talked about this before because I didn't want to push him. I see how much he loves Hope and treats her like his own daughter, but I thought he'd be content to be her step-dad. Not that I'm averse to the idea. This big, brawny, beautiful man never ceases to surprise me.

"Hope doesn't need a piece of paper to make you her dad." I clasp his hand between mine. "She already thinks you are."

"I know, but I want to make it official," he says, mulish. "I've spent my life drifting around and now I've finally found what I'm looking for, I want to make it official."

"If it means that much to you… sure." I lift his hand to my mouth and brush feather-light kisses across each knuckle. "She's lucky to have a dad like you."

"I'm the lucky one." He clears the gruffness from his throat. "Now, are you going to let me get back to work or do I have to punish you later?"

I laugh and stand, brushing off my butt. "Promises, promises."

He waggles his finger at me before making a shooing motion with his hands. "Go."

I blow him a kiss. "See you later."

He doesn't respond, the piece of charcoal already between his thumb and fingers, flying over the page like I've inspired him.

I like the idea of being his muse.

It's nice to have the attention of an amazing guy all on me for once.

CHAPTER FORTY-EIGHT

ALICE

THEN

Prom Night had been excruciating for me. Mom and Diana had fussed over my hair and make-up, but I knew all the hairspray and foundation and mascara in the world wouldn't transform my drab hair and plain features into pretty. Though I had looked better than expected. Mom had made my dress; a simple navy satin sheath with spaghetti straps, that I loved. When I put it on, I felt special, and combined with my hair in a chignon and my eyes highlighted by smoky shadow, I thought I actually looked like a girl who could command the attention of a guy like Cam.

Of course that didn't happen. Apart from greeting me like a pal when I walked into the school gym, Cam had been captivated by his date, one of the popular cheerleaders. What did I expect, for him to take one look at my transformation and suddenly develop feelings? Sadly, that's exactly what I'd hoped and when it didn't happen, it soured the entire evening for me. I barely conversed with my date; he'd asked me as a last resort and I'd accepted because Verdant was a small town and I didn't want the real object of my affections, Cam, to think I was pathetic.

The night had been uneventful. My date had sipped bourbon stolen from his dad from a hip flask, had an obligatory dance with me, tried to feel me up and when I'd rejected him he'd avoided me for the rest of the night.

I know Brooke's night is going to be nothing like that but I'm worried just the same. But my concern has more to do with how Freya will handle her sister's golden night than Brooke having a good time. I volunteered to chaperone the dance to give Freya some privacy to sulk. I knew she would and all through Brooke's preparations Freya had made snide comments or scoffed at her dress until my temper snapped and I banished her to her room.

"What's with her?" Brooke asks before slicking a final coat of gloss over her crimson lips.

"You know what your sister's like. All the attention is on you, she's feeling left out."

I wonder if Brooke will elaborate on the other times she's seen her sister behave jealously. But Brooke's too focused on having a good time tonight and I'm relieved when she shrugs and says, "Her time will come next year. I'm not interested in getting caught up in one of her moods tonight."

"That's my girl." I sling an arm over her shoulder and squeeze, careful not to mess her artfully curled hair cascading down her back. We stand side by side, looking at ourselves in the mirror. Brooke's radiant in an ice blue strapless satin dress with a skirt that flares around her calves, her make-up subtle, her hair glowing gold. She's exquisite and more like Diana in that moment than any other. Her mother would be proud.

Predictably, Freya's mood takes a turn for the worse when Eli turns up, breathtakingly gorgeous in a tux, with a stunning orchid corsage for Brooke. Freya manages to fake it around him, saying he looks great and to have a good time, but I see the signs of strain around her mouth.

When Eli and Brooke head for their limo, I hang back. I won't be far behind in my car because chaperones have to be at the high school hall on time. But I want to speak to Freya. She takes one look at my face and holds up her hand.

"I'm fine. I don't want to talk about this, okay?"

"It'll be your turn next year, honey—"

"But it won't be with Eli," she says, tears in her eyes before she runs to her room and slams the door.

That had been several hours ago and I called Freya once to check on her. She hadn't answered. I hadn't expected her to. I know her jealousy will peter out over the course of the evening and hopefully by the time I get home, she'll want to share a hot chocolate with me while I regale her with tales designed to make her laugh; like how the principal got caught kissing the new gym teacher, and how the football jocks mooned their coach.

However, my plans for a quiet time with Freya when the dance ends are scuttled when Brooke begs me to host the after-party at our house. Eli's mother is having another of her migraines so he can't have the party at his place as originally planned.

I want to refuse. If Freya couldn't cope with seeing Eli and Brooke before the prom, how's she going to react with all the most popular kids in her home?

Brooke asked Freya to join the party if she wanted and Freya had given an offhand shrug before heading to her room. That had been fifteen minutes ago and I'm too busy setting out the food the kids picked up from Eli's on the way over to check on her.

I'm pouring ginger ale into the punch bowl to top it up when I hear the clack of heels behind me. I turn to find Freya in a tight black dress that looks suspiciously like Brooke's, her hair slicked back and caught in a low bun, with dramatically made up eyes and fire engine red lips. She looks way older than seventeen and like she's ready for trouble.

I know better than to ruin her effort by a chastisement, so I settle for, "You look grown up."

"I want to be noticed." She places her hands on her hips, bold and defiant.

I want to say that all the figure-hugging clothes and make-up won't make Eli look at her the way he looks at Brooke. That lusting after her sister's boyfriend will never end well.

But I choose my response carefully.

"I understand where you're coming from, especially as we've talked about this before. But don't you think this is Brooke's night? It's her prom, she deserves to have a good time."

A glint of understanding lights her eyes and miraculously I think I've gotten through to her, before the glint turns flinty. "Every night is Brooke's night. She invited me to join the party and I'm going to."

She flounces toward the back door and I'm compelled to caution her one last time.

"You need to tread carefully, Freya. No good can come of alienating your sister."

"*Your sister*," she mimics, and I'm taken aback by the sheen of tears in her defiant glare. "You have no idea what I'm going through."

She blinks rapidly and her bottom lip wobbles. Before I can comfort her, she murmurs, "You're lucky. Your sister died."

I'm shocked she's speaking about her mother like that but she's hurting, and saying stuff she doesn't mean. I see it in the tears caught on her lashes, in the guilty shift of her eyes. She dabs at the tears with her pinkies, before straightening her shoulders. But her expression is sad rather than insolent, and she gives a little shake of her head before stomping out the door in those ridiculously high heels.

I want to go after her but have no right to lecture after what I did to my sister.

CHAPTER FORTY-NINE
BROOKE

I'm busy the next day, putting the finishing touches on Freya's bridal shower. All the guests—mainly work colleagues and a few old school buddies—have RSVP'd, the flowers have been ordered and the caterer has confirmed delivery time for the food. All that's left is to choose a few corny games to play and I'm sure Hope will have a ball helping me with that.

Once I've ticked my last task off the list I can finally start my research into dementia. I read several articles from health journals online last night but some of them are contradictory so I enlist the help of an expert. One of LA's leading rehab facilities has a neurologist specializing in Alzheimer's, but her specialty is early onset dementia. We spoke over the phone early this morning and she agreed to meet with me this afternoon. I hadn't expected such a fast face to face and as I pull into the facility's car park I hope I'm doing the right thing.

Having too much medical knowledge can be a bad thing and discovering how fast Aunt Alice will deteriorate isn't something I want to know. But I'd like to be better informed and knowing Freya, if I start asking questions about prognosis and medication, she'll get defensive and think I'm criticizing her. This way, I'll be knowledgeable and she doesn't have to feel so pressured being the primary carer.

The facility looks more like a space-age hotel, all sleek stainless steel lines from the outside. Security is tight as it would have to be for patients inclined to wander and I wait at the air-locked front door after buzzing to be let in. When I hear a high-pitched beep I push the door open and enter a pristine foyer, with artfully arranged flowers in tall vases next to leather chairs around glass-topped coffee tables. I give the receptionist my name and who I'm here to see, then step aside. There's the faintest hint of ginger blossom in the air, adding to the hotel-like feel of the place. It's understated elegance makes me wonder if Aunt Alice would be better off in a place like this, surrounded by people in a similar situation, with more than one person who knows how to help her.

From what I've observed the last few weeks, Lizzie spends the most time with Alice, making small talk even if she gets few answers. Freya works all day and has to care for Hope, so she rarely spends more than thirty minutes with Aunt Alice at the end of the day, and Riker barely pops in for the reason he's already told me. Here, she'd be well cared for and who knows, with the right medical attention she may not deteriorate as fast?

It's something I can broach with Freya once I'm more equipped to understand Aunt Alice's condition, though it's a task I'm not looking forward to. Lizzie already told me how insistent Freya is about this. Freya's stubbornness is legendary; I'd witnessed it too many times growing up to want to incur her wrath. Back then I'd done everything I could to avoid her 'moods' rather than stir her up. If I offered help with her schoolwork, she'd turn up her music instead. If I let her have the last slice of pizza, she'd leave it uneaten on her plate. If I wanted to leave a party early, she'd hide so I couldn't find her. Stubborn to a fault.

"Miss Stuart?" A young woman who looks barely out of college approaches me. She's wearing a navy skirt suit, low heels, her black hair pulled back in a severe bun. I'd guess she's an assistant of some sort if not for the stethoscope around her neck and the lanyard dangling alongside it with the name Dr. Aileen Hesham. My dementia expert.

"Pleased to meet you, Doctor." I hold out my hand and she shakes it, her grip firm.

"I don't have much time but we can talk in my office."

I follow her as she swipes her name-card through several electronic panels located next to sealed doors and as we pass through they close quickly with a soft whoosh.

"Here we are." We stop outside a glass-enclosed office that's surprisingly small for a place this upmarket. "I have ten minutes before my next meeting so let's get to it."

I like her no-nonsense approach. She sits behind a huge glass desk that takes up most of the room and I sit opposite.

"Thanks for agreeing to meet with me on such short notice, Dr. Hesham. I'll get straight to the point. My aunt is fifty and suffering from early onset dementia. It came on quite quickly and she seems to be deteriorating rapidly."

The doctor's expression barely flickers. "What exactly are you asking me?"

"Is this normal? Can we slow down the progression?"

She steeples her fingers and rests her elbows on her desk in such a clichéd doctor pose I almost laugh.

"Every patient is different, Miss Stuart, and without having a consultation with your aunt I can't give you definitive answers."

Deflated, I slump into the chair. "My aunt seems to be on a lot of medication."

This surprises the doctor into a barely discernible upward slant of an eyebrow. "Dementia is often treated with cholinesterase inhibitors. They block the actions of an enzyme that destroys an important neurotransmitter for memory. What else is your aunt taking?"

"I don't know." I sound like an idiot admitting it. I should've come better prepared, done some more research so I can ask insightful questions rather than hoping for some miracle answers.

"Dementia can cause agitation in some patients. They become aggressive, hallucinate, and may have ideas of persecution. They also battle with sleeplessness, depression and anxiety. Does your aunt exhibit any of these?"

I nod. "She's drowsy all the time."

"You said she's taking a lot of medication? It may be for anxiety and depression, perhaps a sleeping aid too?"

I don't want to interrogate Hope but from what she said it sounded like Aunt Alice was taking a lot more than that. Only Freya can give me answers and at least I now know where to start with my questions.

"What other forms of therapy is your aunt undertaking?"

"I've only been back home a few weeks but from what I see she's doing nothing."

The doctor's fingers flatten against the desk, surprise evident in both eyebrows rising. "What do you mean?"

"Well, she's living at home with extended family who all look after her."

The doctor's brows knit in disapproval. "She doesn't attend a rehab facility for cognitive stimulation therapy?"

I must look blank because the doctor continues. "CST is a structured program for people with mild to moderate dementia. It's usually conducted in a group and they're mentally engaged with activities like singing, playing word games, talking about current events, cooking from a recipe, that kind of thing. She should also be doing reality orientation training, going over the basics like names, dates and times."

I'm appalled and feel like the worst niece in the world. Why didn't I research dementia sooner? I'd put my faith in Freya, the expert, but it looks like she's too busy with her own life to do all these other therapies Aunt Alice needs. Apart from spending time on her laptop or watching TV, Lizzie told me Aunt Alice does nothing.

Dr. Hesham is staring at me with condemnation, like she's just read my thoughts, so I feel compelled to say, "My sister has been caring for my aunt at home. She's a nurse at a nursing home but I think she's too busy to do all that therapy you just mentioned."

I'm close to tears and the doctor must hear something in my tone because her expression softens. "We do the best we can for our loved ones. So if your sister wants to care for your aunt at home, there are other options like reminiscence therapy that I've found works wonders with my patients."

"What is it?"

"We do it here in groups as part of organized therapy but it can be done one-on-one. You might play music from your aunt's past, show her old photos or treasured items, get her talking about what her school days were like, her work life, her hometown, that kind of thing. It's basically getting her to remember the past, probably fragments at first, but with practice it's an excellent stimulatory tool."

At last, something I can actively do without feeling so damn helpless.

The doctor glances at her watch and rises. "That's about all the time I have. Please don't hesitate to contact me again, Miss Stuart." She hesitates, before continuing. "I think it would be beneficial for your aunt to have an assessment, either with me or another of my colleagues here. We have the reputation of being the best in this field for a reason."

She doesn't sound smug or condescending. She's confident in her abilities and from our short meeting I am too. I agree; I need to discover who diagnosed Aunt Alice in the first place, and she needs to be assessed by someone new, preferably here. I'll broach it with Freya and in the meantime I can get started on the reminiscence therapy. Who knows, it might unleash the password Lizzie and I need to access her diary and discover more things to help her?

"Thanks for your time."

We do the whole door unlocking procedure again down the long corridors before I'm back at reception. Before she turns to leave, she says, "A word of advice, Miss Stuart?"

I nod, the solemnity in her tone scaring me a little.

"Your aunt needs mental stimulation and it's difficult to get that, locked away. Just because she may not be able to verbalize her needs it doesn't mean she doesn't have them."

Feeling suitably chastised and near to tears again, I mumble my thanks before striding toward the door, more determined than ever to help Aunt Alice any way I can.

CHAPTER FIFTY

FREYA

Brooke misses dinner. She had an errand to run and from Hope's weird behavior, alternating between excitement and pretending nothing's going on, I guess they've planned some kind of surprise for me. I've seen Hope this way before, when she wanted to surprise me with a cake for my birthday. She'd been busting to tell me but would shy away at the last moment, practically wriggling with excitement, and she's that way now. I'm relieved, because I still don't trust Brooke one hundred percent and her vanishing on some mysterious errand would otherwise rouse my suspicion.

It's nine forty-five when I hear Brooke's car pull into the drive. She's back. This time of evening is my favorite time of day, when Hope's asleep, Riker's working and Lizzie's either reading in Aunt Alice's room or doing whatever she does online. I usually sit on the back porch listening to the distant crash of waves against the cliffs, sipping a chamomile tea. It's the closest I get to peace these days, switching off the memories and the worry and the guilt.

"Hey, Sis, where've you been?"

"LA," she says, dragging one of the outdoor chairs to place it opposite me before flopping into it. "I need to talk to you about Aunt Alice."

My guard instantly goes up. It's my usual defensiveness rising to the fore because I feel like Lizzie, and now Brooke, have been second-guessing my care of Alice lately.

"What do you want to talk about?"

Brooke shifts in her seat, uncomfortable. "I understand you know what's best for Aunt Alice, and I'm so grateful for all you do in caring for her. But why is she locked away all the time?"

"She's 'locked away' for her own safety. All our patients at work are too."

"But the nursing home must have common rooms for activities and gardens to wander around." Her fingers fiddle with the ends of her sleeves and tension makes her jaw jut. "Aunt Alice has none of that. Ever since I've been home she's cooped up."

"There's always an adjustment period to the medications and they've made her really drowsy. It's best she stays indoors until she's more alert."

Her eyes narrow, and I feel her cool gaze as if she's assessing me. "But surely she can spend short periods of time outside?"

I grit my teeth and try to remain calm. It's all very well for Brooke to care so much now, but where has she been for the last eleven years? "Where's all this coming from? Who did you see in LA?"

"Dr. Aileen Hesham, one of the top doctor's specializing in early onset dementia, and she opened my eyes." A deep frown creases her brow as she folds her arms. "Aunt Alice could be doing so much more."

"Why did you feel the need to sneak behind my back?" My anger is simmering, flowing through my veins like lava. "I could've answered any questions you may have."

She raises her chin, defiant. She's not backing down. "In that case, why isn't she doing cognitive stimulation therapy? And what medications is she on? Does she have hallucinations, sleep issues, anxiety?"

The heat in my veins reaches my face and I'm burning up from the inside out. I need to vent, an outlet for this awful fury rising like a tidal wave that can swamp and devastate. I've been angry with my sister in the past, many times, but have only experienced this fury once before.

I push my teacup away before I'm tempted to smash my fist on it. My muscles are tensed and I'm gasping air to cool down.

She notices my distress and one eyebrow slowly rises. "I don't want to question your decisions, Freya, but why can't you answer me—"

I leap to my feet. "You can't waltz back in here after eleven years and presume to know what's best for our aunt. She's *my* responsibility," I thump my chest, "and I won't have you butting your nose in when you know nothing about it."

I know this isn't the end of it. Brooke has that look, the one I've seen in the past, where she won't let me get away with anything.

"I have no idea why you're being so defensive about this. Dr. Hesham thinks Aunt Alice should have an assessment at her clinic. She has the best facilities—"

"No." I thump the table and my teacup overturns. Brooke's staring at me, wide-eyed, and I know my behavior is only going to push her buttons further, so I temper my outburst with, "Once the wedding is over, we'll sit down and discuss this as a family, okay?"

I see her mulling this. She used to hate confrontation and I'm hoping my placating her to revisit this in another few weeks will do the trick.

After an eternity, she nods, reluctant. "I only want what's best for her. We owe her, Freya. She was our mom and she was amazing."

I try to appear suitably repentant. "I know, and I'm sorry, I get overprotective when it comes to her. After you left and Lizzie was at college, it was just her and me for years. She helped me be a good mom to Hope. She stood by me when nobody else did." I pretend to dash tears from my eyes. "I'm closer to her. I see how fast some patients deteriorate once admitted to our nursing home and I don't want that for Aunt Alice."

A spark of compassion lights Brooke's eyes. "Why didn't you say that in the first place?"

I shrug, grateful she's accepted my excuse. "Because you and I have always had a problem communicating. I guess we need to work on that now you're back."

"You know it's only until the wedding, then I'm off again?"

She made that perfectly clear when she accepted my wedding invitation and I'm counting on it.

"You do what you need to do." I move toward her and lay a hand on her shoulder, giving it a brief squeeze. "I'm glad you're back, Sis, for however long it is."

She covers my hand with hers and we enjoy a rare relaxed moment.

She trusts me.

She's done that a lot over the years. Maybe she shouldn't have.

CHAPTER FIFTY-ONE

ALICE

THEN

I've never been an overprotective parent. I want Lizzie, Brooke and Freya to make their own mistakes, their own decisions, and live with the consequences. But this is Brooke's night and I won't have Freya mess with it.

Seeing her in Brooke's dress, wearing the lipstick I bought Brooke specifically for tonight, is the last straw. I've been patient with Freya. I haven't lectured her; instead, I've given her calm, rational advice because I empathize. But I won't have her ruining Brooke's special night.

I watch from inside, only venturing into the backyard occasionally with a new tray of quiches hot from the oven or freshly baked brownies. The kids aren't doing much, mainly sitting around chatting in groups or dancing to the too-loud music pumping from portable speakers set up around the periphery. Everyone seems to be having a good time.

Everyone except Freya.

I love Brooke for inviting her sister to join her get-together. Brooke's warm-hearted and generous so when the party transferred here she wouldn't have thought twice about asking Freya. She even didn't react when Freya strutted outside wearing her dress; I saw Brooke point at it, laugh and hug her sister, like she wore it better than her. But this is Brooke's crowd, and she's the queen at the center, with Eli her king. I see the two of them put on their prom crowns at times, laughing and jostling and enduring good-natured teasing. Freya doesn't think it's so funny.

Brooke is basking in the adulation of her friends, not in a conceited way but in delightful acceptance they like her as much as she likes them. Eli rarely leaves her side. He's a doting boyfriend and a good kid. I assume they're having sex. The girls trust me but we don't talk about stuff like that, though I made sure the first thing I did when Brooke started dating Eli was to discuss birth control and make her an appointment with our doctor.

She shied away from the conversation, said she wasn't thinking that far ahead, but I know she kept the appointment. They've been dating for a few months now and I hope she's being sensible. I don't pry so I've never searched her room for a pill packet, but I know Brooke weighs decisions carefully, like me, and she'll do the right thing.

Freya on the other hand… she's flirting with Eli's best friend and I wonder if she's doing it to get Eli's attention. Greg seems like a good kid; he's been here a few times when Brooke has held study groups before exams. He's tall, with a ready smile, and plays football with Eli. Freya has never paid him attention before so when I see her sidling up to him, refilling his cup, feeding him brownies, while casting sly glances at Eli, I know what she's up to.

It's warped thinking because in what universe does she actually think Eli will leave Brooke for her? I've been there, done that, and no matter how much I played the attentive friend or loving sister, Cam only had eyes for Diana. Though I can empathize: look how far I'd gone in an attempt to get Cam all to myself. There's no disputing young love and with Freya's heart unwittingly captured by Eli, I can't reason with her.

I've broached the subject a few times but by her behavior tonight she's hell-bent on forging her own path; one that leads directly to disaster. As a slow song blares from some kid's playlist, a few of the couples start dancing. Freya doesn't take much notice until she sees Brooke and Eli plastered together—her arms looped around his neck, his around her waist—then she grabs Greg and drags him into the center of the lawn. She presses against him and starts writhing in time with the music. I see Greg's goofy grin, like he can't believe his luck, but I don't like when one of the boys wolf whistles.

I need to stop Freya before she embarrasses herself as well as Brooke, and I grapple with a plausible excuse to get her back inside. That's when I notice Eli has disappeared, probably to the bathroom, so I seize my chance.

I walk across the lawn, thankful when the songs transition. Greg's disappointed by the change in tempo and my sudden appearance, but Freya doesn't care as her gaze sweeps the backyard in search of Eli. I reach her and grasp her arm.

"Eli's inside. Do you want something to drink?"

Predictably, she believes my lie, her face lighting up at the prospect of some one-on-one time with the object of her affection. The moment we reach the kitchen, I flick the lock on the door and place my back against it.

"What you're doing out there? It's not good."

She widens her eyes in faux innocence. "I'm having a great time. Greg's a nice guy."

"You're right, he is, and that's why using him in the vain hope Eli will notice you isn't proper." My tone is flat, unimpressed. "You're an amazing girl, Freya. Surely you know what you're doing is wrong?"

I notice the shift in her expression from amiable to sly. "You wanted me to move on from Eli."

"I do, but not like this." I press a hand to my heart. "I know what it's like to have the guy I adore not notice I'm in the room because of my sister. I know how it feels, believe me, but what you're doing out there?" I shake my head, glad she hasn't erupted and seems to be listening. "I already told you this is Brooke's night. Let her enjoy it. Please."

I see the change in mood and when it comes it's swift and terrifying.

Her eyes narrow and her expression twists into ugliness. "You have no idea what it's like to be me so don't you dare patronize me by comparing us."

It's not what she says but the way she says it, like she wishes I'd disappear.

Tonight settles it. She has to see someone.

"I'm making you an appointment with—"

"Don't even think about it." She's in my face before I can move, eyes blazing, spittle flying from her mouth. "I'm not talking to a shrink so you can feel better about yourself as a parent." She jabs a finger into my chest, hard. "You're my aunt, not my mother, so butt the hell out and leave me alone."

She storms to her bedroom and slams the door hard enough the windows in the kitchen rattle. I'm shaking, my stomach churning with nerves. Freya needs help but she won't accept it. I've tried the gentle approach, I've tried the direct one, and neither has worked.

I'm at a loss and for the first time since I took custody of these girls I wonder if I've done the right thing.

CHAPTER FIFTY-TWO
BROOKE

I lied to Freya.

I'm not leaving after the wedding, not until I ensure Aunt Alice gets the best care. Freya has done a great job looking after Aunt Alice and I feel bad, breezing in for a short time then leaving again. I want to do more, to ensure my aunt is well taken care of before I go.

Freya thinks I'm butting in. She's the expert, considering her job, so it's not surprising she's defensive when I question her about Alice's care. But I hadn't expected her to explode that last time. I've been patient with her tantrums in the past, and held back many times. What good would it have done to provoke her when I knew she had a short fuse? Besides, I often bit back my opinions because I didn't want to hurt her feelings but now, I'm not holding back. Aunt Alice getting the best care is too important.

Aunt Alice used to bear the brunt of Freya's moods when we were growing up. She'd deflect and distract Freya and more often than not it worked. If it hadn't been for Aunt Alice's gentle but firm guidance I think my sister wouldn't have turned out to be the upstanding citizen she is. She owes Aunt Alice as much as I do.

I accept her rationale for keeping Aunt Alice at home. She'd know how fast people deteriorate when admitted to a nursing home considering she works in one and she doesn't want that for our aunt. But what about all the benefits Dr. Hesham mentioned?

I may have agreed to wait until after the wedding to get Aunt Alice assessed but that doesn't mean I can't make a start on some of that reminiscence therapy the doc had recommended. I need to do my share. Perhaps it's the weight of responsibility on Freya that's made her impatient.

I enlist Lizzie's help in finding our aunt's favorite objects, including anything from the past to jog her memory. Our aunt has never been sentimental so the task is a difficult one but we finally have a few things: a photo of her and our mother lazing around a pool, a small pink toolset she kept for odd jobs around the house, locks of our hair pressed into an album along with our class photos from every year from kindergarten to seniors, and her beloved laptop.

I think it best Lizzie and me don't do it together—it might confuse our aunt more and Lizzie's still overwhelmed with Alice not being her mom—so I take first dibs. I also ask her to keep this between us, after telling her about Doc Hesham's advice and Freya's defensiveness. Considering Lizzie has tried quizzing Freya about Alice's treatment before, only to be met with condescending responses, she agrees to keep this quiet until after the wedding when we can hopefully get more answers regarding Aunt Alice's prognosis.

Evening is the best time for Aunt Alice. Lizzie said the opposite when I first arrived home but I find her too sleepy in the mornings. She still rambles a lot in the evening but she's better than the mornings when she seems drowsy and totally out of it.

I grab the key hanging beside the phone, unlock her door and let myself in. She's dozing and my gaze is drawn to the locked cabinet beside her bed where her medications are stored. Only Freya has a key to open it and for a moment I resent her proprietorial care. I want to see what Aunt Alice is taking because I can match it to what Dr. Hesham said. Maybe the doctor who assessed her initially isn't half as qualified to prescribe treatment as Doc Hesham?

I realize I've become a tad obsessed with my aunt's treatment but I only want the best for her. She deserves it after all she did for me. It's strange, how fast we've come to terms with the lies Aunt Alice told, how she withheld the truth about Lizzie being our sister all these years, not to mention her bizarre disclosure she killed our mom. But I trust Alice. She stood by me when I needed her the most and she must have a rational explanation for her lies.

If she was lucid, I wonder what she'd reveal? The last time she saw me she'd pressed a thousand dollars into my hand and given me a card to access a bank account she'd set up for me. She fully supported my decision to make a new start far away from Martino Bay and I'd loved her for it.

What she didn't know was that I'd come to harsher decisions in the hours I spent alone before that. Decisions involving cutting all ties with my family, including her. I could never return to Martino Bay, not when the guilt of what I'd done sat like a stone in my stomach. I thought they'd be better off without me, but I realize now how much I've missed and how much I could have been helping Aunt Alice.

I also wonder how my life could've been different if I'd had the support of my family after my baby died? Rather than grieving alone, I could've turned to them. I wouldn't have spent the last decade drifting, searching for… something, to make me feel better. Though considering Freya had been pregnant at the same time, it might've been too heartbreaking, watching Freya raise her child.

Blinking back tears, I pick up the first photo, the one of Aunt Alice and my mom sunbathing by a pool, and approach the bed. I touch her arm.

"Aunt Alice, it's me, Brooke."

Her eyes snap open, startling me, as the vacant stare I've come to dread fixes on me. "Brooke," she mimics, more out of hearing me say it rather than any comprehension of who I am. "Sister."

"No, Aunt Alice, I'm your niece." I hold the photo in her line of sight and point to Diana. "This is your sister."

Something akin to fear shifts in her eyes before she averts her gaze. "Too many secrets."

Secrets I would love to get to the bottom of, so I persist. "Diana was my mother. She's Freya and Lizzie's mother too."

A tear seeps out of the corner of Aunt Alice's eye and my heart aches for her, how frustrating it must be not being able to communicate.

"Do you remember where this photo was taken?" I move it into her line of vision again. "It's a pool. Was it your house?"

Though from what she'd told us about her past, she and my mom grew up fairly poor so I can't imagine them having a pool. Her gaze is drawn to the photo again and this time a small smile tugs at the corners of her mouth. "Cam."

This is huge progress. For the first time since I got home she's reacting to her surroundings, understanding me. Then again, I hadn't known about using reminiscing as a tool to hone her memory.

I nod and offer an encouraging smile. "Cam was my dad."

"Brother-in-law. Love. Secrets."

Again with the secrets, something she's repeated every time I sit with her that I've almost dismissed it.

"You loved my dad," I say, hating to think how much pain she must've had to hide, being in love with her sister's husband.

"Loved. Cam."

Another tear seeps out and I feel horrible, dredging up uncomfortable memories for her, until I remember this is part of the therapy Dr. Hesham said could actually help. But I decide to move on to the next object to see if she remembers the toolbox.

"You wouldn't let us girls touch this," I say, holding the toolbox out to her. "We loved the mini screwdrivers, hammer and wrenches, but you wouldn't let us play with them."

"Mine." Her voice is barely above a rasp as she makes a grab for the box, cuddling it against her. "Brakes. Car. My love."

She's merging the photo of my mom with this toolbox somehow. My parents died in a car accident, brake failure. I reach for the toolbox but she grips it tighter so I flick the album open to the first page, with the locks of our hair pressed between the plastic sleeves.

"This is our hair. Lizzie, Freya and me."

"My girls… mine," she says, decisively. "My birthday girls."

I have no idea what that means so I hold up her laptop.

"Secrets." She stabs a finger at the cover. "Birthday girls. Secrets. So many secrets."

Pleased we're still talking of sorts, I continue to delve. "You know you can trust me, Aunt Alice. I'm good at keeping secrets."

"No, no, no." She shakes her head from side to side, suddenly agitated. "Bad secrets. Sister secrets. My Cam. Love. Birthday girls."

I'm losing her. Her fingers clutching the toolbox unfurl and it slips off the bed cover. I catch it before it can slide to the floor and when I look up she's opened the laptop.

Her forehead is crinkled, her mouth pursed as she concentrates, trying to remember the password.

"Here, let me." I type it in for her and she beams when the home page, a photo of her, Lizzie, Freya and Hope, pops up.

I wait, wondering what she'll do, hoping she'll access her online diary and I'll finally be able to make sense of her ramblings. But she sits there, propped in bed, staring at the home page, confusion mingling with frustration in those eyes that were once so expressive. After a minute, she gives up and pushes the laptop toward me.

"Is there anything you want me to look up for you, Aunt Alice? Do you want to watch a movie? Read something?"

A small part of me hopes that the longer the laptop is open the more chance she'll remember something to tie together everything she's been saying.

"Go." She turns her head away from me and I gather up the laptop, clutching it, along with the album and toolbox, to my chest.

"I love you," I whisper, leaning down to press a kiss to her forehead.

I'm almost at the door when I hear the softest response, "Love you too."

For now, it's enough.

CHAPTER FIFTY-THREE
ALICE
THEN

I have no idea if Freya knew I meant it when I said I'd make an appointment with a psychologist or if she finally woke up and realized she could never have Eli, but whatever it was, in the month since prom she's been an angel: she declines several invitations from Brooke to join her and Eli in town, she doesn't spy on them as much when they're around the house and she treats me with more respect. Maybe I should have pushed the issue about seeing a psychologist but with school out for the summer, I'm glad to have some peace and not having to watch her every move.

Brooke has applied to several colleges but they're half-hearted attempts to please me rather than any burning desire for tertiary education. She scored so well, she can be anything she wants to be, but I have a feeling Brooke is more like her mother than she realizes and would rather give up her future for love.

Because there's no doubt in my mind that Brooke loves Eli. He, too, is eschewing college in favor of staying in Martino Bay and joining his parents in the family business, a thriving landscaping venture. The similarities between them and Di and Cam are uncanny. Personally, I hate seeing such talented kids throwing away their futures to stay in a town like this but who am I to judge?

I ruined my future the day I chose vengeance and jealousy over love and I'll never impose my views on my girls. While Eli has worked the last four weeks, Brooke has wasted her days. She knows she'll have to find a job eventually but for the first time in her life she isn't striving for something.

Then she comes home from town one day and rattles my faith in her.

"Aunt Alice, how do you know what true love is? If the guy you love is the one?"

I want to tell her the truth; that you only know what true love is when it's taken away from you. When you can't breathe because that guy has his hands on someone else when it should be you. When you morph into a monster because your one true love has chosen another who you can't help but hate.

But I don't say any of that. "Every relationship is different, honey. One couple's definition of true love will be nothing like another couple's. As for the fabled 'the one', I don't know if that exists, but if the love is strong enough it can make us believe anything."

She's pensive, chewing on her bottom lip, twisting a strand of hair around her finger over and over until the tip turns purplish from lack of blood supply.

"What's going on, kiddo? Is this about Eli?"

She nods, and untwists her hair. "I love him, but something happened today and it's got me thinking."

"What happened?"

She hesitates, searching my face for approval. She must think she gets it because she starts talking. "I was in town today when I saw a guy. He stopped at the lights near the ice-cream parlor and when he looked at me…" The hair winding resumes. "I've never felt anything like it, except that time I got a zap from the power-point with my faulty cell phone charger. Only stronger…" She gives a little shudder. "I love Eli, I really do, but I've never felt like that when he touches me." Crimson floods her cheeks. "It confused me because when that guy smiled, I felt it all the way down here."

She presses a hand against her belly and the color in her cheeks intensifies. She wants answers from me and I'm the least qualified person to give them, considering I know exactly what she's talking about but for me, only Cam made me feel that way.

"It's okay to be attracted to other people, honey. It'll happen throughout your life and it doesn't mean you love Eli any less."

Relief filters across her face. "But it felt wrong somehow."

I cup her blazing cheek. "It was a glance and a smile, honey, you've got nothing to worry about."

"I guess." She shrugs but I can see it's still weighing on her mind. "Is Freya around?"

The last thing I want is Brooke talking to her sister about this. Freya might take it as a sign Brooke and Eli's relationship is headed for trouble and it could give her false hope, when she seems to have moved on.

"If you want my advice, honey, forget about this. It was nothing and you know your sister, she'll only tease you about it."

"Good point."

Brooke leans forward and hugs me. "Thanks, Aunt Alice. You're the best."

"I try." I pat her back, thankful I can help.

There'll come a time very soon when my girls won't need me anymore and then what will I do?

CHAPTER FIFTY-FOUR

FREYA

Riker takes me into town for an early dinner on Saturday night. We don't eat out a lot because of our schedules but when we do I love it because I get to parade my fiancé. He's holding *my* hand. He's staring into *my* eyes. He wants to marry *me*. I bask in the attention. It makes me feel special in a way I never have.

Not that I deliberately seek out ways to flaunt my happiness but growing up I'd felt second best for so long that it's nice to see how far I've come. While Riker can take the credit for some of it, I know it's more than that. Being a good mother to Hope, an accomplished nurse at work, gives me the validation I've craved my entire life. It makes me feel worthy. And I deserve it considering what I've done to get here.

When we get home, Riker opens the passenger door and holds out his hand to me. I take it, and when I step from the car, he murmurs in my ear, "Close your eyes."

"Why? You know I hate surprises."

"I know, but I want to show you my latest creation."

I love when he shares his work with me, when he asks my opinion. "Okay. But why can't I close them when we get to the workshop?"

"Just do it, babe." He presses his lips to mine, and my eyelids flutter shut automatically.

"No peeking," he says, as he covers my eyes with his hands. I walk in front of him. He's guiding me, but as we hit the stone path I know he's not taking me to the barn, he's heading toward the back of the house.

"What are you up to, James Riker Smith?"

"You'll see." His warm breath fans my ear and a shiver of longing shoots through me.

When we stop, I hear Hope giggle and I immediately know this must be the surprise my delightful daughter has been planning with my sister.

There's a loud cacophony of 'Surprise' as Riker lowers his hands and I gasp in genuine shock. The backyard has been transformed into a fairyland, with ivory chiffon and lanterns in crimson, sienna and turquoise strung from tree to tree. A long trestle has been set up, with a lace tablecloth and satin bows at the corners. It's covered in finger food, everything from mini wontons in individual spoons to elaborate twisted lox on rye. A smaller table to one side has colorful cocktails arranged on it, with corny names like 'Bride To Be' and 'Here Comes the Groom'.

It's a bridal shower and, while I may not like surprises as a rule, I'm touched Brooke went to so much trouble to arrange this. It signifies how far we've come and I'm thankful.

Riker spins me around and I see everyone gathered on the porch, work colleagues mostly, with Lizzie, Brooke and Hope fronting the motley crew. Hope's beaming and runs toward me, as Brooke searches my face for approval; she knows I'm not big on surprises, and in that moment I love how close we are again.

I smile and mouth "Thank you" as Hope flings herself at me.

"Isn't this the best surprise ever, Mom?"

I hug her tightly. "Sure is, sweetie. Did you do this?"

"I helped Auntie Brooke, it was her idea."

That's my daughter, honest to a fault.

"Well, it's fabulous. Thank you." I press a kiss to the top of her head.

"There are presents too." Hope points to a smaller table I hadn't spotted yet, tucked beneath the branches of an oak. "But Auntie Brooke said it's probably best you open those later because some people give brides-to-be naughty stuff."

I chuckle. "Your aunt is very wise."

But as the crowd surges toward me, I spy something that belies my proclamation.

Aunt Alice.

She's in a wheelchair, tucked into the corner of the porch.

My euphoria instantly fades. What the hell does Brooke think she's doing? Aunt Alice shouldn't be out here. Why does Brooke think she can make these decisions without consulting me?

As if sensing my displeasure, Brooke waits until my friends have greeted me and drifted off before approaching. I open my mouth to chastise her but before I can speak she holds up her hand.

"I can see by your expression you don't approve of me bringing Aunt Alice out of her room, but Lizzie's watching her so she doesn't wander off. This is a special time for you and she's been a huge part of your life, so she deserves to be here."

My anger fades. "You're right. She should be a part of this. I just worry about her."

Brooke almost sags in relief. "I know you do, but she'll be fine. Now, how about I pour my sister a glass of champagne?"

"Sounds good."

Brooke links her elbow with mine and leads me toward the makeshift bar. I'm overcome by emotion and the conviction we're closer than we've ever been. She's done this for me, thrown a wonderful bridal shower. She came back for the wedding. She cares about me. But she also lied to me.

Can I trust her?

CHAPTER FIFTY-FIVE
BROOKE

Seeing Freya mixing with her work friends, champagne flute in one hand, a mini quiche in the other, with a big smile on her face, I'm glad I did this.

Eleven years is a long time to be away from my sister and despite our differences over Aunt Alice's care lately, re-establishing our bond is still a priority and seems to be progressing. The initial awkwardness between us is fading and witnessing her happiness today makes me wonder if I should've insisted on doing more for her regarding wedding prep, despite her admitting she'd used that as an excuse to get me home earlier. I miss our closeness and throwing her this shower has gone a long way to showing her how much I care.

I wonder if she knows about the baby I lost. Aunt Alice had said she wouldn't tell anyone, including Freya. If so, she's kept that secret for years and has no reason to reveal it now.

But after all the time I've spent with Hope, I wonder if I should tell Freya. It would bond us like nothing else if she learns we both went through teen pregnancies and I know trusting her with my secret would mean a lot to her.

Lizzie has been hovering near Aunt Alice's wheelchair for the last hour, attentive and on guard. Not that I really fear Aunt Alice wandering off anywhere; she's too feeble. It took both of us to get her into the wheelchair. It ratchets up my admiration for Freya, who does it every second day to get her into the shower. Lizzie gives Aunt Alice a sponge bath on alternate days.

My gaze drifts toward Aunt Alice. She's staring at the people mingling on the lawn with unseeing eyes, tapping her hand against her thigh in time with the music. I remember she wasn't a fan growing up, preferring the house to be quiet rather than having the radio blaring, but she didn't mind us turning up our playlists when we were home.

I should use those old playlists as part of the reminiscence therapy. The first night had gone surprisingly well and Lizzie had reported that last night had been okay too, with Alice managing a chuckle at our old high school photos.

I feel vindicated doing this despite Freya not knowing. She may be the expert who nurses patients like our aunt on a daily basis, but in this case maybe she's too close to the situation and isn't seeing things clearly?

I want to keep doing the therapy for the next week and if there's a marked improvement I'll tell Freya what I've been up to. Aunt Alice should be out in the fresh air every day. It would always be under supervision and if she's so frail there's no way Aunt Alice can move out of that wheelchair.

"Hey, Brooke, long time no see." A hand touches my arm and I turn, wishing I'd made more of an effort to memorize the guest list. The tall redhead smiling at me is vaguely familiar but I have no idea if it's a co-worker of Freya's or a friend.

"Hi, how are you?"

She laughs at my generic greeting. "You don't remember me, do you?"

I wince. "Sorry, I've been away a long time."

"Helena. I was in Freya's class at high school."

The moment she says her name I recognize her. Not because Freya brought many friends home back then, but because she'd been at the party the night Eli died. She'd been really drunk, singing some old Springsteen ballad loudly and repetitively. Funny, how such a mundane detail like that has stuck in my head. Then again, I remember every tiny thing about that night because I've gone over it repeatedly in the ensuing years, wishing I'd done everything differently.

"Hey, Helena, good to see you. It's great you and Freya are still close."

"Not so much these days. I travel a lot for work."

"What do you do?"

"I'm a counselor for one of the colleges in LA, but my folks are here so I'm in town regularly."

"That's great."

As our small talk tapers off I expect her to drift away. Instead, she fixes me with an odd pitying stare.

"I was sorry to hear you left town and haven't been back since Eli's death." She shakes her head. "That night was so awful."

Not wanting to dredge up the past, especially with someone I barely know, I mumble an agreement.

"Most of us girls were jealous of you back then," she continues, oblivious to my discomfort. "Eli was gorgeous and such a nice guy. We thought you two were one of those perfect couples who'd be together forever." I don't need to hear this but before I can come up with a polite way to extricate myself, she says, "I was surprised when he returned to the party that night after you two left together, especially seeing how distraught he was." She points at Freya. "I never encouraged your sister's crush on him, but it was lucky she was around that night to comfort him."

Shock renders me mute.

I had no idea Eli returned to the party after I told him the truth, let alone that Freya had spoken to him. She never mentioned anything to me, even after his body was found the next morning and my world toppled.

"We all assumed you'd had an argument..." She shakes her head, genuine sadness clouding her eyes. "I know some of the kids were horrible and blamed you, but these things happen and there's nothing you or anybody could've done to stop him making the choice he did."

Looks like Helena can't help but dole out counseling advice when she's out of the workplace too but I don't want to hear it. I'm too fixated on what Freya has been keeping from me. What did he say to her? Did he hate me? Did he tell her what I confessed?

Now, more than ever, I'm relieved I didn't tell Eli the name of the guy I'd been with that night. I see the way she lords Riker over me; over everyone, really. He's like a prize she's won, like that time at Martino Bay's fair when she shot three bull's-eyes in a row to claim a giant stuffed bear. She'd paraded around all day with that bear under her arm, and these days she wears the same smug expression whenever she holds Riker's hand.

If she ever suspected I'd slept with her fiancé long before she had… no, it's another secret in this family that needs to be protected.

"Anyway, sorry for dredging up the past." Helena gives herself a little shake. "It was nice seeing you again, Brooke."

"You too."

I force a smile but as Helena drifts toward the group clustered around Freya, I'm struck once again by how little I really know my sister.

CHAPTER FIFTY-SIX

ALICE

THEN

It's almost midnight and I'm sitting outside, listening to the waves. I'm not sure whether the distant crashing is comforting but lately, with the girls socializing more, I've found myself out here most nights seeking solace.

Tonight, they're at yet another party and I'm left with too much time to contemplate, to remember. I don't like it. When the girls are around there's noise to drown out my thoughts and now they're eighteen and seventeen respectively I see startling similarities between them and me and Diana. Freya is learning to hide her jealousy better, like I did. But it's there all the same, festering, and Freya is more volatile than I ever was.

I hear a car pull up and I exhale, glad the girls are home. I'm safe from my memories for another night. But my relief is short-lived when I hear a door slam and an anguished cry calling my name. I rush inside to find Brooke, tear-stained and wild-eyed, dragging in breaths like she's run a marathon.

"What's wrong?" I glance over her shoulder and my heart plummets when I realize she's alone. "Is it Freya?"

"She's okay, she's still at the party."

"Then what's wrong—"

"I screwed up."

Before I can ask any more she flings herself into my arms, hanging on so tight I can barely breathe. She's sobbing hard, clutching at me like she'll never let go, and my heart breaks. I don't know what's happened but Brooke is the most upbeat, positive person I know and I've never seen her this distraught.

"Sweetheart, tell me what's wrong." I smooth her back, over and over, in long, slow strokes, murmuring "Ssh," until eventually her sobs peter out.

Only then do I ease her away, desperately hoping Freya hasn't done something to precipitate this level of anguish.

"I did something bad and I told Eli about it because I had to, as we've never lied to each other, but he went ballistic and said some really horrible things so I broke up with him." She hiccups, her eyes swimming with tears. "I've made a mess of everything."

She'll survive this heartache and I can't help but feel relieved Freya isn't the cause of it.

"Hey, it's okay. Whatever you've done, and however you've handled it, it'll be better in the morning when you've had time to gain perspective."

She shakes her head, tears seeping from the corners of her eyes again. "He's not going to forgive me for this. The names he called me… it was so awful I had to break up with him."

I want to ask her what she did but the last thing she needs is an interrogation. She'll tell me when she's ready. For now, all I can do is support.

"Where's Freya? She didn't come home with you?"

"She doesn't know I left. I told one of my friends to let her know." She swipes at the tears still trickling down her cheeks. "I had to talk to Eli so we got out of there."

She shudders and her eyes turn so dark they're almost indigo. "We were talking at the bottom of the cliffs. I begged him to come back with me but he wouldn't budge so I eventually left."

Every property along our long winding road backs onto cliffs but when kids talk about "the cliffs" they're referring to a section out of town known as a popular make-out spot. I'm surprised they went there to talk, but what do I know?

"I messed up really badly," she murmurs, her pain audible. "I'm never impulsive so why did I do something so stupid?"

"We all give in to impulse at times." I reach out and squeeze her hand. "We're human, sweetie. We make mistakes, we learn from them."

And sometimes we pay for them for the rest of our lives.

"Maybe you're right." She drags in a shaky breath and lets it go. "I'll talk to him in the morning when we've had a chance to sleep on it."

"Good girl." I kiss her cheek. "It'll all be better in the morning, you'll see."

Hollow reassurance because I have no idea what she did. I'm assuming it involves another boy. Maybe she kissed someone else? Then again, Brooke and Eli are solid; I can't imagine her doing anything to jeopardize their relationship.

A small part of me still wonders if Freya has something to do with this. She's been so good lately, has it all been a front leading up to this?

I've seen my niece at her worst and I wouldn't put anything past her.

"Thanks, Aunt Alice. I'm going to bed."

"Sweet dreams, sweetie."

I watch her leave the kitchen, my heart heavy. If she's anything like me she won't sleep and will probably still be mulling this problem in the morning. But keeping her distance from Eli for now, gaining perspective, can only help.

I put the kettle on to make another cup of chamomile tea and while I'm waiting for it to boil, I send Freya a text message.

R U OK?

She doesn't answer for twenty minutes. By then I've had two cups of tea and my anxiety makes me crave a third. When my cell finally beeps and I see her *YES, B BACK SOON*, I slump in relief.

Parenting Cam's girls has been a challenge, one I've relished, but on occasions like this I wonder how much easier my life would've been if I hadn't interfered in Diana's. I always think of them as Cam's girls because my sister didn't deserve him and she certainly didn't deserve Brooke and Freya, not after she gave up Lizzie so readily.

I wait up for Freya but her version of "soon" is another fifty minutes. It's after one when I hear a car and when she enters the back door I immediately know something is wrong. She's not wildly upset like Brooke had been but I see it in her eyes. An unease, a furtiveness, that scares me.

I know pushing for answers isn't the way to handle her so I feign nonchalance. "How was your evening?"

"Okay."

She glances at the door behind me like she can't wait to escape, but I can't let her off so lightly, not until I know if she had a hand in upsetting her sister.

"Brooke came home from the party over an hour ago. Did you see her when she left?"

She shrugs. "Not really. There were a lot of people there."

"Did she seem okay to you?"

She rolls her eyes. "Center of attention as usual, so yeah, she was fine."

"What about Eli?"

And there it is, her tell, the barest clenching of her jaw.

"Yeah, he was around, glued to Brooke's side."

She's not telling me everything. Her gaze shifts away for a few seconds before sliding back to meet mine and when it does she's regained control. Her stare is eerily blank, almost catatonic, and I resist the urge to rub my bare arms.

"You'd tell me if something was wrong?"

"Of course," she responds, too quickly. "I'm tired. Can I go to bed or do you want to play another round of twenty questions?"

"Watch yourself, missie," I admonish, but she's already gone, practically sprinting down the hallway toward her room.

I have a bad feeling about this.

Brooke broke up with Eli because of something she did, but I have an awful suspicion Freya's involved somehow.

Hopefully the morning will bring us all clarity.

CHAPTER FIFTY-SEVEN

FREYA

After the last guest leaves, I tuck Hope into bed. She's exhausted from all the excitement and has overdosed on sugar from lime meringues. I'm tired too and once I kiss her goodnight I can't wait to crawl into bed.

Once Riker brought me home for the surprise shower, he hit the road to San Diego, dropping off one of his pieces for a park near the pier, and while I usually love nothing better than snuggling up with him after a long day, I'm glad to have my bed to myself tonight.

However, as I step out of Hope's room and close the door, Brooke is waiting for me.

"I've made a fresh pot of coffee. Want some?"

I don't but she's making me uneasy. Halfway through the shower she kept casting me strange looks, and after a few minutes she took Aunt Alice back to her room and didn't return. I used to think Brooke was predictable once upon a time. I don't anymore. She has this look in her eyes tonight...

"Okay. But just one cup, I'm exhausted."

"Me too."

She leads the way to the kitchen where she's already set up two mugs and the coffee pot. Our friends used to be horrified when we had coffee this late at night but the caffeine never affected us. We could drink a big cup and fall asleep as soon as our heads touched the pillow. The stimulant effect of caffeine was the least of my problems back then.

She sits, pours coffee into the two mugs, and pushes one toward me. "Did you enjoy today?"

"I did, thanks. You and Hope did an amazing job."

She shrugs, as if my gratitude means little. "Have you opened the presents yet?"

"No, too tired, I'll do it tomorrow." I raise the mug to my lips, blow on the surface and take a sip. "Where did you disappear to?"

"Aunt Alice looked like she'd had enough so I took her back to her room."

"That was a good idea of yours, having her there."

"I think so."

She stares into her coffee, not touching it, and I know she's building up to something. The last thing I feel like doing is having yet another discussion about Alice's care.

"I was chatting with Helena earlier." Her tone is almost too blasé and I'm instantly on high alert.

"Yeah? I hardly see her these days, we lead such busy lives—"

"Why didn't you mention talking to Eli the night he died?"

My heart stalls. A chill swamps me. I'm blindsided. I scramble quickly; I've become an expert at that over the years.

"Of course I spoke to him. Most people at the party did."

Her glare is scathing. "I mean after we broke up."

Shit. *Shit, shit, shit.*

"He came back to the party after you two left. I was surprised to see him, especially when he seemed really freaked out."

Her stare is unwavering. She wants answers. "What did he say?"

"That you two had a big fight and you dumped him. I was shocked so I sat with him for a bit."

"And that's it?"

"Why are you dredging up that awful night from so long ago?" I leap to my feet, jostling the table and spilling coffee from my mug.

"Why are you so defensive?" She sips at her coffee, an eerie calm emanating from her. "I'm surprised, that in the horrible aftermath, you didn't mention any of this to me."

"That's exactly why I didn't say anything. You were devastated after he killed himself. What good would it have done for me to tell you how upset he'd been by you dumping him?"

Her accusatory stare bores into me. "You should've told me."

"What difference would it have made?"

She ponders this for a while, finally lowering her gaze to stare into her coffee. "You have no idea how I've spent the last eleven years second-guessing every aspect of that night. What I should have done differently. Regretting our big fight, along with everything else I did."

What does she mean by that? But before I can ask, she bursts into noisy tears and I'm left having to console her rather than grill her.

"You couldn't have stopped him doing what he did. That's not on you, Sis." I pat her shoulder, out of my depth with the level of her grief after all this time.

It had been the same back then, the morning when we learned the horrific truth etched into my memory.

I often wonder if I could go back in time, would things have turned out differently?

CHAPTER FIFTY-EIGHT
BROOKE

I don't sleep that night.

Seeing Freya's reaction to my questions about the night Eli died confirmed what I'd already suspected since Helena told me he'd gone back to the party.

Freya had been the last person to see Eli alive that night, not me.

I've spent eleven years rehashing my last conversation with Eli, wishing I hadn't told him the truth about my mistake with Riker, wishing I hadn't broken up with him because he'd been so disgusted with me he'd lashed out, wishing I'd seen the signs of a guy on the edge, a guy about to self-harm.

The guilt has been insidious and never-ending. I haven't had a relationship since Eli. I've moved around constantly until I joined an international volunteer organization in desperation, hoping that helping others would bring *me* some kind of peace. It hasn't. My five-year penance has been nothing but more of the same; me trying my utmost during the days to distract myself but the nights bringing a smothering guilt resulting in nightmares and insomnia.

Now I learn Freya spoke to Eli after me. What the hell did she say? How long did she spend with him? What did she do to comfort him?

She'd been lying earlier, trying to deflect by trite responses. I may not have seen my sister in over a decade but I can still read her.

She's hiding something.

I wonder… I hate to think it, because Eli had been my world back then, but by Freya's overreaction, did they have a closer relationship than I thought? I hadn't suspected her crush, but how far would she have gone to ingratiate herself with Eli, especially at his lowest? Would she have taken advantage of his heartbreak to get closer to him? Which leads to an even worse thought: had he slept with Freya after I'd broken up with him, and been so consumed with guilt that's what drove him to jump off that cliff?

Another shocking supposition detonates in my wild imagination.

Is he Hope's father?

My head is spinning with my outlandish theories and I hate that she's made me envisage these crazy scenarios.

If she won't give me a straight answer, I know another person who'd been at the party that night.

I slip out of bed, pull on jeans and shrug into a jacket. Thrusting my feet into fluffy slippers, I don't second-guess my decision, even though I know it's a bad idea to seek out my sister's fiancé at two in the morning.

Freya had said Riker would be away in San Diego for the night but I heard his van pull into the drive about five minutes ago. He's probably tired but I don't care. I won't sleep unless I discover if he knows anything about what went down after I left the party that night. He'd been there after we'd hooked up, because I'd seen him drinking with his friends, his eyes following me as I did my best to ignore him and pretend he hadn't had his hands all over me.

I tiptoe down the hallway, only stopping to press my ear against Freya's door. She's snoring in the same way she used to as a kid, soft, snuffling noises. I let myself out the back door and pull it shut behind me, and follow the path to Riker's cottage. I exhale in relief when I see a light still on, casting a golden glow across the yard.

The wind is strong tonight, the sound of the waves crashing against the cliffs louder than usual. I shudder and wrap my arms around my body. I used to love listening to the waves, until I imagined Eli's battered body lying at the bottom of a cliff. Tears burn my eyes but I blink them away. This isn't the time to cry. I need answers and I hope Riker can provide them.

When I reach his door I knock softly, glancing over my shoulder to ensure the main house is in darkness. If Freya freaked out over a few questions, what would she do if she caught me in her fiancé's cottage in the wee hours?

The door opens and Riker's standing there, shirtless, with a towel draped around his neck and wearing low-slung denim. He's lean, every muscle on his abdomen clearly delineated, his chest broad, his pecs defined.

My mouth goes dry. I'm staring but I can't help it. I haven't had a lot of sex over the last five years; being tired and grimy in a place with a water shortage didn't lend itself to getting down and dirty with a fellow volunteer, no matter how cute.

And I would never, ever, cross the line with Riker but for that brief, suspended moment in time I give in to the pleasure of admiring a stunningly beautiful male.

"It's late," he says, sounding more surprised than annoyed. "What's up?"

"This won't take long. Can we talk?"

A slight frown mars his forehead. "It can't wait till the morning?"

"I wouldn't be here if it could."

His frown deepens but he opens the door wider to let me pass. He closes the door, leaving me all too aware it's just the two of us in his cozy cottage, a lone lamp casting everything in shadows.

"What's going on, Brooke?"

His tone's abrupt and I square my shoulders. "The night of the party when we… got together…" Heat flushes my cheeks but I'm not some blushing teen any longer and I need to get this out. "How long did you stick around after I left?"

His eyebrows rise. "Where's this coming from?"

"It's important, just answer the question."

"I was there for about an hour after you left."

"Did you see Freya that night?"

He shakes his head. "It's pretty freaky to think she was at that party too, but no. And even if I did it was dark and I wouldn't have recognized her."

I have no idea how much he knows and I'll have to tell him more than he needs to know if he's to give me the answers I want.

"That night we hooked up, I had a boyfriend."

"Shit, I didn't know." He scrubs a hand over his face as if to erase bad memories. "I wouldn't have touched you if I'd known."

"That's why I didn't tell you…" I shake my head. "What happened that night was all on me." The blush returns, scorching my cheeks. "I told him afterward and he freaked. We had a massive argument and I broke up with him."

His eyebrows are so high now his forehead is a canvas of wrinkles.

"He killed himself by jumping off a cliff that night."

"Fuck." Riker takes a step toward me before thinking better of it. "That's awful."

I nod. "I've lived with the guilt ever since, how what I said that night drove him to it. But at the bridal shower I learned he went back to the party and Freya talked to him." I release a long sigh. "If you saw anything or if she's ever mentioned anything to you, please tell me. I know your loyalties lie with her but it will help give me closure."

He screws up his eyes, thinking, before he finally says, "I remember this guy, tall, dark curly hair, stumbling around the lawn like a madman. He was making a real ass of himself and someone said the prom king had been dumped. There was a girl with him for a while, but then he left. Alone."

Riker had seen Eli. The girl could possibly have been Freya, or maybe not. It could've been someone else who was the last person to speak to him.

"How does this change anything, Brooke?"

"It doesn't," I murmur, emotion tightening my throat. "I don't know why I got so wound up over this, but when I heard I wasn't the last person to speak to him I was hoping for… answers, perhaps, as to his state of mind."

Regardless of who it was, Eli had left that party by himself and had been distraught enough to end his life.

And I will continue to live with that for the rest of mine.

Riker grimaces. "Considering what he did, I'd say that's pretty obvious."

"I know." Unease tiptoes across the back of my neck and I give a little shake to get me out of this funk. "I honestly don't know what I'm hoping to hear after all these years, but I guess I'm so haunted the slightest mention of anything to do with that night turns me into this." I gesture at myself, imagining how deranged I must look, turning up on his doorstep at two in the morning. "Sorry to bother you."

I rush past him but he reaches out and snags my arm. "Hey, it's okay, and for what it's worth, I'm sorry you've had to live with this for so long."

"Thanks," I mumble, making the mistake of glancing up, the compassion in his eyes a beacon for my weary soul. I want to hurl myself against him and have him wrap his strong arms around me. I crave comfort and warmth.

But it can't be from him so I wrench my arm free and make a beeline for the door.

"Brooke?"

I pause and glance over my shoulder. "Yeah?"

"If you ever need an impartial listener, I'm here."

"Thanks." I manage a wan smile before I'm out of there. I close the door and lean against it, a small irrational part of me wishing he'd come after me.

CHAPTER FIFTY-NINE

ALICE

THEN

I watch Roger drive away, my heart breaking for Eli's dad, for my darling girl. As if on cue, Brooke screams, an ear-shattering, piercing screech that has me turning to see her crumple. She heard the news. Her boyfriend is dead and rather than me breaking it to her gently, she's been privy to Eli's father's pain.

I rush toward her and spy Freya a few feet behind Brooke. Freya's indifferent stare flickers between us before she walks away, leaving me to comfort Brooke. I'm not sure if it's because she knows Brooke needs me more in this moment or if she's apathetic to her sister's pain, but whatever her rationale I'm glad. Brooke needs me.

"It's going to be okay, sweetheart." I bundle her into my arms and rock her side to side, my tears not a patch on hers. She wails so loud and long I fear she'll pass out. If I thought her sobs last night were bad, this is so much worse.

She's lost the love of her life, like I did.

And like me, she's had an inadvertent hand in it.

I'm empathic but I can't tell her why I understand so I settle for holding her until she's ready to talk. What seems like an eternity later, she's wriggling out of my arms, her face blotchy, her eyes swollen.

"He died because of me."

"You can't blame yourself." I reach for her again but she scuttles backward. "Couples break up all the time, it doesn't mean…"

I don't want to say the words. Eli killed himself. It's a shocking tragedy and will haunt my poor girl for the rest of her life. I should know. What I did to Cam without meaning to has resulted in chronic insomnia to this day.

"Everyone's going to blame me for his suicide," she whispers, the tears starting again. "They'll say it's my fault."

"How can they, when only the two of you know you broke up with him? You said you left him at the beach?"

She gnaws on her bottom lip so hard I see a speck of blood. "Yeah, I guess."

"Well then, nobody knows you broke up. Not that it makes it any easier, but please don't worry about shouldering the blame on top of your grief."

But I'm wrong.

The first abusive text pings on Brooke's cell about five hours later. Freya's nowhere to be found and while I love that girl like my own, Brooke has to be my priority right now.

The first horrid text, U R A MURDERER, is followed up by a slew more along the same lines, some a lot worse. I end up giving Brooke a sedative because she's distraught to the point of passing out and I confiscate her cell. She doesn't need the vitriol of narrow-minded kids on top of everything else.

How did they find out Brooke broke up with Eli?

Freya strolls through the back door ten minutes later. She's wearing all black—jeans, hoodie, scarf—and looks like a ninja skulking inside. She's been crying: her eyes are bloodshot and her nose is red, and her hand shakes as she swipes it over her face. It does little to wipe the distraught expression from her face.

"Freya, can I get you anything?" She shakes her head and when I open my arms to her in comfort, her gaze skitters away as if she can't meet my eyes.

That's when it hits me. Has she done the unthinkable and spread awful rumors about her sister? Is this her version of the ultimate payback for Brooke?

"Did you know Brooke broke up with Eli last night?"

She considers lying for a second; I see it in her quick glance toward the door, like she'd rather be anywhere than here. But then she finally meets my gaze and nods. "Yeah. They left the party but then he came back and he was a total wreck, raving about Brooke dumping him. Everyone felt sorry for him."

I feel disloyal for suspecting she'd told everyone about Brooke dumping Eli. Then again, it wouldn't be the first time she's wanted to hurt her sister.

"He kept rambling about the break-up but he wouldn't say much more than that…" She shakes her head, sadness clouding her eyes. "He was pretty drunk when they left, then he started drinking again when he came back. I tried to comfort him, I really did."

Devastation twists her mouth. "I just wanted to make his pain go away, you know? I hated seeing him like that…"

Tears fill her eyes. "I was there for him when he needed me most. But then he left. Some of the guys wanted to go with him. Heck, I did too, but he wouldn't let us…"

She blinks rapidly, but it does little to stave off the tears spilling over. "I should've gone with him. I can't believe he's dead…"

That's when Freya falls apart, running across the kitchen to hurl herself into my arms.

"I loved him," she murmurs between sobs. "He was so special. I really loved him and he never knew and now he never will and it feels like my heart is split in two."

I comfort her as I did for her sister hours earlier and somehow Freya's grief feels more intense. I know what she's going through, having to hide her love for her sister's boyfriend, having to mute her grief so others don't pick up on her forbidden feelings.

"I'm so sorry you have to go through this, my beautiful girl."
I placate her with soft reassurances until her sobs fade to hiccups.

When she eases out of my arms, her expression is so bereft I
feel like bawling all over again.

"I'll always love him," she whispers. "I'll never forget how this
heartbreak feels."

She won't. I haven't.

We love the same way, Freya and me. We *feel* intensely and I'll
do whatever it takes to make things better for her.

CHAPTER SIXTY

FREYA

After Brooke interrogating me earlier, I'm on edge. Damn Helena for opening her big mouth and telling Brooke I'd been with Eli the night he died. If I'd known about the bridal shower I would've vetted the guest list to avoid this very thing but either Lizzie or Brooke have gone through my contacts on the family computer and invited everyone.

Regardless, it's too late now. The damage has been done. I think I managed to convince Brooke there was nothing going on between Eli and me but I can't be sure, and that has me worried. She can't learn the truth. It will have devastating consequences for all of us.

I need a distraction so while everyone else is still asleep I open my presents from the bridal shower. I appreciate the thoughtful gift vouchers for spa days, pampering packs, and scented candles. But it's Brooke's gift I'm interested in. Maybe if I see tangible proof of how much my sister cares about me, I won't give in to the irrational urge to smash it to pieces.

I heard her walking around last night. I'm a light sleeper, always have been, so when I heard footsteps down the hallway that paused outside my bedroom I pretended to be asleep. It could only be Brooke because Hope has a much lighter tread and I've known the sound of it since my baby could walk.

At the time I had no idea why Brooke would be creeping around my house at two in the morning so I gave a few fake snores, waited until she moved on, before slipping out of bed to see what she was up to.

I didn't like what I saw.

When she left the house she made a beeline for Riker's cottage. I'd heard him come home; his clunky old van has a noisy engine in need of a service. Despite my exhaustion and relief at having a bed to myself for the night, I'd been tempted to go see him. He grounds me like nobody else.

So what the hell was my sister doing visiting him in the middle of the night?

I dithered, unsure whether to barge over there and confront them or quash my paranoia. I didn't have time to decide because Brooke was only inside for a few minutes, five max. Definitely not enough time for a booty call or whatever other unsavory thoughts crowded my head.

But it's the third time I've caught them together and I don't like it. No matter the time frame, having her seek him out in the middle of the night when he'd barely got home doesn't bode well. There's something going on and I will find out what it is.

The thing is, when we have rare family meals together, I've never picked up on the slightest vibe between them. I've watched for it because that's who I am; time hasn't eroded my self-esteem issues when it comes to my vibrant sister.

Not that Brooke is anything like the girl I once knew. She's quieter, introverted, a muted version of the upbeat sister she'd once been. Eli's death shattered her and despite the years that have passed, it looks like she hasn't recovered.

I saw the vitriolic texts she received in the weeks after Eli's death; nasty, abusive accusations laying the blame for his suicide squarely on her. If it had been me, I would've left town earlier than she had, and I don't blame her for staying away so long.

A small part of me had been glad to see the back of her. I've never admitted that to anyone, but I think Aunt Alice knew. She lavished me with more love, more attention, and that spilled over into her care for Hope too. I felt bad for what Brooke went through and how it severed her relationship with our family, but I'd also reveled in the freedom of not being under my sister's shadow anymore.

Neither Aunt Alice nor I tried to lure Brooke home. Lizzie mentioned it a few times over the years, but I was content to let Aunt Alice take the lead, and she'd always say Brooke had been through enough and it was her choice whether she wanted to come home. I never wanted to revisit the past and I assume Brooke felt the same.

But I've missed her more than I thought and having her home reinforces that. I'm glad I reached out and invited her to my wedding. So the thought she may be conspiring with Riker behind my back irks. It could be another surprise, like the bridal shower, but why seek him out in the middle of the night?

Hating my traitorous thoughts, I find Brooke's gift. It's rectangular, thin, wrapped in pale gold embossed paper with an ivory ribbon curled to perfection. I remember she loved doing this for parties when we were kids. *'Presentation is everything, Sis,'* she used to say, and that mantra spilled into all areas of her life. I've never seen any woman who can take a cheap cotton sundress and bargain sandals and make the outfit look like haute couture. While most teens, like me, were gauche and awkward and trying to find our place in the world, Brooke had been a beacon of style and panache, confident in her skin and likeability. Of course kids flocked to her. Of course Eli found her irresistible.

I may have resented her back then but that doesn't mean I should let residual animosity taint what we've re-established now. Life's too short. I wrench the ribbon off and tear the paper. My breath catches as sentimentality swamps me. It's a photo of the two of us when we were young teenagers, our arms slung across our shoulders, grinning inanely. We look happy, innocent, close.

I've never seen it before. One of the few mementos she must've kept all these years and it makes me treasure it all the more. The frame looks expensive: heavy, wrought iron, with elegant filigree edging. It's a thoughtful gift and typically Brooke.

With fumbling fingers I flick the tabs at the back to release the photo. I peer at it, wondering how different our lives could've been if I'd made the right choices. Would we be closer? Would we have the kind of relationship that invites confidences?

I'll never know because I can't change the past and as I press the photo to my heart, the frame slips and crashes to the floor. The glass shatters and the metal twists in one corner, damaged beyond repair.

Like me.

I swallow back sobs as I run to my room. Poor Brooke; even when she does something nice for me I ruin it. This time had been an accident.

What would she think of me if she knew about those other times?

CHAPTER SIXTY-ONE
BROOKE

I sleep poorly. Riker didn't give me the answers I'd hoped for and I'm still annoyed Freya has never mentioned speaking to Eli the night he died.

The light in my room is brighter than usual, meaning I've slept longer for the first time since I got home. When I glance at my cell I'm surprised to see it's after nine. The last few Sundays Hope has rushed into my room around eight, eager for us to plan a jam-packed day, but Freya must've told her to let me sleep in.

The house is silent as I make my way to the kitchen. There's a note propped up on the island bench.

GONE FOR PANCAKES WITH HOPE AND RIKER.

No sign-off. Freya always thought she didn't need one, her bold block letters enough of a statement. I pour myself an orange juice and wander into the sunroom, where I see Freya has unwrapped her gifts. I check them out, admiring a giant pamper pack filled with lux body lotions, hand creams and bath bombs in a coconut and lemongrass fragrance. I can't see my gift until I reach the table. It's ruined, the glass cracked, with several loose shards askew, the iron frame bent in a corner. It's been dropped and the photo is missing.

Did Freya do this? It looks like the frame has been dropped accidentally but with my sister, I never know. When I found the photo in Aunt Alice's album I thought it would make the perfect gift. I remember the day the photo was taken, a particularly good day when Aunt Alice had taken the three of us into town to our favorite ice creamery. We'd gorged ourselves on pecan sundaes and talked about our plans for the school year ahead. Freya was about to start high school and couldn't wait. She hated that I'd started a year earlier. I'd been secretly glad because it meant I didn't have her tagging after me for an entire twelve months.

When we'd got home afterward, Aunt Alice had wanted to take photos. She'd said her girls were growing up too fast and the three of us pulled faces but agreed. Lizzie had been in some of them but Freya was in every photo with me, trying to outdo me with the biggest grin.

The broken frame must be an accident. Unless… I don't want to believe she'd do this on purpose. Our relationship has come so far since I've been back, but a small part of me can't forget the way Freya behaved in the past when things didn't go her way.

"You saw that, huh?" Lizzie wanders into the kitchen and grimaces as she points at the broken frame. "What happened?"

"Don't know. Looks like it's been accidentally dropped."

"Maybe." Lizzie grabs an apple from the fruit bowl and takes a bite. "You think Freya did this on purpose?"

"No, I don't. You two are closer than close lately, and it's great, but…" She lowers the apple and fixes me with a serious stare. "Remember that jacket you loved as a kid, the gaudy pink one?"

"Yeah."

"I had to hide something in the trash one day." A blush flushes her cheeks. "One of the boys at school had given me this really smutty book and I wanted to get rid of it, so I tried to push it to the bottom of the trash. That's when I saw it."

I know what she's going to say before she says it. Freya must've thrown out my beloved jacket in jealousy; if she couldn't have it I couldn't either.

"The jacket?"

She nods but something shifts in her eyes. "I recognized it because of the color even through two plastic bags, so I dug it out. When I took it out of the bags, it had been ripped to shreds. Slashed a billion times with a knife or scissors or something."

"Wow. Why didn't you tell me?"

"Because I saw the way Freya idolized you and I didn't want to cause trouble between you two." She shrugs. "It was just a jacket."

"Yeah, like this was just a gift." I point at the frame and shake my head. "Does she have anger issues?"

"Maybe it's her way of coping with having you back here after all this time?"

My eyebrows shoot up. "You're defending her?"

She takes another bite of apple and chews it before responding. "I've lived in the same house as her or nearby most of my life and while we saw how she lost her cool after finding out about my parentage, I think she's changed a lot. I can't see her doing something like this deliberately, despite the jacket incident."

Lizzie's right. Freya has changed and I can't see her doing this on purpose, even if she had seen me heading to Riker's last night.

"I know I wasn't around when you left, but Alice told me Freya missed you terribly," Lizzie says.

It's still odd to hear Lizzie call Aunt Alice by her name rather than Mom, but I guess there's no going back now we know the truth.

"She would've had her hands full with Hope to miss me much."

Lizzie tosses her half-eaten apple in the trash and rests a hand on my shoulder. "I know it looks like I'm playing peacekeeper, but I'd hate to see you two at loggerheads when you've finally reconnected after all this time."

I mumble, "I guess," and Lizzie leaves it at that.

But as I glimpse a piece of glass underneath the table, my doubts resurface. Does my sister harbor resentment toward me? And if so, why?

CHAPTER SIXTY-TWO

ALICE

THEN

The last eight weeks have been a living hell.

I hate seeing my girls fall apart and supporting Brooke and Freya through their grieving breaks my heart. Their mutual love for Eli is evident in every teary outburst, in their lack of appetite, in their turning inward and hiding away in their rooms. I don't know what Brooke thinks of Freya's grief; she probably thinks her sister is devastated for her. Then again, I don't think Brooke notices anything as she drifts through the house like a zombie, her arms wrapped around her middle, ashen and listless.

The funeral had been horrific, with Eli's entire high school class as well as kids in lower grades attending, along with most of the town. Brooke had been inconsolable, Freya stoic, and the accusatory glares cast Brooke's way from her classmates had been awful. Kids can be incredibly judgmental and those who'd been privy to Brooke breaking up with Eli at that party appeared to blame her. They should know better, that teens break up and reunite all the time. But they stared at Brooke like she'd physically pushed Eli off that cliff and she had to deal with her classmates' judgment on top of her sorrow.

Because of how her so-called friends treated her at the funeral, Brooke hid at home afterward. She stayed in her room, she lost a lot of weight, and the few times she ate I heard her throwing up. Her pallor terrified me and she had dizzy spells that confined her to bed. She consumed my attention and I knew I was letting Freya down because she was grieving too, but it wasn't the same, having the boy you coveted die, to going through what Brooke had to.

It has been two months to the day since Eli died and naïvely I didn't think things could get any worse.

They have.

I'm sitting in the reading nook with Brooke, the first time I've coaxed her out of her room in days. I made blueberry and choc-chip pancakes, a weird combination but one she's loved since she was little. She's barely taken a mouthful, but she stares at her plate like it holds the answers to her pain.

"Try to eat some more, sweetheart." I rest my arm across her shoulders, shocked by the boniness beneath her tattered T-shirt.

"I'm not hungry," she murmurs, before shrugging off my arm and placing the plate on a nearby side table.

"You have to eat—"

"Why? So it'll make me feel better?" She spits the words out, as if they're as unpalatable as food these days.

I hate seeing her in so much pain. "I know you're hurting, but give it some time, you may feel better—"

"I'm pregnant," she says, her voice cracking, her hands shaking as she covers her face. "Time won't fix that."

I gape, curses whirring through my head, before I close my mouth and try to think of what to say in a situation like this. Brooke looks like a walking skeleton. Dark circles rim her lifeless eyes and she's exceptionally pale. My poor baby is in no fit state to bring a child into this world.

"Are you sure?"

She gnaws her bottom lip and nods. "Eli and I had a scare once before and I bought a few tests back then. I just took one and it confirmed it."

I'm reeling. How can Brooke bring Eli's child into this world while she's still shattered over his death? But this has to be her choice. She's been through enough without having me impose my will on her too, so I lay a comforting hand on her shoulder. "What do you want to do?"

This time she doesn't shrug it off and after a few moments, she lowers her hands so I can see her face.

"I need to have it."

Need, not want, and *it*, not the baby. If her emotionless tone doesn't alert me to her ambivalence her words are a giveaway.

"But I can't keep it," she adds, vehemence in her declaration.

I'm confused. Why would she want to carry to term only to give her baby away?

"I can't end a life, not after Eli, but I can't keep the baby either because it would be a constant reminder…" A lone tear trickles down her cheek before she raises her tortured gaze to mine, beseeching me to understand. "Will you help me?"

"Of course, sweetheart, anything you want."

I need to think, to come up with a way for all of us to move forward. It won't be easy but I want to do what's best for my family. I've never believed in that old cliché "love conquers all" because it doesn't; I'm living proof of that. Brooke needs a chance to put the recent horrors behind her and if giving up her baby will help her do that, I'm all for it.

But then I think of Eli and how both girls loved him. A baby that's a part of him would be so special…

I'll make the arrangements for adoption but deep down I hope Brooke will change her mind when she gives birth.

CHAPTER SIXTY-THREE

BROOKE

Freya doesn't mention the broken photo frame and when I ask her about it, she's embarrassed and shrugs it off, so I don't push it. She's pinned the photo to the fridge with a magnet as if trying to appease me. It does, in a way. I like seeing that photo; it reminds me of why I've come home and the bond we've re-established is important to me.

But because I'm unsure if Freya broke my gift deliberately or not, I don't tell her what I'm doing today. I'm tiptoeing around her, avoiding yet another awkward confrontation. If we get the answers regarding Aunt Alice's care that I'm hoping for today, I'll tell her then.

"Are you sure we're doing the right thing?" Lizzie is nervous, her thumbnail chewed to the quick, a habit I thought she'd conquered as a kid. "This feels wrong."

"Freya's done a great job with Aunt Alice but it can't hurt to get a second opinion." I glance in the rearview mirror where our aunt is currently napping. "You saw how much more animated Alice was outside at the bridal shower, and the reminiscence therapy is definitely working."

"Yeah, but not taking her medication can have major ramifications…" Lizzie shakes her head and lifts her other thumb to her mouth.

"It's one day and she'll be under the care of one of the eminent dementia doctors in the country." I reach across the console and pat her arm. "It'll be okay."

"I hope so." Lizzie lowers her hand and clasps it with the other, turning her head away to stare out the window.

I hope so too, because I'd never put Aunt Alice in jeopardy deliberately. But Freya isn't giving me answers regarding Alice's care—she'd even fobbed me off when I'd asked for our aunt's medical records—so she's left me no option but to go over her head. I've deceived my sister, which doesn't sit well with me, but if Aunt Alice gets the care she deserves it'll be worth it.

For my plan to work, I had Lizzie insist she learn how to administer Aunt Alice's medication and we'd fooled Freya into showing her. Lizzie told her Riker was planning a surprise weekend away after the wedding as a quickie honeymoon and Lizzie had to know what to give Alice. Freya had been reluctant—she' s a control freak when it comes to our aunt's care—but had agreed.

Freya gave Lizzie a duplicate key to the medicine cabinet and agreed to let Lizzie administer this morning's dose. She'd been adamant about supervising but a convenient phone call from Helena—I'd asked her to do me a favor, no questions asked, and she'd agreed in exchange for us to catch up for dinner one night soon—meant Freya had been busy while Lizzie gave Aunt Alice her meds.

Only she didn't, and I now have a list of everything Aunt Alice is taking, and Dr. Hesham can assess her without the influence of meds while Freya is at work. I don't like lying to Freya, but this is too important.

When I pull into the LA facility's car park, I find a spot near the door. Lizzie's tight-lipped after I park and kill the engine, but she gets out and fetches a wheelchair. I swivel in my seat and gently tap Aunt Alice's leg.

"We're here, Aunt Alice."

Her eyes fly open and for a moment I'm startled by her manic stare, before a film clouds over. She doesn't speak as she looks around and remains silent as we help her into the wheelchair, take her inside and wait for her appointment.

Dr. Hesham wants to assess her alone before reporting back to Lizzie and me, so when a nurse calls Alice Shomack I wheel her in, give the doctor a list of her meds and retreat to the waiting room. Lizzie has vanished in search of coffee and when she returns I take the cup she offers, chugging down the putrid brew because my mouth is dry.

"I'm not sure I want to hear how bad she really is," Lizzie says, sipping at her coffee. "At least with Freya being the primary caregiver, I can pretend she's not so bad."

She raises stricken eyes to mine. "I still think of her as my mom."

"I know." I lean into her, slide my arm around her waist and hug her tight. She rests her head on my shoulder and we stay that way until the nurse comes out to call us in to see Dr. Hesham.

The nurse takes us past her office and into a large, bright room with various machines, a huge clock taking up most of one wall, and board games stacked within shelves of a monstrous bookcase. I'm sure we're both holding our breath and as we step inside I'm not sure what to expect, but it isn't Aunt Alice sitting at a table, moving letters around on a word game, her brow furrowed in concentration but beaming like she once used to when she read my end of semester grades.

Dr. Hesham approaches us and holds out her hand to Lizzie. "Aileen Hesham, pleased to meet you."

Lizzie shakes her hand. "Elizabeth Shomack, but everyone calls me Lizzie."

The doctor nods and looks at me. "How are you, Brooke?"

"Fine, thanks."

It's a rote response because I'm far from fine. I want to know my aunt's prognosis and what we can do to help.

"Please, take a seat." The doctor gestures to three seats in the opposite corner of the room from Aunt Alice.

Once we're seated, Dr. Hesham says, "It's probably easier if I tell you what I found and you confine your questions for the end."

Lizzie and I nod. I try to get a read on the doctor but her face is carefully blank. They probably taught her that in medical school, with the bad news she must have to deliver frequently.

"Firstly, your aunt is a delight. She submitted to all the tests I administered and didn't appear aggressive in the slightest, which can be common with patients who come here for the first time. They become disoriented and scared." She shoots a glance at Aunt Alice before refocusing on us. "I'll email you the test results but I'll summarize briefly. Yes, she's exhibiting signs of early onset dementia, but she's not as advanced as you led me to believe, Brooke."

Heat flushes my cheeks, embarrassment making me practically squirm. I want to yell, "This isn't my fault, I'm doing the best I can," but that won't endear me to the doctor.

"The thing is, I've taken a look at her medication and I don't think she needs all of it."

I shoot Lizzie a glance and her high eyebrows match mine.

"That said, I don't observe her day to day. She may be anxious, depressed and hallucinating usually, and she happens to be having a good day." A tiny groove dents her brows. "Why I asked you not to give her meds today was to observe what happens. While she still has a cocktail of drugs in her from what she's taking daily, not taking meds at the usual time may exacerbate symptoms and that's what I expected to see today."

The groove deepens. "You mentioned your sister has been the primary caregiver for your aunt, is that right?"

I nod, wishing Freya were here so she could hear all this firsthand rather than Lizzie and me having to relay it to her, and I feel guilty all over again for resorting to subterfuge to obtain a second opinion.

"I'd like to talk to her and see if I can access your aunt's previous medical records. In the meantime, I would suggest cutting back on some of the medications."

The doctor hesitates, her astute gaze swinging between Lizzie and me, her intense scrutiny disconcerting. "Without seeing your aunt's records I can't give an accurate diagnosis, but I will say this. A lot of her symptoms can be caused by side effects of medication. I've seen it before, when a doctor not well versed in early onset dementia misdiagnoses without getting the full picture."

I'm stunned. Aunt Alice's symptoms could be due to her meds? Is Freya aware of this? Or is she so close to Aunt Alice she's oblivious to changes in her condition?

"Brooke, are you all right?"

I blink and refocus to find Dr. Hesham studying me with one eyebrow arched.

"Yes, thanks, this is a little overwhelming, that's all."

Lizzie's wearing the same shell-shocked expression I am but there's something almost furtive in her gaze that I'll explore later.

"Actually, I think you've made significant progress with your aunt's care today," the doctor says. "Bringing her in is the first step and I hope I'll see Alice again soon. I'm fairly certain I can help."

"Thanks," I say in unison with Lizzie, and we give an awkward chuckle.

As the doctor heads over to Aunt Alice to say goodbye, Lizzie leans in close. "Do you think Freya's aware of this?"

"I have no idea."

But I intend to find out.

CHAPTER SIXTY-FOUR

ALICE

THEN

We move to LA where nobody knows us and rent a small apartment. I find a place for Brooke to stay. It's an old mansion on the outskirts of the city where other pregnant teens are housed. She's free to come and go as she pleases, as are all the girls, but as expected she retreats into herself. She doesn't socialize with the other girls. She barely acknowledges me when I visit. She doesn't ask how Lizzie's doing at college and she rarely mentions Freya. It's like leaving Martino Bay and all it represents for her has cleaved her memories in two: she wants to forget the past and is lackadaisical about the present.

I worry about her every day. I wish I could make this easier on her but I can't. I try to distract her with the glossy magazines she used to love poring over with her friends, with the latest release by her favorite fantasy author. Nothing. She thanks me with a tight smile then turns to stare out the window, her preferred pastime these days. The larger she gets, the more introverted she is, until she's barely saying a word by her due date.

I visit often but I forbid Freya. The last thing Brooke needs is to see her sister.

Like everything else in her well-ordered life—apart from this unplanned pregnancy—Brooke goes into labor on her due date.

When I get the call I race to be by her side. My beautiful Brooke is stoic throughout the long twelve hours. She moves around, she has a shower, she rocks over a big blow-up ball and when she's fully dilated she lies on the bed, ready to push on command.

I made her watch birthing videos with me but the guttural groans ripped from deep within her throat are nothing like the women we saw on the DVD. She's a red, sweaty mess, making heart-rending noises, and I wish I could make this easier for her.

I hold her hand. I whisper comforting nonsense. And when the midwife asks her to pause as the baby crowns before giving an almighty push, I'm there.

But as Brooke falls back on the pillows, exhausted, there's no sound and I see the nurse bundle the scrawny baby into a towel and shoot me a frightened look.

The baby is blue.

"Let me see my baby," Brooke whispers, plaintive, but I shake my head and reach for the baby.

"It's better this way, sweetheart. He's at peace."

With that, I whisk the baby away but not before I see Brooke's face crumple, and try not to cry at the devastation in my niece's eyes.

CHAPTER SIXTY-FIVE

ALICE

THEN

I comfort Brooke as much as I can. But it's useless: all her favorite magazines and chocolates and soaps in the world won't erase her loss and she just sits in an armchair by her hospital bed, staring out the window for hours at a time.

With her baby gone, Brooke would usually be discharged quicker than most but I speak with the nurses, who agree to give her extra time to grieve in the sanctity of the hospital. I encourage her to take walks with me and on the third day she agrees. We always turn right out of her room and I see the way she averts her tear-filled gaze from the sign that points left toward the nursery.

She doesn't speak and my attempts at conversation usually fall flat after the first few tries, until I give up and settle for silence. But she's uncomfortable when I'm around, like she wants to grieve in peace, so I only stay for a snatched hour here and there.

Brooke is discharged on the seventh day, a week after her world imploded. I want to point out to her that she'd planned on giving the baby up for adoption anyway, that she'd probably still be grieving for his loss if he'd lived. But I don't, because what good can come of it?

She's not coming home and I don't blame her. Martino Bay holds nothing but haunting memories of Eli's death and the misplaced responsibility she feels. Better she makes a fresh start far from ghosts of the past.

But as we stand at the entrance to the bus depot, I wish I could change everything. I wish I could take away this darling girl's pain.

"I don't know when I'll be back, if ever," she says, the dark smudges under her eyes almost violet, and stark against the pallor of her face. "I can't go back…"

"It's okay, sweetheart." I bundle her into my arms and she stiffens, as if trying to hold herself together, before melting into my embrace for a brief moment.

She pulls away quickly and her bottom lip is wobbling. "What will Freya and Lizzie think—"

"Don't worry about them. You need to focus on yourself." I cup her cheek. "You've been through a terrible ordeal, Brooke. You need time to heal, to recuperate. Be kind to yourself and if you ever need me, you know where to find me. In the meantime, there's a thousand dollars in that envelope I gave you and I've set up a bank account in your name so you don't have to worry about money, okay?"

"Thanks," she says, jumping when a voice over a loudspeaker announces the next departures for Albuquerque, Las Vegas and San Francisco.

I don't know where she's going. I'd rather not know, because I'll be tempted to visit and she doesn't need that right now. A clean break is better. I know, because it's what I did after I lost Cam and leaving Verdant, moving to Martino Bay, was the best thing I ever did. A fresh start to soften the pain of the past and fuel optimism for the future.

"I love you. Don't ever forget that." This time when I pull her in for a hug she sags against me, my coat muffling her sobs as I smooth her back, crying silent tears.

Our eyes are red and bleary when we pull apart and I manage a watery smile before I squeeze her hand one last time. She doesn't return my smile and I don't blame her. She's on her own now and while it's the best thing for her, she must be as terrified as I was embarking on my new life.

But I don't have time to mourn Brooke's absence because a day later, I'm beside Freya when her baby is placed in her arms.

"What are you going to call her?"

Freya stares at the tiny squishy face and her smile is beatific. Freya can do this. She can be a mom. I had my doubts, but watching the love bloom on her face makes me sag with relief. I just wish Brooke could've experienced this same joy her sister is, but life is cruel and I hate that one niece is ecstatic, while the other is devastated. The death of a boy, the birth of a girl. Yin and yang. Two halves of a whole.

"I thought I'd loved Eli," Freya whispers, not tearing her gaze from the baby. "But I was wrong. This is love. This tiny, beautiful, perfect baby girl gives me hope for the future."

Freya slowly raises her gaze. "I'm going to call her Hope."

"A beautiful name for a beautiful girl." I brush a fingertip across the baby's forehead, my eyes misty. "I'm so proud of you."

"It's been a long nine months," she says, unable to tear her gaze from her baby's face. "So much sadness and now this tiny miracle." She blinks several times but it doesn't stop a tear from gently plopping onto Hope's forehead. "I wish Eli were here to share this joy with me."

Me of all people know it's futile wishing for things that can never be. "You need to focus on your beautiful girl now."

"I know," Freya murmurs, kissing Hope's forehead. "But remembering Eli at a time like this is fitting, don't you think?"

Freya doesn't want to hear what I think. She should never have coveted her sister's boyfriend and it's time to set the past to rest. Brooke can never know. It would break her heart even more.

"I think you're going to be a great mom and I'll help you as much as I can."

She smiles at me, radiant in a way I've never seen her before. "Thanks, Aunt Alice. For everything."

Tears burn the back of my eyes but I can't cry. Because if I start I may not be able to stop. I'm happy for Freya, I truly am, but I can't stop thinking about Brooke's loss and how she'd react if she knew about her sister's joy.

"How are you feeling?" I press a hand to Freya's forehead like I've done many times in the past. When she was a teething toddler, when she had croup, when she picked up a nasty flu in her last year of grade school.

I've had my worries with Freya over the years but seeing her take to motherhood is a challenge I'm looking forward to.

Nothing can erase the past. I can't change what I've done, but I know Diana and Cam would be proud of their daughter and the love she'll lavish on their granddaughter.

"I'm feeling fine, Aunt Alice, stop fussing."

I've never seen Freya so focused, all her attention on Hope as she cradles her gently. "I'm a mom." She sounds wondrous as she raises the baby closer to her face and breathes in. "I'll protect Hope with everything I have. My baby... my precious girl..."

The tears I'm battling spill over. I'm so happy for Freya, yet I can't help but wish things could've been different for Brooke.

CHAPTER SIXTY-SIX
BROOKE

I know Aunt Alice still has a cocktail of medication rattling around inside her even without taking her pills this morning, but if what Dr. Hesham said is true and those meds can cause her dementia symptoms I know I've only got tonight to try and delve deeper.

Freya will be back to administering the pills tomorrow morning and tonight is the most lucid Aunt Alice has been since I came home. Lizzie had been amazed at how Aunt Alice made the odd observation on the ride back from LA and when she'd recognized home as we turned in the drive, Lizzie had been floored.

It makes us both consider the meds are playing a part in our aunt's deterioration and we need to discuss it with Freya. She'll hate our underhanded tactics in getting Aunt Alice independently assessed but she can't refute medical evidence and I know that ultimately, she loves our aunt as much as we do.

"Do you need me?" Lizzie asks, once Aunt Alice has eaten. Even her appetite seems to have improved tonight as she manages a small fillet of steamed fish and roast vegetables.

"I'll be fine." I cast a glance at the closed door. "If you could keep Freya busy, that'd be great."

Lizzie's somber as she nods. "She's with Riker at the moment but I'll be on the lookout in case she wants to come check on Alice."

"Thanks, I'll let you know how I get on."

"Good luck." Lizzie pats my shoulder and then she's gone, leaving me alone with my aunt.

I want to see if her ramblings have meaning tonight, if she says anything specific and if so, use it to access her diary. I want answers to so many questions.

When Lizzie closes the door, Aunt Alice's eyes open and she fixes them on me.

"Brooke," she says, with a faint smile, and I'm buoyed by her recognition. "Good girl."

She always used to call me this and I'm encouraged.

"Hey, Aunt Alice, how are you?"

She scrunches up her face and I laugh. "That good, huh?"

She taps her temple. "Too foggy up here."

"We all have those days."

I can't believe we're actually conversing. It may not be rocket science but she's responding coherently, which is more than she's done before.

She stares at me until a frown appears. "Why are you here? You're supposed to be gone."

"Freya's getting married—"

"No. No, no, no." She shakes her head side to side and I start to worry when she thumps her temple with her fist. "What about the baby?"

"Hope's okay."

She stops her head thumping and stares at me again. "Hope. Yes." She snaps her fingers. "A baby to unite the family."

Considering I didn't know about Hope's existence until I returned home I have no idea how Hope is meant to unite us all.

"Do you feel like writing in your diary today?"

It's underhanded, but if I can watch her enter the password I can replicate it later.

"No. Too many bad memories." She presses her fingers to her lips, a wary glint in her eyes. "Diana got what she deserved but my poor darling Cam... then there's you and Freya... so many secrets..."

She's gazing at some point over my shoulder and I glance at where she's looking only to see a blank wall.

I assume Lizzie's maternity is one of the secrets she's referring to between her and my mom, but I'm shocked to hear her say Diana deserved to die in that car accident.

"Did you hate Diana because she gave Lizzie away?"

Aunt Alice doesn't answer and I'm about to repeat the question when she nods. "I hated her for many things. Jealousy is bad." She points to her heart. "It eats away at this until you're left with nothing but memories and the sins committed."

"What sins?"

I feel bad interrogating her but who knows when I'll next get the opportunity?

"You don't want to know." Her eyes fill with tears and I feel worse. "Car brakes fail every day... no one suspected... I didn't do it... not really... but maybe I did..."

She turns away to stare out the window as I assimilate what she's admitted.

Had my sweet, docile aunt tampered with the brakes on my mom's car? Her laptop password BRAKEMYHEARTCS3 suddenly makes a lot more sense. But to actually kill her sister? It's outlandish, but the more I ponder the more I think this could be the secret that haunts her.

I need to access that diary.

Though what will it prove? I would never cause my aunt pain, not in the condition she's in. So what if I discover she killed my parents? It happened twenty-eight years ago. I'm not going to tell anyone.

However, I can't help but think if she's hiding one secret there could be more.

CHAPTER SIXTY-SEVEN

ALICE

THEN

We return to Martino Bay: Freya, me, and baby Hope.

She knows about Brooke losing her baby. I had to tell her the truth. She grieved for her sister but it was brief, because she had her own bundle of joy to care for. Freya has always been self-centered and I knew once she had Hope she wouldn't care about anything.

Freya's an attentive mother and she enrolls at a nearby college and completes a nursing degree while I care for Hope.

The years pass. Brooke sends the occasional email from various Internet cafés around the country: Denver, Memphis, New Orleans, Miami. She's subdued, broken, and I know her life is a shadow of the gilded life she once led. She says she has no intention of returning to Martino Bay and I don't push it.

Lizzie finishes college but does nothing with her art degree. She comes home and moves back into the main house. I love having her home. She's a sweet girl and treats me like a queen, always has. I contemplate telling her the truth about her parents adopting her out and how she came to be mine but I don't want to mess with our relationship, not when it's so good.

Everything is fine, until the postcard arrives.

Hope picks up the mail from our roadside box every day after school and she runs into the kitchen, brandishing the rectangular piece of cardboard.

"Who's Brooke?"

I'm dicing onions on a chopping board near the sink while Freya's changing out of her work clothes. She's been working full-time at the local nursing home since Hope started school two years ago and she loves it as much as the patients and co-workers love her.

It never ceases to amaze me she chose nursing as a profession. She was the least nurturing kid I know growing up. But whatever her motivations I'm glad she's happy and stable and far removed from the girl prone to moods.

"She's your aunt." I place the knife on the board and turn to face Hope. "She travels a lot and that's why you've never met her."

Hope glances at the postcard and her nose crinkles. "Does she know about me? Because this is addressed to you, Mom and Aunt Lizzie."

What can I say? That I've deliberately kept Hope a secret so not to rub salt into Brooke's wound? That Freya has a child when she doesn't?

I settle for, "We don't correspond much. She's sent me the occasional email, and this is the first time she's sent a postcard."

Thankfully, Hope accepts my answer. "I've never seen a postcard written on before. It's so old-fashioned."

"Then you should keep it as a souvenir." I hold out my hand for it. "After I've read it, that is."

Hope shrugs and hands it over. "She doesn't say much."

Hope's right. I read Brooke's brief missive.

JOINED A VOLUNTEER AGENCY.
OFF TO STH AMERICA, PARAGUAY.
WILL BE OUT OF TOUCH FOR A WHILE.
LOVE TO ALL.
BROOKE XXX

A kiss for each of us, but not Hope. As I stare at my great-niece helping herself to milk from the fridge, her tongue poking out between her lips as she concentrates on not spilling a drop as she pours, I experience a rare moment of being conflicted.

Have I done the right thing in keeping Hope away from her aunt? I've always valued family and this feels wrong. Maybe getting to know Hope would help ease Brooke's pain? But then Hope glances up at me and grins, the sparkle in her eyes so like her mom's, and I know I'm right. Knowing Freya's daughter, seeing her sister's happiness, would only accentuate Brooke's loss.

Then later that morning, an email arrives from Brooke and I'm conflicted all over again.

Hi Aunt Alice,

I thought the postcard would be enough before I'm out of contact for goodness knows how long. But it's not. I've got so much to say and no one to say it to but you. You've always been there for me and I love you for it.

I'm not saying this to make you feel bad, but just to offload. So here goes.

I'm lost.

Not literally, but emotionally. I'm sitting on a grubby plastic chair at Dallas/Fort Worth Airport watching people depart. There's a lot of foot traffic today and it looks like everyone's in a hurry to get where they want to be. Not me.

I'm drifting as I have been the last five years, since I saw the blue squished face of my baby being whisked away. There isn't a day that goes by where I don't blame myself for the death of my precious baby boy. I should've never fallen pregnant in the first place, but knew I had to carry to term as punishment for what I'd done. Eli died because of me and no matter how many times you've tried to reassure me, everyone's right. I deserved the blame.

Volunteering abroad is an impulsive decision but one I can live with. I want to escape, to be surrounded by people who need me as much as I need them. I want to do good, to make a difference. It's my penance and I hope you understand.

I do miss you, Freya and Lizzie but I still can't face returning. Too many memories, too much pain. Thanks for the last update. I'm surprised Freya is a nurse. Do you remember that's what I wanted to be in junior high? It feels like she's living my life while I'm a fugitive on the run, moving from town to town, doing menial jobs, avoiding relationships, totally and utterly lost.

I wish I could call you. But a part of me doesn't want you to hear the longing in my voice and how much I miss my old life in Martino Bay, but I guess I gave that up the moment I made the wrong choice. It defines me.

Thanks for the money you regularly put in my bank account. I rarely access it. I chose this life; I need to live it. But communication will be limited where I'm heading, a tiny remote jungle village near the Amazon, so if you want to talk, it's now or never. I tried calling earlier but got voice mail. Hearing your voice brought back a host of memories, all of them good. I love you.

There's a mom with a beautiful baby boy here and I can't look away. I want to tell her I had one of my own and though I wouldn't have kept him, I would've liked to know he was healthy and happy somewhere with parents who love him. But he died and my life is nothing how I imagined. And I have nobody to blame but myself.

I know I've offloaded a lot here but I felt like I had to. If you call me back within the next ninety minutes, we'll get to chat. Otherwise, I'll see you when I see you. Say hi to Freya and Lizzie for me.

Take care. Xx

My cheeks are damp with tears and I jump when a hand lands on my shoulder.

"Don't call her back," Freya says, sadness in her voice.

"What harm can a call do? She sounds awful."

Freya blinks rapidly, like she's battling tears. "I miss her too, but how will calling her back help?" She shrugs. "You heard her, she's heading to South America and she'll be gone for years. Why make it harder on her by hearing your voice?"

"Don't be so callous," I snap and Freya rears back. I never talk to her like that.

"I'm not being callous, I'm a realist." She presses a hand to her chest. "A phone call will change nothing. She's leaving, why not let things be?"

I pick up my cell, flipping it over and over, weighing my decision. I have my reasons for not wanting to call Brooke back. Our lives are perfect just the way they are. But I'm a softie. Hearing Brooke's voice, conversing with her, is a far cry from the occasional emails we've exchanged over the years and it will undo me completely. I'll beg her to come home and it's unfair to put that kind of pressure on her; it's not my decision to make.

"Don't you miss her at all?"

To my surprise, Freya bursts into tears, noisy sobs that startle me. I've never seen her cry like this; she's too reserved usually. It's disconcerting.

"That was a stupid question and I'm sorry." I wrap my arms around her.

She clings to me, her tears soaking my shoulder, as I smooth her back. When her sobs subside, she pulls away, my pragmatic niece once again.

"I guess we're alike, you and me."

"How so?"

"We've had to learn to cope without our dazzling, beautiful sisters at some point in our lives," she says, using her fingertips to dab at the moisture under her eyes. "We love them but along the way we also wish they were never born."

Her candor surprises me and I nod, curious to hear what else she'll say in this oddly vulnerable moment.

"Everything we've been through, everything we've done, defines us." She shakes her head, sorrow darkening her eyes. "So many times growing up, I wished Brooke wasn't around, and now that she isn't... I never expected to feel this lost without her."

Emotion clogs my throat. I've never seen Freya so vulnerable. "I understand. And I wish things could've turned out differently, but I want you to know how proud I am of you, how you've matured into a strong, independent woman capable of love."

Tears shimmer in Freya's eyes. "Thanks, Aunt Alice. Hope is my world but it would be nice to have my sister in it too."

"I know, and some time in the future, she'll be back."

Until then, I have to hope I'm doing the right thing.

CHAPTER SIXTY-EIGHT

BROOKE

The next morning, Freya administers Aunt Alice's meds again and an hour later she's back to being drowsy and disoriented. It's proof of what I suspect and what Dr. Hesham inferred. The medication is making my aunt worse.

I'm not putting up with it any longer.

I bide my time all day by sitting by my aunt, trying to crack her diary password. It's one of those stupid online sites that when you click the "forgot password" links and they email you, you need to enter the old password to create a new one. Crazy, considering you wouldn't need to use that link if you remembered it in the first place. An IT expert could probably get around it and I'm considering taking the laptop into town to do just that, when Aunt Alice sits bolt upright in bed and yells out, "Birthday girls. My girls. Happy birthday."

This is nothing new, she's said some variation of this before and I push the laptop aside to go sit on the bed and comfort her.

"It's okay, Aunt Alice. It's not my birthday yet but I promise you I'll be around when it is."

Three months away and I'm not going anywhere until I know she's receiving the care she deserves.

"My baby Brooke," she says, calmer now as I ease her back against the pillows.

She's staring at me, unseeing, and I hate that she's reverted to this when she was so much more alert yesterday. I press a kiss to her forehead. "Rest up, I'm right here."

This seems to placate her and her eyelids flutter shut. I've wasted enough time trying to guess the password and I've only got another hour to do the online research regarding her meds before Freya gets home and I confront her.

I type "Can medication side effects mimic dementia symptoms?" into the search engine and thousands of hits pop up. I click on the first link from a respected medical journal and start to read. I'm not sure whether to be reassured or appalled.

Freya has been a nurse for six years, not including the practical hands-on experience during her degree. Not only that, she works with dementia patients. So how can she not know the cocktail of meds Aunt Alice is taking can actually exacerbate her symptoms rather than prevent them?

According to this journal, medications can wreak havoc on memory, language, attention, behavior and many cognitive faculties. The biggest culprit is anticholinergics, which treat many things including anxiety, sleep disorders, depression, allergies and high blood pressure. Other meds like benzodiazepines and corticosteroids are also linked to cognitive difficulties and considering how many drugs Aunt Alice is taking… I'm not surprised Dr. Hesham expressed concern.

What draws my attention the most is that medication side-effects may masquerade as dementia, so if loved ones exhibit symptoms like confusion, delirium, memory loss, changes in mood, poor reasoning and speech difficulties, don't automatically assume it's dementia.

It makes me wonder if Freya jumped to conclusions about our aunt's diagnosis and increased her medications, which in turn exacerbated her symptoms? But Freya can't prescribe medications.

A doctor must treat Aunt Alice. I need to find out who initially diagnosed her and get hold of her records ASAP. I spend the next sixty minutes reading but the other articles are similar to the first. They virtually say the same thing but at least I'm armed with information now.

I hear Freya and Hope come home. They go about their usual after school/after work routine and I bide my time. What I have to say to Freya has to be done in private. I wait until Hope's bedroom door closes, meaning she's had her snacks and is about to tackle her homework—I can't believe how much work a ten-year-old has to do at home these days compared to when I was a kid. Aunt Alice is still napping so I slip out of the room and lock the door. I hate the scrape of the key in the lock. If her meds aren't making her worse and she really does need high care I want her moved to a better facility where she won't be under lock and key, free to move about in a carefully gated area.

Freya's in the kitchen drinking a glass of water. Her shoulders are slumped and she's frowning, the fine lines around her eyes exaggerated in the dim lighting. She looks like she's shouldering an invisible weight. I hope it's not guilt for mismanaging our aunt's condition.

"We need to talk."

She startles and some of the water sloshes out of the glass. She's jumpy and when she glares at me I see genuine fear in her eyes.

"What about?"

I point to the back door. "Let's do this outside so we can't be overheard."

She follows me out the door. I walk some distance until we're halfway between the clifftop and the house.

"Why does Aunt Alice take so many medications?"

Predictably, she bristles, her shoulders squaring, her jaw clenching. "Because she needs them. Why are you questioning me on this? I'm the expert."

"I need to see her medical records."

She makes a disparaging pfft sound. "You won't be able to make head or tail of them."

"I think you'd be surprised." I hate that it's come to this, me doubting her expertise when it comes to caring for the woman who devoted her life to raising us. "I've been doing some reading. The side effects of certain medications can mimic dementia."

She has the audacity to laugh. "The medications are helping her, not causing her problems. Besides, she was diagnosed by our best physician at the clinic."

I hadn't planned on telling her about yesterday yet. I wanted to give her the benefit of the doubt, the chance to consider my point of view, to explain if necessary. Instead, her arrogance in belittling me isn't right. But I know Freya. I need to tread carefully or she'll shut down completely.

"I'm not questioning your judgment. You've done an amazing job caring for her, but you may be surprised to learn when Aunt Alice didn't take her medications yesterday she was more lucid than she's been since I came home."

All the color drains from Freya's face. "What do you mean?"

"Lizzie didn't give her the meds because I arranged for her to be assessed by that dementia physician I mentioned to you before, and the doctor says the combination of meds Aunt Alice is on may be exacerbating her symptoms—"

"How dare you!" she screams, anger flushing her face. "I'm her carer. *Me*. I know what's best for her, not you, and certainly not some quack I've never heard of."

I love my sister and I accept her faults, but her quick-fire temper and defensiveness when questioned is annoying.

"Sis, I'm home now, and you don't have to do this all on your own."

"You're only home for the wedding and then you'll be gone." She snaps her fingers. "And I can't fucking wait."

I'm stunned. She's never sworn at me before.

"That's harsh—"

"Everything was fine until you came back, so stop your half-assed diagnosing and back off."

Usually I would. I hate conflict and I don't like seeing Freya riled up. But Aunt Alice's care is too important and if there's the slightest chance my sister has made a mistake, with Alice's diagnosis or meds, I need to make a stand.

"I'm not backing down, Freya. We need to resolve this."

For a split second I see her eyes go eerily blank and her hands clench into fists, like she's going to come at me. Disdain twists her mouth into a grimace, before she turns and sprints toward the house, leaving me chilled to the bone.

CHAPTER SIXTY-NINE

ALICE

THEN

I rarely hear from Brooke over the next five years and every time she emails, infrequently considering she's out of Wi-Fi range unless she's in a town, I experience a pang of heart-breaking guilt that renders me useless for a day.

I should've called her back that day before she left for South America. I should've told her I loved her and begged her forgiveness for messing with her life when she needed me most.

Now I fear it's too late.

Something is not right with my head.

I wake up groggy. I forget the simplest of things, like paying the gas bill or buying milk at the grocers. I'm confused when Lizzie and Hope talk at the same time, and following their conversations is increasingly difficult. I walk into a room and forget what I want. And memories of my past are blurring in a frightening way.

I'm worried. If Lizzie has noticed anything she's not saying, but my sweet girl has never been one to rock the boat. She spent four years at college pursuing an art degree yet returned home to work at the local elementary school for a short time, before quitting to run an online baby business. I expected her to spread her wings, travel the world, but she preferred working from home. I never complained because I love her earnest devotion to me. It almost makes it easier to bear lying to her every day of her life.

I've contemplated telling her the truth, especially now I'm not myself. But what would it achieve other than alienating the one person I truly trust to look after me if I've got some horrible disease?

I trust Brooke too, but she's not here. As for Freya, she's so self-absorbed she wouldn't notice if I fainted at her feet. She's getting married and has been floating since Riker proposed to her two weeks ago. He's a good guy and I somehow feel safer with him moving into one of the cottages on site.

When he first started dating Freya I couldn't fathom why a worldly guy like him would see anything in my homebody niece. But as the months passed and I watched them together, I've come to value his presence. He has a calming effect on her and that makes me happy. He's an old soul, one of those unflappable men to depend on, and I've enjoyed getting to know him over a coffee in his workshop every morning.

I wander into the kitchen. Freya's cooking fajitas for dinner, the sizzle and aroma of beef strips sautéing in oil filling the room. I stare at the island bench, covered in small bowls of grated cheese, guacamole, sliced onions and peppers, and wonder why I came in here. Maybe I'm thirsty? Hungry?

Frustration makes me want to thump something. What's happening to me?

I must make a noise because Freya glances over her shoulder. Our eyes meet and I want to tell her I'm not myself, to ask what's wrong with me and can she see it. She smiles and I'm momentarily comforted. I'm so proud of the woman she's become. She's a tireless worker, a great mom and she'll make a devoted wife. Riker is lucky to have her.

"Hope you're hungry," she says, gesturing to the spread on the island bench. "I'm cooking your favorite."

I like fajitas? I thought I hated Mexican food. Too much spice gives me indigestion. Brooke's the one that likes anything spicy… and in that moment I remember why I sought Freya out.

"Did you send the wedding invitation yet?"

Freya nods and switches off the stove. "Yeah, the moment you mentioned Lizzie told Brooke about the wedding and she might come home, I sent it off to the volunteer organization's head office in South America."

"Good girl. It's going to be great having Brooke home and all my girls together again."

I don't understand the cunning glint in her eyes. "Yeah, it's going to be great."

"I've missed her…"

"Me too," Freya says, dishing the sizzling beef onto a platter. "When I was a new mom I would've loved to share Hope's firsts with her: the first time Hope sat up, rolled over, pulled to stand, walked. Her first word, her first day at kindergarten, her first day at school. But you insisted life would be harder for Brooke if she came home so I cut off contact to make it easier on her. And I understood. Brooke was grieving the loss of her baby while I was raising mine, so it would've been too hard on her."

She fixes me with a look I can't interpret. "But a small part of me resents you for keeping us apart."

I know Freya is talking. I see her mouth moving and I hear the jumbled words, but I can't make sense of anything, a second before I slide into darkness…

As we leave the nursing home where Freya works, I stumble and her arm shoots out to steady me.

"Why did that doctor ask me so many questions?"

"You haven't been well, Aunt Alice, so I scheduled an appointment with Dr. Chilthorn. He's our most experienced physician."

"He's too old. That doctor looked about one hundred to me."

Freya laughs. "He's seventy-five and very experienced."

I shrug. "I don't like quacks and that one looks like he should be a patient in that place, not a doctor."

Freya smiles and squeezes my arm. "Good to see your sense of humor hasn't diminished. He says you're fine to remain at home but you'll need to take some medication to help you remember things, okay?"

"I don't need help." I yank my arm out of her grip and stop, staring at the row of cars in confusion.

"Aunt Alice, we're parked over here."

I glance at several SUVs, unsure which is ours. I hate this intermittent disorientation. It's worsening and I hope I'm okay by the time Brooke gets home.

Freya takes hold of my arm again. "This way."

I'm docile and compliant as she leads me like a child. She buckles me in, and as I look out the windshield, I can't remember where we've been.

"What's happening to me, Freya?"

Her smile is kind, her touch comforting. "Don't worry, you'll be fine."

I hope so, because I have so much to tell Brooke when she returns.

CHAPTER SEVENTY
BROOKE

After confronting Freya, I want to hide in my room and regroup. I don't know what to make of my sister's overreaction. I need to think, to figure out a way to get those medical records. But my plan to hibernate is thwarted the moment I set foot inside and my niece spies me.

"Hey, Auntie Brooke. Want to see what I learned in science today?"

With her sparkling eyes and animated expression, how can I say no? This girl melts my heart and no matter how moody her mom is I'm glad I got to establish a bond with my gorgeous niece.

"Sure thing, sweetie."

She slides off a stool and points to the hallway. "I've made a start on my science project, it's in my room."

"Lead the way."

I do a funny little bow and she laughs. I follow her to her room, where her desk is littered with markers, cotton, wire and Styrofoam.

"Ta da." She throws her arms wide. "What do you think?"

She's constructed a rudimentary solar system, using a bent wire hanger and bits and pieces. For a ten-year-old, it's magnificent.

"I think it's fabulous."

She beams and flings herself at me, and I luxuriate in the feel of her warm body pressed against mine. She's about three months younger than my son would've been and it's times like this I grieve all over again for what I lost.

It doesn't matter I was giving him up. I wanted to have the chance to hold my baby, to kiss him, to say goodbye. Instead, I have nothing and my sister has this amazing girl.

"I'm having trouble making Earth, Mars, and some of the smaller planets to scale," she says after she pulls away. "Got any ideas?"

We chat about her project for a few minutes, when she changes the subject completely. "Hey, I asked Mom when your birthday was and she told me, and I was like wow, you, Aunt Lizzie and Mom have birthdays really close together. How freaky is that?"

"Yeah, your mom's only eleven months younger than me, and Lizzie a year older…"

I trail off as what Hope said sinks in.

Lizzie, Freya and me.

Birthdays close together.

Aunt Alice has repeatedly rambled about her girls and birthdays. Is the password to her diary our names and birthdays? It's closer than anything I've tried before. It's definitely worth a try.

"You're incredibly artistic, Hope, and I can't wait to see what you come up with next. Thanks for sharing your work with me." I drop a kiss on the top of her head. "I'm popping in to see Aunt Alice, okay?"

"Sure."

She gives me a wave and is quickly absorbed in her project again. I race to Aunt Alice's room, unlock it, and slip inside. She manages a wan smile before turning back to the TV, turned down low on some quiz show I've never seen. Her laptop is in its usual place on a side table and I pick it up, my hands shaking as I flip it open and the screen lights up.

I type the first four letters of the online diary site into the search engine and it immediately pops up, considering the amount of times I've tried to access it. I try various combinations of FREY-ABROOKELIZZIE along with our birthdays. I try the full years, abbreviated versions, swapping our names around.

When I hit enter for the fifteenth time and see a green tick, I can't believe my eyes.

I'm in.

I should feel bad for reading my aunt's private diary but I don't. I want to see how this all started and what her early symptoms were, how she coped, and if anything I learn can bring her peace.

The entries are divided into years, the first one the year my parents died and Aunt Alice became our guardian.

I click on the first entry and begin to read.

CHAPTER SEVENTY-ONE
ALICE
NOW

Brooke is home.

My sweet, caring girl. She and Lizzie are so alike in their gentle temperaments.

Nothing like that other one.

I made a mistake in trusting Freya once. She appears to have redeemed herself over the last ten years but is it all an act? She thinks I don't notice things because of my confusion. She uses words like early onset dementia that don't mean much to me. I forget my own name most days and I never want to leave this room I'm in.

But then Brooke takes me outside one day. We travel in the car, and my mind is clearer than it's been in a long time. I see some lady in a white coat, who asks me a billion questions and makes me do dumb things like tell the time and point to places on a map. I'm not very good at it but she's nice and I don't feel so bad.

The fear starts as we return home. My chest tightens as Brooke turns into the driveway. Now I've been out of that room I don't want to go back. But I'm safe there. I know it. But my head's always worse when I'm in that room, like looking at the world through a kaleidoscope and not being able to make sense of the shapes.

I want to tell Brooke something. It's important. It hovers at the edge of my consciousness, within reach but nebulous, and it floats away over and over.

Something about her birthday… or is it mine? Or the other one's?

She's always on my laptop like I once was. That thing was my savior after my sister died and I was responsible for her girls. I had no one to talk to. I was so lonely. No friends, no boyfriend, no family. I needed to get out all my pent-up feelings. I poured out all my thoughts, my fears, my guilt. Keeping a record in a journal kept me sane.

Is that why Brooke's on there too?

Is her sister bad like mine?

I wish I could help her. But my thoughts are jumbled. Nothing is clear.

This is hell.

And nothing less than I deserve for what I've done.

CHAPTER SEVENTY-TWO
BROOKE

It's a long entry but I have to start somewhere and the faster I read, hopefully I'll get the answers I crave.

I used to laugh at Diana for keeping a journal all through high school. Every night she'd be in bed, scribbling in that thing, like she had so many important things to say. I never saw the value in it.

Until now.

Toby has just left. I met him at the supermarket of all places and I foolishly invited him into my home because he's nice and reminded me of Cam. But the girls didn't like him and I'm not ready. It's too soon to let anyone into my heart, when it still belongs to Cam.

But I'm so frustrated. I have no one to talk to and if I don't let out some of these feelings locked inside I'll go crazy. If I'm not already.

Even now, months after I accidentally killed the love of my life, I can't believe it. I may have hated the way Cam danced to Di's tune, but at least when she was around he was too.

He should've never been in that car. Not Cam, never him.

Even to the end, she thwarted me. Bad enough I had to put up with being second best my entire life, she took the one thing I wanted most in this world.

My grief is still raw, all-consuming. Cam should be here, raising his daughters with me. That was the plan. And with time, he would've grown to love me. We were close once and if Di hadn't come home after GIVING AWAY HER BABY, Cam would've been mine.

Now, I'm raising Brooke, Freya, and Lizzie. Cam was meant to co-parent with me but he's gone and I'm stuck doing it alone. But I can't begrudge him that. None of this is his fault. And I love these girls because they're a part of him.

The investigators ruled the car accident just that. Old car, old brakes. But I hate the uncertainty that even though I didn't follow through on my plan to tamper with Di's brakes, I might've somehow inadvertently done something when I touched them. It's a guilt I'll have to live with, even though the one thing I wanted most—Di's death—actually happened.

I'm rich, thanks to Cam. I sold their house to move here, to Martino Bay, and I have control of the girls' trust funds Cam's parents set up before they died. But all the money in the world doesn't make up for my loss.

Cam, I love you and I always will.

I never thought I'd be a mom to your three girls at twenty-three but here I am. I promise you I'll do my best. I'll love them like they're my own, because they're yours.

You and me, Cam, forever.

I rear back from the screen, my breathing ragged. I scrub a hand across my face but it doesn't change the print dancing before my eyes. My sweet aunt, who raised me, loved me, had an obsession for my father, hated my mother, and had tried to kill her because of it before growing a conscience.

Sadness tightens my chest and I breathe slower, waiting until I regain control to keep reading. I skim through the next week of entries, more of the same, lamenting the loss of Cam and citing every reason why she hated Diana. I can't equate her level of vitriol with the caring aunt I know and love. It doesn't make sense.

The entries peter out, only the occasional one for the first few years of her guardianship. She chronicles our life in Martino Bay, the odd guy she hooks up with, mundane stuff. My eyes start to ache as I speed-read each entry, until I spy a momentous date.

The day my baby died.

My breath hitches but I force myself to read.

I swear my heart stops when I see Brooke's baby. She's blue, unresponsive, and the midwife looks panicked. She bundles the baby and passes her to me and I allow Brooke one glance before I'm gone.

It would make life easier if the little one hadn't lived. It will make what I'm about to do a non-issue.

I gasp as I re-read those lines over and over, my mind unable to compute one little word.

She.

Aunt Alice told me I had a boy.

Why lie?

I brace for what's to come and continue.

I rush her into the nursery where several nurses get to work on reviving her immediately. It doesn't take long and when I hear my great-niece's first lusty cry I sag against the wall in relief.

I hate lying to Brooke.

It kills me, it really does.

But at no stage when she said she wanted to give up her baby did I entertain the thought.

I'm not my sister.

When I first learned the truth about Lizzie I vowed no Shomack baby would ever go through what she had.

So I lied.

I told Brooke the adoption was all arranged, but it wasn't. I know someone who's only too happy to have something of her sister's. Someone who's so like me in our mutual envy of our sisters, someone who knows what it's like to be second best.

While Brooke is nothing like Diana, I know this is the only way to calm Freya down. She loved Eli how I loved Cam and losing him changed her irrevocably. Now, she'll have a piece of Eli forever, just like I have Cam in his girls.

Of course Freya loved my plan.

She'll have something of Brooke's that is irreplaceable.

She'll have won.

It breaks my heart to see Brooke grieving for her lost baby boy but it's for the best. She never wants to return home and that's fine by me. Even if she does, it won't matter. Freya's been living with me in LA, "having her baby" before we return to Martino Bay. No one will know the truth but us. And it has to stay that way. I can't bear the thought of Brooke thinking badly of me. I love her, but this is for the best. She doesn't want her baby, Freya does.

End of story.

But it's not, and as tears spill from my eyes I stand, place the laptop on the chair, and move toward the bed.

A red mist films my eyes, blurring with the tears, making sight impossible. I'm shaking with rage, and nausea churns my gut.

Aunt Alice has fallen asleep and as I stand over her, reeling from what she's done, I want to kill her.

CHAPTER SEVENTY-THREE

FREYA

I'm flummoxed, at a complete loss.

What am I going to do about Brooke?

She won't give up on this obsession with Aunt Alice's care. Why else would she be badgering me for the medical records? I can't have anyone but Dr. Chilthorn treat Aunt Alice. He's pliable and unreliable. If someone else takes her bloods and does a full screening…

I have to do something before it comes to that.

Ideally, I would up her dosage until she drifts into a permanent sleep. But those kinds of things are picked up through toxicology by a medical examiner and I'm not giving up my life before I get everything I've ever wanted.

I'm due to marry Riker and have the happily-ever-after Brooke always wanted.

If Aunt Alice says something to jeopardize that…

I can't believe Lizzie and Brooke pulled that stunt by not giving her the medications. Alice has enough in her system to not have clarity from one day's missed dosage but I'm still scared. I know I've acted impulsively in the past and let my anger control me but I can't afford any slip-ups this time around.

Hope barrels into the kitchen and skids to a stop. This kid never walks, she always runs everywhere like she's got places to be and people to see.

"Hey, Mom, I showed Auntie Brooke my science project, she thinks it's cool."

"That's because you're cool." I give her a quick hug, my mind still fixated on my dilemma.

"She's not leaving after the wedding, is she?" Hope perches at the island bench and rests her chin in her hands. "Because I don't want her to go and you should ask her to stay."

As if. I'm counting down the days until Brooke leaves. I can't have her meddling any further. And I feel bad for dosing up Aunt Alice. But I had no choice. The moment Lizzie mentioned emailing Brooke about her concerns for her mom, and she told Brooke about the wedding, I had to take action.

When Brooke leaves I can cut down Aunt Alice's dosage again. I've been doctoring her food with a variety of sedatives since she first voiced her opinion on Brooke returning and it hadn't been difficult getting old Doc Chilthorn to diagnose her with early onset dementia. His examinations are rudimentary at best and, as a co-worker, he's been freely signing off on the required scripts ever since.

When I started this I didn't want to harm Aunt Alice, just make her dopey enough she couldn't let slip any secrets to Brooke. If she hadn't taken her meds yesterday it had been a close call. That can't happen again.

"You're daydreaming, Mom." Hope rolls her eyes. "Tell Auntie Brooke she has to stay."

"It's her choice, sweetie." I manage to inject enthusiasm into my voice when I hate it every time Hope waxes lyrical about Brooke. It plays into every one of my old insecurities and I can't contemplate they may have some invisible biological bond proving nature over nurture.

"I think she's the best." Hope folds her arms, the stubborn glint in her eyes so reminiscent of my sister a physical ache spreads in my chest.

I know Hope doesn't mean it literally. My daughter loves me and has from day one. But to hear her say Brooke is the best…

I have to come up with a way to keep Aunt Alice silent until Brooke leaves.

CHAPTER SEVENTY-FOUR

BROOKE

I don't know how long I stand over Aunt Alice.

I lose track of time as I assimilate the shocking news I've just learned.

Not only did the aunt I've adored my whole life almost commit murder, she stole my baby and gave her to my sister.

It's diabolical, like some ridiculously elaborate plot out of the soap operas she'd watch when we were kids. She'd always have healthy snacks waiting for us when we got home from school, and I thought they were to keep us quiet while she sat glued to the latest saga. Little did I know her life mimicked some of those crazy screenwriters' creations.

I can't fathom how she thought this was remotely okay. She tries to justify it in her diary by implying she's like Freya, the slighted sister, the second-best sister, but I'm not buying it. Aunt Alice has mental issues and that's one trait she definitely shares with my sister.

My baby.

Sweet, delightful Hope is *my* child.

My throat tightens and I drag in deep breaths as spots dance before my eyes. I can't pass out. I need to keep reading. Because I now know why Freya maintains such tight control over our aunt's care.

If Aunt Alice had an attack of guilt with me coming home after all these years and wanted to come clean, Freya's carefully constructed life would fall apart. I know my sister. She'll never let that happen.

Everything slides into place. Her keeping Aunt Alice under lock and key, administering a plethora of drugs, not wanting an independent assessment… I wonder if Alice has dementia at all or is Dr. Hesham correct in implying her symptoms are caused by an over-consumption of meds?

I have no idea if my conspiracy theory is correct so I need to keep reading. If Aunt Alice has mentioned anything in her diary regarding forgetfulness, new symptoms, that kind of thing, I need proof before I go making wild accusations.

Scowling, I return to the screen, trepidation making me feel sick. Entries are few and far between after Aunt Alice and Freya return to Martino Bay with *my* baby. Riker gets a mention when he comes on the scene. He's obviously captured my aunt's heart as well as Freya's because she raves about him. There's a few months gap until the next entry, just after Freya announces her engagement.

I'm happy for my girl. She'll get the happily-ever-after I craved but never got. I have my doubts about what a great guy like Riker sees in someone like her. I've looked for signs he's not genuine but haven't spotted any. Yet I can't help but sense there's more to him wanting to marry Freya than meets the eye.

Their courtship has been speedy so why does a guy who's spent his life moving around suddenly want to settle down? And why marry? Him moving into the cottage is commitment enough. It's a gut feeling I have that he has an ulterior motive of some kind and I spend time with him every morning to see if he's genuine… yet I can't fault how he treats Freya and Hope. That's what endears him to me the most, the way he is with my great-niece.

Seeing Freya so happy has got me thinking… it's time for Brooke to come home. I know Freya is scared I'll reveal the truth but I would never do that. Yes, guilt still consumes me most days for what I did. But Freya is a good mother and keeping Hope in the family rather than giving her away like Brooke wanted to do has been my goal all along.

But I feel sorry for Brooke. She deserves to be a part of this family rather than drifting the way she has for the last decade or so. She's a good girl and deserves a lot better than the hand she was dealt.

I worry about her. I hope returning home won't dredge up the past for her. It's eleven years since Eli died, the town has changed, but some people have long memories. I'll try to protect her as best I can.

But I'm worried about more than my niece's homecoming. Lately, I haven't been feeling well. Food has become tasteless and I'm forgetting the simplest of things. I sense Freya watching me closely. She keeps asking if I'm okay and it's bugging the hell out of me. But she's a good girl. She's taken over all the cooking and serves up different meals every day. She insists I eat even though I've lost my appetite and it seems to be dwindling daily.

Maybe it's a virus of some sort. Whatever is making me feel so awful I need to get over it, because Brooke is finally coming home and I can't wait to see my girl.

I blink rapidly at my aunt's sentiment. She seems to genuinely care about me, but I will never, ever, forgive her for what she's done.

Interesting, that she started feeling unwell after news of my return broke. I'd been surprised to receive Lizzie's email expressing concerns about Aunt Alice and mentioning Freya's nuptials, closely followed by the wedding invitation, so of course I'd agreed to come home.

Maybe Freya had been hoping I wouldn't? Would Aunt Alice still be okay if I hadn't made the decision to return?

I need to confront Freya but I'm wary: what is she capable of? I want to shove her so hard she can't get back up. But all I have are these diary entries and with Aunt Alice's mind the way it is, what's to stop Freya dismissing all this as a figment of her imagination, the ranting of a demented woman?

Hope's birth certificate is probably doctored too, naming Freya as the mother, so even if I could locate it, that won't prove anything.

Hope and I need to get DNA tested.

That's the only way to have irrevocable proof Hope is mine.

And then what? The last thing I want is to traumatize my daughter. She's a wonderful child and learning the truth about her twisted aunts isn't going to be good. But I can't leave her in Freya's care. Not after this.

I also need to prove Freya's been poisoning Aunt Alice by over-medicating. Once I have any kind of evidence, I can blackmail her into granting me full custody of Hope.

It's a convoluted plan that depends on so much.

Or there's a simpler way...

I know what happens when I push Freya's buttons. She won't like me knowing the truth. She'll hate it. And she'll act accordingly.

As the glimmer of an idea takes shape, I wonder if I can do it.

It's risky. It's bold. And it could have severe consequences for us all.

But Hope, *my* daughter, is worth it.

CHAPTER SEVENTY-FIVE

FREYA

I feed Hope leftover lasagna for dinner. I barely fork a mouthful of mine. I have important work to do once she's in bed, involving researching untraceable poisons. Thankfully, Brooke doesn't appear for dinner and Lizzie's visiting an old college buddy in Palm Springs. Riker's working on a surprise for me, a wedding gift, and has made me promise I won't go anywhere near his workshop.

I'm angsty, my stomach knotted with nerves, until Hope eats, has a bath, reads for the requisite thirty minutes before lights out. I'm never more grateful that she falls asleep quickly and when I hear her breathing even out I close the door.

I can't use the computer in the den to research. Even if I clear the search history there are experts who can trace anything and if there's any doubt surrounding Alice's death, who knows what will be investigated in this place. But using her laptop won't raise any red flags. Anything searched on her device can be explained away by the hallucinations of a woman with dementia.

I unlock her door, pocket the key, and enter. Surprisingly, her laptop is open but nowhere near her bed. It's on the movable table near the TV, well out of reach.

I hear her snuffling snores as I cross the room and spin the screen around to face me. It's in resting mode but comes alive when I touch the 'enter' key.

That's the moment my life as I know it ceases to exist.

I never had any fear Lizzie or Brooke would access Aunt Alice's online diary because it was password protected. I knew because when I heard Brooke was coming home for the wedding I checked. I tried many combinations and came up empty, so how the hell has Brooke figured it out?

Unless... I glance at my aunt's slumbering form. Had she unlocked it the day Lizzie had skipped her meds? Has she done this deliberately to thwart me after all these years of pretending to be on my side?

The anger is a slow burn. It doesn't come in a rush. It starts in the pit of my stomach and spreads outward, inch by inch, until I'm burning up.

I need to get out of here before I do something I'll never be able to explain away.

I run from the room, from the house, and it's only when I'm outside taking great heaving breaths to ease the constriction of my chest do I realize I forgot to lock Alice's door.

Then again, who cares? The best outcome for me is if she stumbles out of that room, gets lost, and walks off the edge of the cliff.

The cliffs... they've always been a draw for Brooke and me. It's our go-to place where we do our best thinking. Her bedroom door had been open as I'd run from the house, the room empty. If she's read Aunt Alice's diary, I bet she's in shock and what better place to think than our cliff?

I jog as I follow the path leading to the back of our property. My lungs tighten as I break into a sprint and I'm panting by the time I catch sight of her. She has her back to me. It would be so easy to run at her and push...

I stumble over a rock and stub my toe. I'm always clumsy near the cliffs. A curse spills from my lips before I can stop it. She hears me, and turns, and in the wan light from a half-moon she looks like a demon.

She's mad. Her shoulders are rigid, her back ramrod straight, her hands clenched into fists. There's no doubt: she's read the journal.

"Thought I might find you here," I drawl, needing to play for time so I can gauge what she's going to do. "Been snooping, Sis?"

I half expect her to come at me, there's so much hatred in her eyes. Instead, she shrugs. "Aunt Alice's diary made for interesting reading, if that's what you mean."

I snort. "She's delusional. I don't know what she's written in that thing but it's probably all invented."

"Really? So the fact she gave you my baby is a lie?"

I try not to react but I can't help taking a step toward her. It's the tell she's waiting for, her grin smug.

"Apparently you wanted to be like me so much you thought you'd steal my baby?"

I grit my teeth to stop from responding, but I've waited my whole life to tell her exactly what I think of her. I can't resist.

"I never stole anything. It was Aunt Alice's idea. She came to me and laid it all out, how bad she felt when our mom adopted out Lizzie and she didn't want the same thing happening to your baby. So I went along with it. I'd go into hiding too, when the baby was born she'd tell you it had died to stop you hunting for it later, and I'd raise it."

"Hope's not an it!" she yells, her mouth twisting with fury. "She's my baby and you stole her."

"You gave her away." The anger is building and I let it come. I welcome it. I embrace it. "You never deserved her, like you never deserved Eli." She blanches and I take another step forward, determined to make her suffer, like all those years I suffered growing up in her shadow. "I loved him a hell of a lot more than you and I would've never treated him the way you did on the night of the party."

I jab a finger in her direction. "You broke his heart with your slutty behavior that night and luckily I was there to pick up the pieces. He needed me. He wanted me…"

Until he didn't, and that moment of rejection is something I'll have to live with forever.

"What did you do?"

Brooke's tone is flat, brittle, and I'm surprised by her question. She hasn't asked what I meant. It's almost as if she knows… but she can't. Nobody does. Aunt Alice suspected but she was too gutless to ask the question because she knew she wouldn't like the answer.

But I'm done hiding. Because I know how tonight will end. I've known it from the moment I spotted Brooke out here. People are going to say she couldn't handle the stress of being back here, that she wanted to join her beloved in the same way.

It's the only possible outcome.

"Eli came back to the party and I comforted him, but it wasn't enough so when he left I followed him." I point to the left. "He actually walked almost all the way back here, obviously with the intention of begging you to take him back. I couldn't let that happen so I took my chance."

I remember the night so clearly, the night I lost the love of my life. Aunt Alice once said something similar happened to her and it didn't register until I had to go through the same gut-wrenching agony of losing Eli.

"I told him the truth, that I loved him, that he could be with me because you weren't worth it. I tried to kiss him, but he pushed me away. That made me mad…"

"You killed him," Brooke whispers, taking a step back. Good, one step closer to the edge. "He didn't jump because of me."

"Not everything's about you," I sneer. "Great deduction though. No, he didn't jump. I came at him again and when he pushed me away I fought back. He was drunk, I wasn't, so when he lost his balance…" I make a swooping action from high to low with my hand. "I didn't mean to do it. It was an accident."

"Bullshit." Her eyes glow in the darkness. "Even when he lost me he still didn't want you, so you pushed him."

I shrug, my calm infuriating her more by the way she starts shifting her weight from side to side. "I might've, I don't remember."

"You're a liar," she hisses, placing her hands on her hips like she's some kind of avenging angel. "But you know what, Sis? You're not the only one who lies."

I falter, unsure what she means.

"Remember when I said Riker and I barely spoke at that party?"

I hear a dull roaring in my ears. "Yeah, he said it too."

"We both lied."

She's triumphant, her shoulders squared, lording her secret over me until I can barely see straight.

"We had sex that night," she says, emotionless, her grin a leer, as the roar intensifies, deafening me to everything but her cutting words cleaving me in two. "I felt guilty so I came clean to Eli. He went ballistic and started calling me some nasty names I probably deserved so I broke up with him."

"You lying bitch—"

"Now, now, Sis, that's a severe case of pots and kettles, don't you think?"

I take three steps toward her. I'm almost close enough to shove her. She doesn't flinch. "Want to know the best part?"

My skin prickles with dread, electricity lighting every one of my cells with incandescent rage.

"Remember when I first discovered I was pregnant and told Aunt Alice I took a test because I'd had a pregnancy scare with Eli and had a spare one lying around?"

I can barely nod I'm trembling so hard, fury warring with fear.

"I lied." She leans forward, her grin taunting me. "Riker took my virginity."

The truth crashes over me in a sickening wave as I relinquish the tenuous control on my rage. It floods me, lending me speed, lending me strength, as I lunge at her. She screams and tries to sidestep, but I'm too fast. We grapple and she screams again as I pull her hair, snapping her head back so hard I hear a crack.

We shuffle toward the edge, the guard rope no match for two women hell-bent on destroying each other.

"I'm going to end you, just like I ended your pathetic boyfriend, and then I'm going to marry Riker and raise *your* daughter."

It's my turn to grin as she slips, but I realize my mistake a fraction too late.

Somehow Riker is there, and I'm not sure if he's trying to save me or push me, my momentum carrying me forward as Brooke slides under me, and then I'm falling…

CHAPTER SEVENTY-SIX
BROOKE

The scream as Freya falls fades as I cover my ears. I lie on my back on the hard ground and rock from side to side, wishing I could eradicate the memory of what just happened.

I didn't push her. I was tempted; there'd been a moment as she'd first lunged at me when I wanted to sidestep and send her plummeting with a shove in her back. I wanted to reclaim the life she stole from me.

Ironically, now I can, but who's going to believe she jumped? Freya has a daughter, a fiancé, and is about to be married. Nobody is going to believe she committed suicide. And poor Hope, having to live with the stigma, having to learn the truth from me...

I squeeze my eyes shut and continue rocking, reaching for answers that aren't there, when two hands grab me. My eyes fly open to see Riker squatting next to me, concern etched into his face.

"Are you okay?"

"Not really. Freya..." I choke up and he helps me into a sitting position.

"I tried to stop her. It wasn't your fault."

"You did?"

He nods. "Yeah, I saw you two fighting and I started running toward you but as I reached out to grab her she'd already gone over." He shakes his head. "I can't believe she's so unhinged."

I'm not sure if he means by what just happened or in general. He reached us too late, which means he didn't hear what I revealed to push Freya to the edge.

I have to tell him.

I have to tell him I drove her to it deliberately.

How I left that laptop open for her to find, knowing she'd be driven to drastic measures to keep her secrets.

That I knew she'd go searching for me out here when I wasn't in the house.

That I taunted her with the one thing guaranteed to drive her crazy.

It had worked, too. Discovering Riker is Hope's father pushed her over the edge; literally. I've achieved what I set out to do.

Get rid of my lunatic sister so she's never near my daughter again.

I want to tell Riker the truth. About Hope's paternity, about everything. But shock is setting in. I see it in his eyes, in the blankness of his expression, in the slackness of his mouth. He just watched the woman he loves plunge to her death. Now is definitely not the time for him to learn he's Hope's father.

"We need to call the police," I say, as he holds out his hand and helps me stand. "I need to tell them the truth."

His gaze locks onto mine. "And what's that?"

"Exactly what happened—"

"No." His lips compress and he shakes his head. "Hope needs you now more than ever. You can't be dragged through an investigation, possibly facing a manslaughter charge, or worse."

He grips my upper arms so tight I wince and he eases his grasp. "We tell them Freya's been under a lot of pressure, what with your aunt and the wedding. We tell them I said I needed more time and I wanted to call it off. Then you found her tonight… down there…"

I don't want to lie. I've had enough of them to last a lifetime.

But he's right. Hope's going to be distraught losing Freya. She'll need Lizzie and me to get her through this. And when it comes time to tell her the truth about our real bond, I want her to trust me and love me enough that it's a shock I can help her adjust to.

"Brooke, you know it's the only way."

I'm so sick of this family and its secrets, but as I stare into his eyes, willing me to trust him, I give in.

Freya killed Eli.

She poisoned Aunt Alice.

She stole Hope.

She would've killed me.

She doesn't deserve to have control over what happens to me from beyond the grave, so I'll do what Riker says. I'll do what the women in this family do best.

I'll lie.

CHAPTER SEVENTY-SEVEN
BROOKE

Most of Martino Bay turns out for the funeral of one of their beloved. If the eulogy didn't paint Freya out to be a saint, the many well-wishers who offer me condolences leave me in little doubt. Her countless hours volunteering, her tender nursing care for the elderly, her hands-on mothering, nobody has a bad word to say.

And Riker, Lizzie and I stand there, accepting and grateful, when we knew a different side to the lauded Freya.

It may be hypocritical but I actually shed a tear. I loved my sister once. We were close. I included her in everything, in my circle of friends, in my hobbies. We loved choc-chip cookies and sunbathing in the backyard and reality TV. We caught the school bus together, we did our homework together at the library, we were closer than most siblings.

She repaid me by stealing my daughter.

Aunt Alice has filled in some of the blanks. Many of her memories have returned now she's off the meds. Dr. Hesham thinks it's unlikely she has early onset dementia and that with time she may make a full recovery. I'm not so sure.

There's an emptiness in Aunt Alice now, a vacancy behind her eyes. She remembers the past and how much Freya coveted everything I had, how she resented me, how her 'moods' as we called them occasionally erupted into uncontrollable rages. I think she blames herself. I feel sorry for Aunt Alice, but I don't know if I can ever forgive her for what she did.

I'm not sure if Lizzie believes Riker and me. After all, she's lived with Freya a lot longer than I have and our sister never demonstrated suicidal tendencies before. But she wants to do right by Hope too and I'll tell Lizzie the truth once the furor dies down.

After the graveside ceremony everyone comes to our house for the wake. Toasts are made, sandwiches are eaten, tears are shed and then it's finally, *finally*, over as I stand in the sunroom, staring toward the cliffs, hating all they signify.

When the last person has left, a doddering old doctor who apparently diagnosed Aunt Alice in the first place, I go in search of Hope. She's in her room, lying on her side on top of the bed covers, her gaze fixed on the solar system she created.

"Is it okay if I come in, honey?"

She nods and my heart breaks as I glimpse the tear tracks staining her cheeks. I sit on the side of the bed and place my hand on her waist. "We're so proud of you today."

Another tear slides out of the corner of her eye and she doesn't respond for a long time. "Why?"

"Because you were brave. It's hard losing someone we love." I stroke her hair, offering scant comfort but it's the best I can do for now. "And I want you to know I'm here for you whenever you need me, okay?"

Her eyes seek mine. "You're not leaving?"

"No, sweetie, I'm never leaving you again."

She perks up at that and pushes into a sitting position. "Really?"

"I'm here for you, forever."

When she flings herself at me and I hold her tight, I know I've done the right thing in perpetuating the lie Freya killed herself.

It's the only way I get to make amends, and that's raise my daughter.

We both cry a little and when she's done I lower her to the pillow. "Want me to bring you in a hot cocoa with extra marshmallows?"

"Yes, please." Her smile is watery but it's a smile just the same and my heart expands with love.

"Be right back." I press a kiss to her forehead and leave the room, closing the door behind me.

As I enter the kitchen to heat up the milk, Riker's there, pacing from one end to the other.

"Hey, you okay?"

"Yeah, long day." He grimaces and runs a hand through his hair, sending it spiking in all directions. "How's Hope?"

"Coping better than I expected. She's a fighter."

He eyeballs me. "Just like her mom."

His stare is intense, unambiguous, and in that instant I realize he knows.

"How did you know?"

"The moment I laid eyes on Hope I knew she was mine," he says, his tone gruff. "She's the spitting image of my sister. The resemblance is uncanny."

"When was that?"

"About eight months ago. I was selling a few pieces at the local market when they came by my stall and I swear my heart stopped when I saw Hope. Freya was with her, so we started chatting. I had to know more so I asked her out, then on our first date I found out Freya was your sister."

He taps his head. "It blew my mind, because with Hope's resemblance to Kel, I wondered if you'd had my kid, dumped it on your family and done a runner. So I cozied up to her to find out more."

I'm stunned. He's known from the beginning?

"It didn't take long for me to figure out that's not what happened, that for some inexplicable reason Freya was passing Hope off as her kid." His nose screws up. "I've never been completely comfortable around Freya. She had this way of putting on a front when I could tell she felt entirely different on the inside, and she never wanted to talk about you. I asked her once and she got really upset. That was our first argument. And I didn't like the way she talked to your aunt sometimes, like she had something over her, which I guess she did, considering they were passing off Hope as hers. So I decided to stick around."

Still reeling from his revelation, I shake my head. "Is that why you proposed?"

He nods, sheepish. "I got a paternity test done with one of those online companies, using hair from Hope's brush. Once it was confirmed I'm her father, I knew I couldn't leave her. I didn't love Freya but I was willing to do whatever it took to keep my daughter safe and if that meant marrying your sister, so be it. And when Alice suggested inviting you to the wedding and Freya freaked out, I knew I had to talk to you and see what the story was."

"Why didn't you say something?"

"Because I didn't know if I could trust you either." He holds his hands out, palms up, like he's got nothing to hide. "For all I knew handing Hope off to your sister was what you wanted and I didn't want to tip you off until I knew more."

"This is nuts."

I press my fingertips to my temples. It does little to alleviate the pressure building in my head.

"You have no idea what it did to me in here," he presses a fist to his heart, "when I saw you and Hope together. You're a natural and she gravitates toward you…"

He shakes his head, his expression tortured. "It gutted me to know the truth and be so damn helpless to do anything about it. Until that night on the cliff."

I stiffen, every muscle in my body clenching.

Has Riker just admitted to murdering Freya?

Those last few moments before she fell are a blur. We were grappling, I lost my footing, Riker was there, but I thought Freya was already pitching over the cliff. I thought it had been momentum.

Was it something more sinister?

I want to believe this man is inherently good, that everything he's done has been for Hope, that he loves our daughter as much as I do.

But in that moment, I wonder if he's as good a liar as the rest of us.

As he envelops me in his arms, I know I'll always have doubts about him. And after learning the truth about Aunt Alice and Freya, I'll have trouble trusting anyone again.

But I can do this.

Hope is depending on me.

It's time to step up for my daughter.

My daughter.

I don't know what the future holds, but if I ever have a child again I hope it's a boy so a girl won't have to contend with a sister.

Some of the girls in my family don't have a great track record with sisterhood.

A LETTER FROM NICOLA

I want to say a huge thank you for choosing to read *My Sister's Husband*. I hope that you enjoyed reading it as much as I enjoyed writing it.

If you'd like to be kept up to date with all my latest releases, please sign up at the following link. Your email address will never be shared and you can unsubscribe at any time.

www.bookouture.com/nicola-marsh

Writing is such a wonderful job and none more so than when the glimmer of an idea pops into my head and develops into a full-blown story I can't wait to tell.

I know this sounds crazy but I wrote *My Sister's Husband* in eighteen days.

Insane, right? But I couldn't stop the words pouring onto the page as Brooke, Freya and Alice demanded to have their stories told.

I had so much fun bringing these characters to life and if you loved *My Sister's Husband* I'd be grateful if you could write a review. Even a few simple words of appreciation makes such a difference helping new readers to discover my books for the first time so please take the time to leave a review.

I love hearing from my readers – you can get in touch via my Facebook page, Instagram, Twitter, Goodreads and my website.

Thanks for taking the time to read *My Sister's Husband*,
Nicola

@NicolaMarsh

www.nicolamarsh.com

NicolaMarshAuthor

@nicolamarshauthor

ACKNOWLEDGEMENTS

Having a book published is rarely a solo effort so thanks to the following people:

Jennifer Hunt, my fabulous editor at Bookouture. You make the process of draft to print seamless and your insightful edits push me to get the best out of every story. Thank you so much!

Noelle Holten and Kim Nash, publicist extraordinaires, who put their heart and soul into marketing every book. Thanks for getting my books into readers' hands.

The entire team at Bookouture, I love your transparency, your dedication and your passion for books. I'm grateful for my domestic suspense novels to be published with you.

Kim Lionetti, my agent, who supports me through every book.

Soraya Lane and Natalie Anderson, my writing champions, who keep me focused on the next big idea.

My parents, for not giving me a sister like the twisted ones portrayed in this story!

Martin, who thinks everything I write is gold. Your support is invaluable.

My beautiful boys, who fill my heart with love. You're the reason I strive harder with every book.

For the bloggers and reviewers who take the time to read my books and spread the love. I appreciate all you do. A special shout-out to Marnie Harrison, who read *The Scandal*, my first foray into the domestic suspense genre, and told the world how it kept her up all night reading. And for making a video about it when she never does! Marnie, it's always nerve-racking for an author waiting for that first review, especially in a new genre, so your kind words about my book really helped.

My loyal readers, thanks for buying my books. Each purchase enables me to keep writing more stories I get to share with you, so thank you!

Printed in Great Britain
by Amazon

57263078R00190